400 LIGHT-YEARS FROM ANTARES...

I recall every minute, every second, as we two sat and talked in a Victorian room stuffed with mummified people who saw and heard nothing.

"You called me Pur Dray," I whispered. I swallowed. "You must know I hold only being a Krozair of Zy as of importance. Tell me, Madam Zena Iztar, tell me, for the sweet sake of Zair!"

"Now," she said, her voice in its hard practicality made me sit up. "The Savanti have set their hands to the work they consider proper for Kregen, for they are of that world and are a last faint remnant of a once mighty race. You have heard of them as the Sunset People. The Savanti have at heart the well-being of humans like yourself. As for the Star Lords, their plans are different, wider and more universe-embracing, and I shall tell you only that you will have to make a choice one day, and the choice will be the hardest thing you have ever done."

"Put me back on Kregen and I will choose!"

"They were big! And they were close!"

THE
TIDES
OF
KREGEN

by

ALAN BURT AKERS

Illustrated by
Michael Whelan

DAW BOOKS, INC.

DONALD A. WOLLHEIM, PUBLISHER

1301 Avenue of the Americas
New York, N. Y.   10019

Published by
THE NEW AMERICAN LIBRARY
OF CANADA LIMITED

The Saga of Dray Prescot

The Delian Cycle

I. TRANSIT TO SCORPIO
II. THE SUNS OF SCORPIO
III. WARRIOR OF SCORPIO
IV. SWORDSHIPS OF SCORPIO
V. PRINCE OF SCORPIO

The Havilfar Cycle

I. MANHOUNDS OF ANTARES
II. ARENA OF ANTARES
III. FLIERS OF ANTARES
IV. BLADESMAN OF ANTARES
V. AVENGER OF ANTARES
VI. ARMADA OF ANTARES

The Krozair Cycle

I. THE TIDES OF KREGEN

First Printing, August 1976

1 2 3 4 5 6 7 8 9

PRINTED IN CANADA
COVER PRINTED IN U.S.A.

Table of Contents

List of Illustrations

A Note on the Krozair Cycle

With this volume of his saga, Dray Prescot is hurled afresh into brand-new adventures on the planet of Kregen, that grim and beautiful, marvelous and terrible world four hundred light-years away beneath the red and green fires of Antares, under the Suns of Scorpio.

Dray Prescot is a man of above medium height, with brown hair and brown eyes that are level and dominating. His shoulders are immensely wide and he carries himself with an abrasive honesty and a fearless courage. He moves like a great hunting cat, quiet and deadly. Born in 1775 and educated in the inhumanly harsh conditions of the late eighteenth century English navy, he presents a picture of himself that, the more we learn of him, grows no less enigmatic.

Through the machinations of the Savanti nal Aphrasöe, mortal but superhuman men dedicated to the aid of humanity, and of the Star Lords, the Everoinye, he has been taken to Kregen many times. On that savage and exotic world he rose to become Zorcander of the clansmen of Segesthes, and Lord of Strombor in Zenicce.

Against all odds Prescot won his highest desire and in that immortal battle at The Dragon's Bones claimed his Delia, Delia of Delphond, Delia of the Blue Mountains. And Delia claimed him in the face of her father, the dread Emperor of Vallia. Amid the rolling thunder of the acclamations of "Hai Jikai!" Prescot became Prince Majister of Vallia and wed his Delia, the Princess Majestrix. One of their favorite homes is Esser Rarioch in Valkanium, capital of the island of Valka of which Prescot is Strom.

Far to the west of Turismond, the western continent of this grouping of continents and islands called Paz, lies the inner sea, the Eye of the World. There Prescot as a swifter captain became a member of the mystic and martial Order of Krozairs of Zy. He says he values his membership of the Krzy more highly than any other of his honors.

After a series of adventures on the continent of Havilfar, during which he fought in the arena of the Jikhorkdun and became King of Djanduin, idolized by his ferocious four-armed Djangs, Prescot managed to stay alive to thwart the plans of the Empress Thyllis of Hamal. In the Battle of Jholaix Hamal was defeated and an uneasy peace ensued. Prescot and Delia and the children returned to Esser Rarioch in Valka looking forward to a happy and contented life.

Thus ends the Havilfar cycle. This volume, *Tides of Kregen*, opens the Krozair Cycle. Kregen is a world too rich in passion and action to allow a fighting man like Dray Prescot to rest for long. Once more, then, Prescot is launched into fresh adventures, but this time there is a hiatus which, I believe, might easily break a man of lesser fire and spirit than Dray Prescot, Krozair of Zy.

Alan Burt Akers

Chapter One

The Star Lords' warning

When two wizards begin quarreling it is time for sensible men to take cover,

"You young fambly, Khe-Hi!" Evold Scavander spluttered and fumed, his bewhiskered peppery features fairly glowing with baffled fury. "You lord of mumbo jumbo!" I fancied he would explode at any moment. He sneezed, powerfully, and Khe-Hi-Bjanching took a smart step backward, waving a hand before his young and handsome face.

"Now, old man, admit you have no powers to penetrate—"

"Powers! Powers! I've had more powers than you've had loloo's eggs for breakfast!" Evold swiped away at his face with a huge square of silk, all bright orange and red and brown. "I tell you, you arrogant puffed-up wizard of Loh, I put no store by this tomfoolery of appearances—"

"I saw, Evold, you ninny! I *saw!*"

"You saw the remains of last night's dopa, you young whippersnapper." He sneezed again, a veritable gusher of effort. The handkerchief swiped fretfully. "I'm the wizard to the Prince and don't you forget it!"

"To the Prince you may be anything, old man, I do not doubt. But a wizard!" Here Khe-Hi-Bjanching, that young and superior Wizard of Loh, laughed most sardonically, cutting old San Evold to the quick. "I grant you do have a power, aye, a mighty fine power of drowning a man in your sneezes! But as a wizard you would do well sweeping out the zorcadrome."

"I'll—I'll—"

"What? Cast a spell and turn me into a toad? Well, go on. Try."

9

"That mumbo jumbo is for you young fools. I know what I know."

They were really going at each other now, there on the terrace of my high fortress of Esser Rarioch in Valkanium. Only by chance had I come on them, being troubled in mind and going to find old Evold Scavander. When two wizards quarrel it behooves a mere man to be circumspect about taking himself off, but I stood for a short space in the shadow of a pillar watching them, the pressure on my spirits a little relieved by their antics.

Khe-Hi-Bjanching waxed more vociferous, his white gown with the crimson rope around his waist a blaze of radiance in the streaming light of the suns. "And I know we have had a visitation. If you do not instantly let me pass to report to the Prince he'll have your head off and have you hanging by the heels from the highest battlements of Esser Rarioch."

"The Prince would not condone such barbarities. He'd as lief trim your height by a head."

They went on like fighting cocks. With shrill squeals my younger twins, Segnik and Velia, scampered around the corner. They could run well now and were involved in some activity that made them oblivious to the quarrel. By the time they realized what was going on, a realization matched to their understanding of funny old San Evold and clever San Khe-Hi, Turko the Shield appeared, his face grim, to seize them up with two muscular heaves, one under each arm. He did not see me and he carried the twins off with a gentle concern that pleased me, despite all their squawking for Unca Turko to let them watch the fight.

Turko the Shield, a mighty Khamorro whose superb body and muscles could break men and destroy armed and armored foemen, felt that altogether sensible desire to place as much distance as he could between himself and a couple of wizards about to do each other mischief.

This quarrel appeared to me to be the outcome of the perfectly natural friction to be expected. Evold, who was the wisest of the wise men of my island Stromnate of Valka, shared the fears of the old when confronted by the eager zest of the young. But Evold had served me well and he ought to know he would never be cast off. Khe-Hi-Bjanching had yet to prove himself.

Turko's rumble, carrying off the younger twins, faded, and I smiled. Oh, yes here in my wonderful island of Valka in my high fortress of Esser Rarioch I could smile because I was with my Delia and my children; I could smile even though I knew with a pang of misgiving just what the Wizard of Loh meant when he talked of an apparition, of an appearance. This, then, explained the trouble that lay on my spirit. Although I had not seen the apparition this time, I had felt it and its evil power, malefic and altogether horrible in that high palace of light and laughter.

The twin Suns of Scorpio flooded their jade and ruby lights onto the high terrace; the bees buzzed in the flowers; the whole scene in that clear limpid air was one to dizzy the senses with beauty. Young Yallan halted at the end of the terrace, the hefty jar of water on his shoulder shaking and slopping as he hesitated to dare to pass. Yallan worked in the kitchens—he was not a slave, for neither Delia nor I will allow slaves in our lands—and he was paid well. He was a man, an apim, for we did not consider the carrying of heavy jars of water up the flights of steps a girl's work. He saw me and he slopped more water.

The time for fun had gone.

"Sans, Sans," I said, stepping forward. I used a gentle voice, but they both switched around smartly, knowing just who it was who spoke to them, and instantly started in hurling their sides of the argument at me. I held up a hand. They fell at once to silence.

"For the sake of Sweet Merrilissa, let young Yallan past. He spills the water, and it is a heavy task to carry it up."

"Yes, my Prince," they said, together, looking at Yallan as though he had sprouted horns. Yallan swallowed, walked past and turned and said, "My thanks, my Prince. Shall I call the palace guard? When two wizards . . ." He looked troubled.

"They merely riddle a puzzle, good Yallan. I thank you for your thought."

"Well, my Prince," he said, looking doubtfully at the two wizards, still standing on tiptoe and glowering at each other.

San Khe-Hi half turned his head, stared at Yallan and said with very much of a snake's hiss in his voice: "Be off, or I shall turn you into one of the little insects that crawl upon the floor!"

Yallan let out a screech and fled. He spilled drops of water as he went, but he did not drop the jar.

I said, "That was unkind, San. Unkind even if funny."

"There are important affairs of state, my Prince, that you must know—"

San Evold choked and sneezed. "Important! He wakes with a sore head from dopa and sees visions!"

"Not so, Evold. I know whereof Khe-Hi speaks. I have had visitations before, apparitions."

The Wizard of Loh nodded his head, the sunslight catching that blazing red hair and sheening brilliantly. "I told you so, you old dodderer! Go back to your chemicals and your cayferm and your silver boxes!"

But San Evold Scavander was not the wisest wise man in all Valka, just to be foisted off by a youngster, even if that young man was one of the famed and feared Wizards of Loh. He looked at me closely and he no longer sneezed.

"You speak sooth, my Prince. I know that. Then I would like to know more—all there is to tell. For there must be danger here." Then, unable to resist a last dig at Bjanching, he added: "For if danger threatens in Valka, I would not like to repose much confidence in this young fambly, for all he claims to be a Wizard of Loh."

"I'll show you!" began Bjanching.

I silenced them.

"Tell me what you have seen, San. All of it. And quickly."

He knew that tone of voice. As you know I had picked up this Wizard of Loh in the island of Ogra-gemush, when Delia and Merle and Bjanching and I had been put to the test of the two doors by that unhappy King Wazur of Ogra-gemush. He had heard me and he had seen me in very different circumstances from these wonderful surroundings of Esser Rari-och, so he answered up quickly and succinctly.

"I awoke with the sure knowledge that a Wizard of Loh in lupu had appeared here. I could sense the locus. I saw him, not a strong manifestation; but I know he was evil."

"Aye," I said. "Aye. Unless I am mistaken that is the manifestation of the Wizard of Loh called Phu-Si-Yantong."

Bjanching drew in his breath with a hiss. I had spoken to him of Yantong, enough to acquaint him with that devil's evil intentions toward not only me and my family here in Valka, but also of his insane ambition to rule the whole continent of Havilfar and the island Empire of Vallia also, of which my Delia's father was Emperor.

"The malefic force was great," said Bjanching. He was a young man, the only young Wizard of Loh I had seen up to then. Sometimes his spells did not work. He was eager and willing to learn, and highly contemptuous of those who put no store by his powers. "He was in lupu at a great distance."

"The greater the distance the better," I said. Lupu is that trancelike state into which the Wizards of Loh can place themselves and so see and observe over distances. Phu-Si-Yantong had given orders that I was not to be assassinated, for he planned to use me in his evil schemes. From time to time he kept an observation on me. Now that I had my own Wizard of Loh I wondered if I might use Bjanching in more practical ways.

I looked at him. He was well aware of his enormous good fortune in being still alive and, into the bargain, of having a standing at my court in Esser Rarioch.

"Tell me, San. Is it possible to counter these intrusions in some way?"

"Yes, Prince," he said quickly. Too quickly, for his face clouded and he thought, then said: "It depends on the strength of the wizard."

"He is very powerful. With no disrespect to you, I hazard the guess he is the most powerful Wizard of Loh outside Loh itself, at least as far as I can judge."

"Then I can set up a defense which will slow him down. I can fool him, for a space. After that . . ."

"He has purely physical ambitions. He wishes, quite insanely, to assume powers of overlordship in as many countries and nations as he can contrive. I think that weakens him."

All this time San Evold had been spluttering and sneezing away in a minor key. Now he burst out: "Well, by Vox! Why do you not take a great armada and crush him, my Prince?"

I smiled. "The question is, San, where is he? What are his powers? I do not forget he is in alliance with two evil men I know: Vad Garnath of Hamal, a man who would benefit the whole of Kregen by dying, and the Kataki Strom, the personification of devilment."

"Katakis." Khe-Hi-Bjanching pursed his lips. "They are bad business, by Hlo-Hli!"

"Then begin at once, San. Call on my chamberlain Panshi for whatever you require. I would have my house cleansed of these visitations. One day Phu-Si-Yantong may appear with a greater desire than mere observation." I turned to Evold. "And, San Evold, you would greatly oblige me by rendering assistance to San Khe-Hi."

Evold's old stained smock quivered. He sneezed. But he got out, "Right gladly, my Prince," well enough. I knew I could trust him, and he would provide a useful check on Bjanching until I was fully satisfied as to that young Wizard of Loh's credentials.

As they went off, to go by way of the long hall of the images to that lofty room given over to San Evold as a laboratory, I was pleased to see they had forgotten their quarrel. Already they were talking as wizard to wizard, in their two very different disciplines, anxious to hatch out a likely scheme to foil this Opaz-forsaken Wizard of Loh who was trying to play dirty tricks on their ruler.

I sighed. Truly, I had to be thankful to Zair for the quality of my friends and companions.

That made me itch for Seg—for Seg Segutorio had taken his wife Thelda and their children and gone flying off to pay a call on his homeland of Erthyrdrin. That was a visit long overdue. As for Inch, he was up in his Black Mountains of Vallia working like a beaver on a new dam that would bring prosperity to one of his valleys and its people.

There was nothing I could do about Seg and Inch, for I never forgot they had their own lives to lead, both being Kovs of Vallia, and for the moment there was nothing more I could do about foiling that rast of a Phu-Si-Yantong. So, throwing off these cares that were, after all, only dreamlike in quality, I went off to find Balass the Hawk and my eldest son Drak and see how they fared. I was most interested in Drak's education. He was growing up now, he and his twin sister Lela, and while my Delia had indicated very firmly that she fully intended to take care of Lela's education herself, it was my responsibility to see about that rapscallion Drak. I had not smothered him with titles and honors, as so many powerful men of the Empire suffocated their sons. Delia and I had created the rank and title of Amak in Valka. This was, in Hamal, the lowest rank of nobility. We possessed a tiny island just off the north coast of Valka, a place no more than a dwabur across and three dwaburs long. It was called Vellendur. So with a small and deliberately low-key ceremony we had created our son Drak the Amak of Vellendur. The people there were apims, a simple fisher and weaving folk, who had sent as many stalwart sons—aye, and daughters—as they could when we had freed Valka from the evil grip of the slave-masters and the aragorn.

An ample gift had seen to many of their wants and they were grateful for what had been done for them, for they had suffered when the aragorn had ridden in, powerful and haughty, to drag away their people into slavery. So now Drak was the Amak of Vellendur. I fancied he was pleased. But I'd told him in no uncertain terms that he wasn't to begin to get puffed-up ideas of his own importance, and his allowance was kept very low. Delia handled that, I felt it was perhaps a trifle too low and so from time to time I would slip him a handful of valens, or buy him a zorca colt or a stavrer pup. When Delia found out she was angry, but I thought that Drak was learning the lessons he must learn for life not only on Kregen but on any world where men traffic together and there are lords and those who are not lords.

Balass the Hawk, that fierce hyr-kaidur, was giving Drak all the benefits of the higher arts of swordsmanship as it affected Balass. He'd been a hyr-kaidur in the arena of Hyrklana with me and was a supreme secutor. This meant he understood the ways of sword and shield. For others of the arts of war we went to others of my friends and companions.

So, going down the stairs that led to the walled-in sandy enclosure where Balass sweated away, I paused, looking out under the steaming rays of the twin suns.

I felt shock.

It was quick—far too quick, by Zim-Zair!

Against that opaline radiance floated a dark shadow. I saw the widespread wings, the squat head, the raked-forward talons. This bird of prey was not large enough, or shaped correctly, to be a flutduin, the superb saddle bird we in Valka were adopting slowly. This was a bird I had seen many and many a time during my life on Kregen, this planet four hundred light-years from the world of my birth, this glorious world of Kregen under Antares which held all of life I held dear.

This marvelous world of Kregen held also the Gdoinye, the messenger and spy for the Everoinye, the Star Lords.

I stared up at the silhouette of the bird and the Gdoinye flicked his wings and so dived directly for me.

My hand jerked spasmodically to the rapier scabbarded at my side. But, even then, I wondered of what use mortal steel would be against this gorgeous scarlet and gold raptor. The bird wheeled before me with a harsh and raucous cry. I knew that if anyone looked on this scene they would not see the bird, for the Star Lords, who had brought me across the interstellar gulfs, protected their servants, although they took scant heed for my hide.

"Dray Prescot! Idiot! Fool! Onker!"

"Aye!" I shouted back. "I am all of those things, for I do spit you through!"

The bird screeched again, windblown laughter or a mere bird's cry I knew not. "You are a high and mighty man, these latter days. You are a noble, a prince, a Prince Majister, no less."

"These things have come to me through no seeking of mine." I hurled the words at the Gdoinye but I know now that I spoke of my humility with pride, with foolish pride.

"Nonetheless you hold high position here in Valka, and in Vallia, no less than in Strombor or with your clansmen of Segesthes. And, Dray Prescot, are you not also the King of Djanduin?"

"You know it, you cramph of a bird."

"You are the cramph, onker, for you forget why you were brought to Kregen at all."

"I never knew, you get-onker!"

The bird screeched again, and this time, I swear, the mocking amusement at my own stupidity sounded clearly in the cry.

"You were never meant to know. And you think you may defy the Star Lords, you puny human mortal?"

I made no reply. The Star Lords, who could hurl me away from Kregen and all I loved back to Earth four hundred light-years off through space, had never bothered themselves about my welfare, only calling on me to perform tasks for them. But they had not troubled me for a very long time now. Although it would be foolish to say I had forgotten them, their eternal menace had drifted into the back of my mind. Now I was being reminded of my true position.

"Have I failed you yet?" I spoke quickly as the Gdoinye swerved, all a shimmer of scarlet and gold beneath that streaming opaline radiance from the twin suns.

"You fail at your peril! There is work to your hand!"

"And if I refuse?"

"You may not refuse, Dray Prescot. You are not a pawn nor yet are you the master of your fate. Think on, Dray Prescot, think on these things."

The Gdoinye said *swod* and not pawn, but I knew damn well what he meant. But I did not know what he meant by saying I was not a pawn. I had struggled against the Star Lords in the past and felt I had gained some advantage over them; I fancied there was a great deal more to learn before I could banish them from my scheme of things.

"You are a great man, Dray Prescot, with your string of titles and your lands and money and power. The Star Lords exact strict obedience from those they select to serve their ends."

"You nurdling great onker!" I bellowed. "What are these ends and what are the Star Lords trying to do here on Kregen?"

This time I was certain the damned bird laughed at me in a great cackling cry and a ruffling of feathers. He bore up and his pinions beat widely and he soared up and away. As I stared up after him his departing cry wafted down, hoarse and mocking.

"The Star Lords are most considerate of you, Dray Prescot. They send me to warn you, to give you time. Think how puissant are the Star Lords, and how generous!"

Then he was a mere dot against the radiance and then he was gone.

Feeling in a foul mood I went down to the sandy arena. Drak was thwacking away at Balass, making his shield gong. Every now and then Balass would reach out and touch Drak with his wooden sword, just to remind him and make him jump about a bit.

"Father!" said Drak, leaping back most agilely and turning to me. "Father! I saw a monstrous great bird, all red and gold, in the sky, making a most terrible noise."

I just stared at him.

"There was no bird, Drak," said Balass. "I saw nothing."

"No," I said, most heavily. "No, Drak. I saw nothing."

Chapter Two

Shanks against Valka

Delia was swimming when I walked into our private walled garden high on the flank of Esser Rarioch. Below the far wall the expanse of the Bay was visible, with a small portion of the city of Valkanium and ships sailing to and from the harbor with white sails burnished by the sun's glow. I stood for a while on the flags watching as Delia lazed through the water.

Every time I look at my Delia, my Delia of the Blue Mountains, my Delia of Delphond, I feel that thump of blood at my heart, that constriction of my throat. I may be accused of many things on two worlds, and if I am accused of saying the name of Delia more often than most, then I defend my right to that—no! I do not defend! I scorn anyone cloddish enough not to understand the glory and the magic and the love her name evokes—my Delia, my Delia of Strombor, my Delia of Vallia!

Thinking these savage and chauvinistic thoughts I walked down the wide shallow steps into the garden until the flower-covered wall concealed all the vista below so that Delia and I were completely alone in our own private garden.

She saw me and waved a bare arm and dived and swam under the water to the marble edge of the pool. I waited for her and bent to lift her out while she caught me cunningly and pulled, dropping back. With a mighty splash we both went in.

I spluttered and tried to catch her, but she was eellike, flashing, glorious, and for a while we swam and played and I forgot the cares of government and high politics and the snares and entrapments of my enemies.

That gorgeous brown hair of Delia's with those enraging

chestnut highlights floated on the water as she lay on her back, kicking with her feet. She splashed me, so I splashed back, and we met, breast to breast, without struggling, and sank down into the blue water. When we came up for breath she said: "And have you seen Segnik and Velia, Dray? They both deserve a spanking for what they did to poor Aunt Katri."

"They only hid her wool, dear—"

"They must learn to behave themselves."

"Yes."

We climbed out and sat on the grass to sun ourselves dry. The glory of the suns fell on the garden and on the fairest flower within that garden—well, I well not maunder on. All this made me feel the agony of what might befall if the Star Lords called on me again. I meant to speak to Delia. But how to explain to your wife that you had never been born on the world where she was born? How to explain that you came from a speck of light in the sky four hundred light-years away, a world that possessed only one sun? Only one moon?

How tell that on that world lived men, apims, Homo sapiens, and there were none of the other races of men that made Kregen so marvelous and horrible a place? How could she be expected to believe? One sun only? A solitary moon? Only apims? She would shake her head and laugh and push me in the pool.

I said: "I may have to go away again."

It was brutal.

She turned to me.

"You mean it?"

"Yes."

"Oh, Dray! Can you tell me? Long ago I made up my mind never to ask. I remember the strangeness of our first meetings, the time I spent in the Opal Palace of Zenicce, and the time you said you had spent with our clansmen. Dray! I am frightened to know, and yet, and yet I must know. . . ."

"I will tell you, Delia, my heart, one day. I promise."

"And how you made yourself the Strom of Valka, and yet there was no time, for we marched through the hostile territories of Turismond, with Seg and Thelda, and that awful Umgar Stro, and—"

"Hush, hush. It will not hurt you, save for the parting."

"That is like a death."

"I know."

Banal words. But then, banal words mean so much when the hearts of those saying them tremble so in agitation and unspoken apprehension.

We spoke then of the ordinary familiar things of our life, those items of consuming importance to us. Segnik and Velia must be spoken to. Lela was to visit friends in Quivir, where that rip Vangar Riurik, the Strom owing allegiance to me as the Kov of Zamra, was throwing a party. For Drak I had other plans, and as I spelled them out Delia nodded, her sweet face downturned and her hair spreading in a glowing brown and golden flood. She knew from our experiences together that what I suggested was not only sensible, it would give Drak the best of all possible chances on this terrible world of Kregen. We spoke of the new watercourses to be sculpted into the gardens, and I slowly suggested that we change the plans to a pump to bring water up higher still, a wind-driven pump, so the kitchen staff might be relieved of one burden. Delia agreed at once.

She lay back, glanced under the suns and rubbed her bare tanned stomach. "I am hungry."

"Yes, and I have a meeting with my Elders after the meal. . . ."

"After! Why didn't you invite them?"

"I wanted to be with you and the twins."

"Oh."

So we stood up and, our arms around each other, went slowly up out of that scented garden back into the high fortress of Esser Rarioch and, after one of the essential meals of Kregen, got to the business of running the country.

There was much to discuss but I will not weary you with a recounting of the measures we took, for although they were of consuming interest to me then—and still are, by Zair!—they were much of the stuff of government in many places and worlds, I dare say. Zamra was still giving us a little trouble over the question of slaves. I ruled—if that is not too strong a word to use—from my palace of Esser Rarioch in Valkanium, the capital of Valka, not only Valka herself, but Zamra and the other islands also. These included Can Thirda.

So far no one had agreed on a new name for the island since it had been pacified after the troubles and then given to me as a gift by the Emperor, I had vetoed Prescotdrin and Draydrin, regarding the latter as downright ugly. I thought then that I would never have a land named after me, in which I was wrong, as you shall hear. I wanted Deliadrin. My word carried much weight, of course, the chief opponent being Delia herself.

She rather fancied Can Drak, but then again perhaps Leladrin would be nice, or maybe . . . and she would pause and put her chin on her fist and gaze around the table, her laughing eyes sizing us up, one by one, until those solid, respectable—aye, and some ruffianly too!—men of mine would shuffle their feet and then, despite all, smile broadly in response. I think we had a good life then. I know it. I knew, very positively, that I did not wish to leave.

So we discussed and decided on the cares of statecraft until a messenger burst in, wild-eyed, disheveled, thrusting past the guards who had the sense to let him pass.

"My Prince!" he bellowed. Blood stained down his face, brown and cracked, oozing where the sweat ran across the bright wound. "Leem Lovers! They have razed Fossheim! The village burned—burned—" He staggered and would have fallen but a guard caught him and quickly carried him to a seat.

Delia brought wine herself. He swallowed painfully. "My Princess—"

"What of Fossana?" I said. I spoke more roughly than I intended, for the man braced up in the seat, staring with wild eyes.

"The island—" He choked and swallowed and began again. "We fought. There were ten of us, ten and a Deldar—lookouts—we fought—Deldar Nath the Shiv—they were devils, devils! Fishheads! They cut us down!"

Tom Tomor ti Vulheim, an old blade comrade and a man with whom I had happily fought when we took Valka from those damned aragorn, was already running for the door, the sword on his hip banging. He was yelling. Tom, whom I had made take the name of Tomor from the battle we had fought under Tomor Peak, and who was the Elten of Avanar, was now the general of my armies of Valka. I could trust him to take what were the immediately necessary measures against these fishheads, these weirdly repellent diffs sailing around the curve of the world from the other grouping of continents and islands of Kregen to rape and plunder and burn.

The full significance of this latest assault was not lost on us. We were to the north of the equator, and the Leem Lovers sailed up generally from the south, to attack the continent of Havilfar and its associated islands down there. They had penetrated to the north of Havilfar and over to the west up the Hoboling Islands. For them to have come this far north could only mean they had stepped up their activity. Why they had done so still remained a mystery. Our immediate task was to drive them back and prevent their making a base on the sweet little island of Fossana.

Delia glanced at me and I saw that she was moved.

There was more than mere agony over the despoiling of one of the islands which looked to us for protection. For the island of Fossana, to the south and east of the island of Valka, had been marked out by me as so charming and delightful a spot that the title of Amakni of Fossana should be the proud title of our daughter Lela, to match her twin brother Drak. But Delia had put a slender finger to her lips and shaken her head and said, "Not yet, my great grizzly graint of a husband. You always rush into things headlong. Let Drak have the glory for a space, for he will ..." And then she had paused and bit her lip.

So I finished for her: "One day, if we were ordinary people, he would take my place."

But, speaking thoughtlessly, she had forgotten that by virtue of a dip in the Pool of Baptism in the River Zelph of far Aphrasöe, she and I were assured of a thousand years of life.

The fuller implications of that situation must wait their rightful place in this telling of my life on Kregen.

For now Delia was indicating to me that, had we let Lela become the Amakni of Fossana, she might have been there now, when the shanks came in their swift strange craft. She might have ...

I said, "We must drive them out of Fossana rapidly. I believe they seek a secure base here." I looked down on the swod and his blood-caked face. "You have done well to reach here. Your name?"

"Barlanga, my Prince. I took our patrol flier. I ran from them—I flew away—" He choked and then got it out. "My comrades were dead. I was the last. I should have—"

"No, Barlanga. You did the right thing. Now we know and may fall on these devil shanks with great force."

Then I was out of the conference chamber and yelling.

Very few burs after that the fliers took to the air, all the airboats cramed with fighting men, raging to hurl these hated shanks, these evil Leem Lovers, these fishheads back into the sea where they belonged.

"We were slow, by Vox!" Vangar ti Valkanium, my chief of fliers, grumbled away as he gripped the rail of the high deck, peering over the head of the timoneer at the controls. Men massed forward on the main deck of the flier, armed and armored men, raging to get at the shanks. This flier was one we had acquired in the old days and so far she had failed us less often than others. Those fliers I had taken from Hamal, built for the Hamalians themselves, formed an elite squadron and they were well ahead with Tom Tomor in command.

I fretted at the delay, but I said, "We must have sure knowledge before we attack, Vangar. The onslaught on Fossana could easily be a ruse. These devil fishheads are not fools."

"You are right, Majister. I meant we were slow assembling and forming and taking to the air."

My ugly old face does not smile easily when I am not with Delia and the children. "We did well, Vangar, and you know it. Does the title of Elten then sit so heavily on you?"

"You have created me an Elten, my Prince; that is the least of my worries."

The air streamed past, whirling the banners and pennons high, blowing the bright arbora feathers in helmets into riotous color. Up there on a gilded staff my flag flew, the yellow cross on the scarlet ground, that battle flag fighting men call Old Superb. It felt good to have that war banner flying there. Ahead the sky remained clear and blue and the sea below lapped deep and calm. Ahead lay horror and battle and sudden death.

The parting with Delia had been brief, for I had kissed her and then run to don my trappings of war. She had insisted I

wear armor, and not only to please her but because it was a
sensible precaution I wore a breast and back. The short scarlet cape flared in the wind of our passage. The old scarlet
breechclout was wrapped securely and pulled in with a
broad plain lesten-hide belt with a dull silver buckle. I do not,
as you know, care to have straps around my chest or shoulders, and generally hang my varied collection of swords from
whatever number of belts is necessary around my waist. I had
a rapier and main-gauche of fine Vallian manufacture. That
particular sword which Naghan the Gnat, a superb armorer,
and I had made in imitation of a Krozair longsword hung
scabbarded down my back under the cape. These were
weapons enough, but in addition I had belted on a fine
thraxter that had come into my possession after the Battle of
Jholaix. As for headgear, I wore a plain steel cap with a rim
of trimmed ling fur and with a rather more flaunting scarlet
tuft of feathers than I would ordinarily relish. The thing had
a most Tartar air about it, but Delia had insisted I wear some
helmet, and the tall scarlet tufts of feathers would show my
men where I was.

That made me glance at Turko, massive and muscled,
where he stood with the enormous shield he would bear in
action to protect me. Where Turko the Shield went, men
knew, there went Dray Prescot, Prince Majister of Vallia,
Strom of Valka.

As the aerial armada pressed on I had time to consider,
somewhat ruefully, that Valka's own fleet of great sailing
fliers could not hurtle across the wind as we were doing. I
had assigned them to defense of the island. One day I must
return to Havilfar and go to Hamal, that puissant Empire under its evil ruler, Thyllis who was now crowned Empress, and
discover the final secrets of the silver boxes that powered,
uplifted and directed the fliers.

Our fleet of airboats pressed on. Now we flew over the
scattering of islands called the Nairnairsh Islands, from the
huge numbers of nairnair birds that made of every rocky
headland a cawing, fluttering colony of white and brown
feathers. I could see a few small ships sailing, fishermen, local
traders, and I looked—thankfully in vain—for a sight of the
tall, winglike banded sails of the shanks.

"Not far now, my Prince."

Balass the Hawk stood at my side, fully armored, his visor thrown up, grim and yet splendid, with his hawklike black face a great comfort to me.

The wind bluster cracked Old Superb above our heads. The suns glittered from armor and weapons. I turned and, looking ahead, said, "Not long now, Balass."

In those days I felt no admiration for the true courage of the shanks, of the shanks, those fishheads who sailed in their superb craft around the curve of the world, sailing from their grouping of continents and islands to sack and destroy the fair cities of our continental grouping of Paz. These shanks, these Leem Lovers, were superb seamen. Yet I knew, as an old sailor, that after their immense voyage across the open sea they would need a secure base, a good anchorage, a place to careen and refurbish their ships, a place to get their breath back after the voyage. Fossana would be such a place. They must not be allowed to make a base so close to Valka. . . .

"We must stop them here," I said, still looking across the sea, willing the voller to fly faster and bring us to the battle quickly. "They must not be allowed a chance to fester here."

A voice spoke at my back, a voice that made me go cold from the very first syllables.

"We will fight them, Father, and we will win!"

Slowly I turned around.

Young Drak—my son—Drak—stood there in brave panoply, all scarlet and gold, staring up at me with a set and defiant expression across his face. He knew what he had done. He had no fear of the terrible shanks, but he was most uneasy about my reaction.

With him—Delia!

She smiled at me.

My heart leaped. She wore a scarlet breechclout, a breast and back, and a helmet very much like the one she had insisted I wear. She carried her rapier and main-gauche scabbarded to her slender waist, and I knew how well she could use them, the Jiktar and the Hikdar.

"Delia," I said. "You should not have allowed him."

"He is like you, Dray. A wild leem. And is this not to be his portion in life?"

"Aye."

Oby stood there also, accoutred, smiling away at me, rel-

ishing his part in the coming battle. As a young rip he had a
most dubious effect on Drak. Young Oby had mended much
of his wild ways when he had been my assistant in the arena;
now his passion was all for vollers and the mysteries of aerial
navigation, but it was clear he intended to get into the coming fight.

"And Naghan the Gnat?"

"I am here!" shouted Naghan and, in truth, there he was,
loaded down with choice specimens from his own armory,
smiling away like a loon. I shook my head.

"Mad, the lot of you. . . ." I looked past Naghan. "And
you, Tilly, you are here also."

"Yes, my Prince," said Tilly, her glorious golden fur glowing in the light of the Suns of Scorpio, for Tilly was a most
delicious little Fristle fifi.

A mewling and harshly screeching roar told me that Melow the Supple had also come with us. I stared at Melow and
the ferocious manhound stretched her neck up, then put out a
fearsomely clawed hand to keep her son Kardo from beginning one of the interminable fights he was always into with
Drak. Well, I welcomed Melow and Kardo, for the jiklos are
terrible and ferocious, mighty in their strength. Although
really human beings, they have been changed so that they run
on all fours and possess the fighting ferocity of the leem.

"Melow, your son Kardo will be with Drak?"

"Yes, Dray Prescot. For that is where he wills he should
be."

"And you will be with the Princess Majestrix."

Melow lolled her red tongue between those horrific jagged
teeth, and I felt a little more easy. Mind you, once I had this
circus home I would let them know just what my true
thoughts were on this foolhardy rushing into danger. Didn't
they understand the sheerly awful power of the shanks?
Didn't they realize they could all be killed?

A lookout shouted from forward and I swung around to
look ahead. A cloud hung in the sky athwart our passage, a
cloud that must have grown with incredible swiftness, for
only murs before the sky had been clear.

A dun shadow swept across the glittering sea below and in
an instant we plunged into the cloud. Dank tendrils of vapor
brushed us, clinging and unpleasant. Vision was reduced so

that I could see only those faces near me; beyond the quarter-deck the ship vanished.

Shouts and yells arose. That cloud—how could it have formed so quickly?

The voller jerked. I knew that feeling. The flier lurched and skidded sideways. Her nose went down. We were falling.

"Those Opaz-forsaken cramphs of Hamal!" yelled Vangar, incensed that once again his duty as chief of fliers was to preside over a crash.

"Silence!" I bellowed.

In the ensuing hush we heard the wind bluster and roar as we fell. Slowly the haze cleared and we dropped free of the cloud. I looked up. The rest of our fleet was winging swiftly on, arrow-straight for Fossana. Now it would all be up to Tom Tomor, and it would be to him the responsibility would fall. I looked down. An island below showed creamy surf breaking on a beach. Massive trees crowded close, and there were at least three village clearings visible. Men were running below. Men like myself, apims, and also weird forms with grotesque fish heads, scaled and armored, running with vicious tridents flashing in the suns, weapons stained with the blood of my people.

"*Shanks!*"

The voller hit the sand. Ahead the wooden palisade of a village offered shelter. Everyone leaped from the stranded voller, running fleetly for the village. Heads appeared over the stockade.

A flight of arrows rose and I cursed. Then I realized the arrows curved away, falling into a body of fishheads who were trying to cut us off.

"Run!" I bellowed.

Straight for the village gate we raced. The valves were dragged open. We tumbled through the opened portal and the villagers slammed the heavy lenken logs back with a thunk. Iron bars dropped. The headman came running up, distraught, wringing his hands. Simple fisher folk these, used to landing fine fat fish in their nets, and now they faced man-sized fishheads raging at them, armed with tridents, swords and bows, their plunder from the sea revenging itself horribly on them.

He knew me.

"Majister! Majister! Monsters—they—"

"Man the walls! Keep your heads down!" I shook his shoulder. "It will be all right, Koter, all right."

"Yes, Majister, yes—but the fishheads—"

We could hold this place until my fliers returned. We must hold this place! Nothing else would do. Nothing.

The Leem Lovers were in force, roaring in to attack, hurling spears and tridents, shooting arrows. My men replied with the cool precise shooting Seg Segutorio had drilled into them. These men were Valkan Archers, but they used the great Lohvian longbow and they could outshoot the compound reflex bows of the shanks. Spare supplies of shafts had been brought from the flier, for Jiktar Orlon Llodar in command of the regiment was an officer in whom I reposed confidence. He did not have his full regiment with him, for half had been embarked on another flier, packed in like fish in a barrel. With three pastangs of sixty men each we must hold off an unknown number of fishheads.

I leaped up onto the parapet around the stockade. The village possessed a stockade because these islands were often the scene of raids from Pandahem, or from a dissident nation of Segesthes beyond Zenicce, or, in the old days, from the slavers and aragorn. Along the beach the voller lay stranded, and shanks were already clambering and running there. I cursed. From the trees other shanks were running. The devils must have beached their ships and marched overland. There had not been a sign of a shank ship as we crash-landed.

A circuit of the stockade brought me back to the parapet over the main gate. This faced along the beach, as I have said, and not out to sea or inland. Defensive considerations dictated that choice. A small protected harbor held a few fishing boats, little better than dories. The circuit of the walls had shown me we could hold. A stream trickled down from the forest so we would have water, if the Leem Lovers did not divert or dam the stream.

"Now, Jiktar," I said brusquely to Orlon Llodar. "Now is the chance to show that the Second Regiment of Valkan Archers can do better than the First."

Before Llodar could answer, young Drak, who had followed me around most carefully, sniffed. "I would like very much to see that," he said. I glared at him. As you know,

Drak is the Hyr-Jiktar—colonel in chief—of the First Regiment of Valkan Archers. Lela was Hyr-Jiktar of the Second.

Orlon Llodar smacked his buff-sleeved arm across his breastplate. He wore a bob there. "We shall, my Prince, and with due respect to Prince Drak, outshoot the finest the First could offer this day."

"I believe you. These yetches of fishheads will try to fool us. They will feint an attack on one flank and then drive in on another. All faces of the stockade must be kept under observation at all times. Have a party of swordsmen handy to rush to the threatened wall. And watch out for their Opaz-forsaken tridents. They are vicious."

"My Prince!" he bellowed, in the old soldierly way.

Barbaric and savage are my warriors of Valka and they love little better than a rousing fight, but we had been knocking drill and discipline into them. They would have full need of all their courage and skill now.

But we could hold. With determined and skillful leadership we could defy the Leem Lovers. I was determined enough, Zair knows, and as to skill . . . well, this bore the appearance of a militarily simple defense of the fortified place. If they tried to burn us out . . . I bellowed for the headman, one Remush the Trident, for he was a noted fisherman, and got him to organize fire fighting parties of his people with all the buckets and containers they could find. This was the village of Panashti on the island of Lower Kairfowen. I fancied these names would be remembered henceforth, filling men's mouths.

"I wish, my Prince, that my pastangs were at full strength." Jiktar Llodar stared with venom at the shanks as they massed at the forest edge.

"All the more glory, Jiktar, for those who are here."

That was cheap enough, Zair knows, but it fitted the occasion.

The gate looked sturdy in construction, with square towers and a walkway across the gap. "Here, Planath," I said, pointing. "Raise the standard here."

Planath Pe-Na, my standard-bearer, was a Pachak and a man of exceptional virtues. He rammed the standard pole into a crevice in the wood and then lashed it upright. Dead or alive, Planath would stay by the standard. I turned to

Kodar ti Vakkansmot, the chief of my corps of trumpeters. "Give a few good bracing calls, Kodar. Rouse the blood in 'em!"

"Aye, Majister."

The lilting peals of the trumpet sounded over the small stockaded village of Panashti on the island of Lower Kairfowen. I fancied the men would brace up at the sound, grip their weapons more firmly, glare the more murderously at their antagonists.

The blueness stole in quietly. It muffled the bright, brilliant sounds of the trumpet. It wrapped its baleful coils around me. I saw the blue radiance churning everywhere. The world was slipping away, I was falling, the whole world turning into the semblance of a giant Scorpion, come from the Star Lords to carry me far and far away.

Chapter Three

I defy the Star Lords

I, Dray Prescot, of Earth and of Kregen, knew what was happening to me.

This obscenity had taken me before, many times, snatched me away from pleasant home life with those I loved and hurled me into fresh adventures in Kregen under Antares. Even more balefully still, it had thrust me contemptuously back to the world of my birth four hundred light-years off through the depths of interstellar space.

"No!" I shouted.

I was falling, in actuality. For the blueness lifted, the radiance dwindled a little and I felt myself falling and in the next instant the ground smashed up iron hard. I was winded. I tried to yell again, to shout my defiance of the Star Lords and their commands.

I heard voices—Delia's voice, Drak's, others—shouting; through the misty blueness I saw forms above me; hands grasped my arms and legs and I was carried, swaying and swinging above the packed earth. A shadow blotted my sight of the forms dimly visible through the blue mist. I thought I must have been carried into one of the huts. The blueness grew again. "No! I will not leave! It is unthinkable!"

The blueness twirled about me, the Scorpion shape grew and grew and then, in very final truth, I was falling.

I was encompassed in a floating blueness. Everything turned blue, roaring and twisting in my skull.

"I will stay on Kregen!" I screamed it out, and I knew with a feeling close to despair that my scream gushed voicelessly from my mouth. I tried again. "I will not leave! More! I will not leave *here*!"

The sensations of falling persisted now with dread finality. The blueness coiled in my eyes and head; I could not speak, could scarcely breathe; a weight oppressed my chest. All manner of thoughts flitted like black bats through my mind. I felt the ground again, dust and heat, and the abrupt hammer of conflict bursting painfully through into my skull.

All the sensations I had come to except of a transition smashed at me. I was naked. I lay in the dust. And nearby a battle took place.

The Star Lords had contemptuously ignored my feeble yells of defiance. They had not banished me to Earth, for as I opened my eyes the glorious mingled lights of Antares fell about me, but I was no longer within the stockaded village of Panashti. I was no longer near Delia and Drak and all my other friends there.

On occasions before I had attempted to defy the Everoinye and instead of being banished to Earth had been dumped down, naked and unarmed on some unknown spot on Kregen, there to sort out a problem for the Star Lords. Always before I had obeyed. I knew that the quickest way to rid myself of the immediate obligation to the Star Lords was to obey their injunctions and to settle the problem at hand. Then, always, before, I had been able to go about my own business.

This time was different.

I sat up on the dusty ground and saw a sickeningly familiar sight.

A mass of crazed Relts ran and fell and were slaughtered as the shanks pursued them. I sat under the shadow of a voller parked beside two other vollers at the edge of a gulley in the dusty ground. I would have to stand up, all naked as I was, and run forward, into the fight, possess myself of a weapon and so defend these people against the Leem Lovers. This I could do. This was the way of it, the way of my life on Kregen. I was expected to take up arms at once and rush in to save the life of the one person—perhaps two, if a mother and child were involved—in that melee whom the Star Lords wished preserved.

What they were planning with the people whose lives I thus perpetuated I did not then know.

I didn't care, didn't give a damn.

This time I was Prince Majister. This time my wife and child were penned in a tiny rickety wooden village under savage attack from monsters from around the curve of the world.

Against the skyline beyond the struggle I saw twin peaks, forested, shaped like sugar loaves. They bulked there against the blue. I knew them. I knew where I was. This was the island of Vilasca. Vilasca, barely twenty dwaburs from the Nairnairsh Islands, and south of them the island of Lower Kairfowen. And, on that island, the village of Panashti!

I leaped up.

Barely twenty dwaburs. A mere hundred miles! A fleet voller might take less than two burs—much less—to cover that distance—a little over an hour. There are forty Earth minutes to a bur. If the flier was speedy . . .

Over there across the dusty earth where the Leem Lovers had swarmed ashore to catch these people all unprepared a vicious and bloody struggle raged. This island of Vilasca did not owe allegiance to me; I was not its Strom or Kov or any other noble. I felt desperately sorry for those people, but there was no question, no hesitation in my mind. My duty lay elsewhere.

The voller controls felt warm under my hands. I thrust the levers hard over. Again I forced the speed lever all the way across, hard against the stop. The voller leaped into the air, screaming away, curving to the east and south. Twenty dwaburs to go. . . .

As I shot over the beach and left that struggle I looked down.

What I saw shocked a fresh and awful knowledge into my brain. I saw the fighting down there, the wicked shapes of Leem Lovers as they went about their business of slaughtering the people of Vilasca. Among those shanks I saw the hideous forms of shtarkins. No one then knew the name these fishheads gave themselves; we called them by a variety of names of which shant, shank and shtarkin were only three. But the ones I called shtarkins were not fishheads. As I looked down I saw the reptilian heads, the snakelike features, the hard, unfishlike scales closely set, the wide eyes and the trap-mouths set flatly in wedge-shaped heads, a flicker of forked tongue darting through as they fought. Snakeheads!

The voller bore me up and away and I left those fearsome fighting shtarkins to slaughter the good people of Vilasca.

The shtarkins employed the tall asymmetric bow instead of the short compound reflex bow. I had no real knowledge of the asymmetric bow, but the thing shot an arrow fully as long as a great Lohvian longbow and was reputed accurate to prodigious ranges. Seg would have had his keen professional instincts immediately aroused. The arrows, cloth yard shafts, were tipped with long serrated heads. I saw one burst clean through a running woman, and as she fell my hands twisted the levers to bring me down.

But a vision arose, a vision of another woman falling beneath the arrows of the Leem Lovers. And that woman was Delia. With agony, with remorse, but decisively and with bitter determination, I smashed the levers back and shot the voller up and away.

I had selected this airboat as the fastest of the three, and my faith in my own judgment was proved as I cleaved the air, heading east and south. Somewhere far over the northwestern horizon lay the main island of Vallia, that great and puissant Empire of Vallia of which Delia's father, my children's grandfather, was Emperor. They would have to buckle to, now that they were thus cruelly beset.

As for the Star Lords—I would see them abandoned to the Ice Floes of Sicce before I would abandon Delia and Drak!

So I shot on. Looking back, I suppose the Star Lords, having always seen me operate in obedience to their commands before, held their hand. Once before I had taken a flier and left the scene of my labors to raise an army. That had been in Migladrin, when Turko and I had flown back to Valka to bring those fighting men of mine who had won the Battle of the Crimson Missals. But then I had not left a scene where immediate action had been necessary. Always before, when I had been hurled all naked into a strange part of Kregen, I had jumped up and obediently gone into action to save the lives of those the Star Lords wished preserved.

This time I had turned my back.

A bur ticked by, then a quarter of a bur.

Below me the sea clumped with the Nairnairsh Islands.

Not long to go now! My men must resist. They must hold

out until I was once more back among them to lead them to victory.

So puffed up with pride are the princes of the two worlds.

A shadow fleeted across me. I looked up. The scarlet and gold messenger of the Star Lords swung up there, circling lazily, riding the air currents. He was watching me. I did not shake my fist. I ignored him.

Frail hope!

He stooped, swooping down on the voller. He screeched.

"What is this thing you do, Dray Prescot?"

I said nothing.

"Onker! You destroy yourself!"

I flared back at him. "You great nurdling onker! Do you think I can leave my wife and my child in mortal danger for you?"

"Yes."

I hurled abuse at him, shaking my fist, screaming. The voller surged on. And there, below me the village of Panashti!

I slanted the voller down headlong through the air.

The shanks had put in an attack, for bodies sprawled before the stockade. Activity in the forest edge indicated a fresh attack at any moment. I had to be there, leading my men, fighting to protect my Delia and my son!

Even as the Gdoinye swooped in fast, I saw the scaled and fishy forms leaping forward with a shower of arrows to cover them. And, among the arrows, there blazed forth fire-arrows. Pots of fire were being hurled. Wisps of smoke lifted from the huts as the fire-arrows struck, as the pots of fire burst. Men and woman ran with their water buckets to douse the flames.

Almost there! I was yelling and shouting and beating my fist against the speed lever. I scarcely heard the Gdoinye.

"Onker, Dray Prescot! This is not for you! This is not the way of the Everoinye!"

"Get away, rast!" I bellowed. "I am needed below!"

Part of the stockade was burning. The shanks were making a determined attack there. They were running with ladders made from cut branches. I saw men struggling, the flash and wink of steel. Faintly through the wind's rush I could hear the bestial screams and shrieks. My fist beat the lever, I shouted and the Gdoinye swerved in and alighted on the very gunwale of the voller. I had never seen him so close before. He was truly magnificent, full of throat where the golden feathers encircled him, his scarlet feathers ruffling in the slipstream. His predatory black talons fastened on the wood and canvas of the voller. His black eyes, lit with inhuman intelligence, regarded me implacably.

"You are to be given another chance! Dray Prescot, getonker! You are to serve the Star Lords. They grant you a boon, a boon never granted to you before."

"Keep your boons, nulsh!"

The burning corner of the stockade was down. The shanks were smashing in with axes. Men were running. My Valkan Archers were running up to reinforce this threatened corner. The swordsmen were already in violent combat inside the palisade. More and more fishheads were clambering over the ruin of the walls. I screamed in baffled fury and swung the voller to alight directly on their heads. I would smash down from the sky clean on top of them. That should give my men a chance to rally.

The moment was coming. I measured the drop and checked the speed of the flier.

In a knot of struggling men I saw the glittering armored figure of Balass the Hawk, striking fishheads down. Turko the Shield appeared from a hut, struggling—struggling with Delia! She was trying to run after Drak—and Drak was racing headlong to hurl himself into the fray!

I shrieked—I, Dray Prescot, Lord of Strombor and Krozair of Zy—I shrieked like an insane man.

Melow the Supple and her son Kardo appeared, raging, striking down fishheads with the awful venom of the manhound. Their jagged teeth ran green with the spilled blood of the Leem Lovers. All the others were there, battling desperately to protect Delia. The voller slowed, for if I smashed headlong into the shanks I'd as likely kill myself as well as them. Any minute now. I perched up on the gunwale just abaft the windscreen, ready to leap into the fray.

Turko still held Delia and his great shield deflected two arrows that caromed away, spinning.

"Remember the great gift the Star Lords bestow on you, Dray Prescot, you onker!"

And then the scarlet and gold bird shifted and changed and flowed and the blueness of the Scorpion enfolded me.

Falling ... Falling ... Dropping down and down ...

I felt the dusty earth at my back. I heard the shrieks and cries of battle and I knew that this battle was not the one into which I wished to plunge but that other, strange, uninteresting, unwanted battle on the island of Vilasca.

I sprang up.

Then, instantly, I realized this great gift of the Star Lords.

For the very first time on Kregen I had been transported and had not arrived naked. I wore all my battle gear, the trappings in which I had flown off to fight the shanks.

"I curse you, Star Lords! This small thing is no great gift to me! I defy you! *I defy you!*"

Without a thought, without a prayer, I sprang into the second voller.

She went up at full lever, and I did not even bother to look back.

Again I set her toward the east and south and this time I did pray, pray that I could arrive in time to see my Delia and Drak alive, to hold my dear Delia in my arms once more.

A ripping sound brought me around, the rapier instantly in my fist. The long barbed serrated head of an arrow thrust up through the floor of the voller. I cursed the thing and thrust the rapier back.

Bending to pick up the arrow, dragging it through, I thought to assuage the pangs of agony tearing at my mind by learning what I might of the shtarkins.

The hateful voice croaked by my ear as I straightened up.

"The Star Lords are most wroth. You have sinned mightily."

The Gdoinye perched on the rim of the voller. His feathers glittered in the light of the suns, glittering golden and scarlet in that streaming opaline radiance.

I said nothing. I whipped the longsword from my back, hefted it in that cunning Krozair grip, swung it full-force horizontally.

Had the Gdoinye been a mortal bird he would have been sheared in two.

He skipped lightly away and the great blade hissed through thin air.

"You have made a mistake, Dray Prescot, and now you must pay. No man defies the Everoinye!"

"I do! I, Dray Prescot, onker of onkers, defy any man who seeks to destroy my Delia!"

"Then are you a doomed man!"

The Gdoinye vanished. The blueness swelled. The enormous form of the Scorpion swooped upon me, radiant blueness washed all around me, washed me away, washed my senses away so that as I fell I fell soundlessly and hopelessly, for the very last words of that inhuman bird were: "Back to Earth, Dray Prescot, get-onker of onkers, back to Earth—to *stay!*"

"No man defies the Everoinye!"

Chapter Four

Soldiering, science and secrets

Back to Earth—to stay!

What a fool! What a fool!

Yet I could not have done other than I had.

I should have helped those poor devils of Vilasca. The island owed allegiance to Trylon Werfed, a man I knew only moderately well, a man against whom I had heard no whispers of plots against the Emperor. I should have jumped in and helped them beat off those damned Leem Lovers and then I could have taken voller for Delia.

But I am me, Dray Prescot, as thick-skulled a man as ever lived on two worlds. As I made my way back to civilization I reflected that I could not have done other than I had, and to pretend otherwise was folly. Dangerous folly. I admitted that I must have grown mighty proud and aloof in all these ridiculous titles and ranks I had amassed through no fault of my own. Well, leave out that I had deliberately made myself King of Djanduin. That is true. But the reasons for that decision were rooted in Khokkak the Meddler at first, and then in a sober understanding of a duty laid upon me. No, I had grown fat and comfortable and supine and now I must pay the price of arrogance and pride.

But to stay on Earth—to stay!

I reflected on that. The Star Lords had dumped me down all naked and miserable in Morocco, which was in a fine old state of unrest. The locals were standing up for their rights, and the French from Algeria, which they had taken in the 1830's, were trying to take over there. By virtue of my tutor Maspero and the genetically coded language pill he had given me in Aphrasöe, the Swinging City, I could understand and

41

speak the languages of people with whom I came into contact. The Moors—although that is hardly the correct term for the Sherifs, for the Moors were a light-skinned people—would no doubt have cut up a European dumped among them naked and defenseless. But I was enraged, and I used fury as a weapon to drown my maniacal despondency. I simply treated them as I would a people among whom I found myself on Kregen.

It has to be said that if a man can survive on Kregen he can find survival much easier on this Earth. I exclude from that the refined life of cities which in its artificiality can destroy more surely than sword thrust or ax bite.

With language no barrier it was easier, of course. Even as I talked with these dark-bearded, hawk-faced warriors of the desert, after I had shown them I was not a man to be lightly killed, I could still hear the hissing shrills of the shanks as they swarmed to the attack. "Ishtish! Ishtish!" they skrieked as they charged forward. And as my men shot them down or struggled hand-to-hand with them, so my archers shouted: "Vallia! Vallia!" Or: "Valka! Valka! Prince Dray!"

Well, I was a prince no longer. I was a foolish European among the Arabs and I had to fend for myself. I made my way to Fez and from there to the sea where I took passage for Marseilles. Once there I arranged with London for funds. I do not reveal the name of the bankers who looked after me. I had saved the founder of the bank from a nasty experience on the field of Waterloo; now his sons merely took me for my own son. But they were a closed-mouth lot. I do not think a great deal can discompose a tight-fisted, crafty, elegant banker of the City of London.

Through canny investment by these same people I was now a wealthy man. Of course, it meant meant nothing.

Every day those dread words echoed in my obstinate skull: "Stay on Earth—*stay!*"

I had to take it for granted that Delia and Drak and the others were safe, that they had repelled the attack from the village, and that Tom had come sweeping back to look for his prince and so brought my fighting men down in their regiments to save the day. I had to assume that. Any other course would leave me more of a madman than I already was.

The bankers, cool, assured men though they were, looked at me askance as I did business with them. I took myself off to become a solitary. A year passed, then another. Despair clawed at me. But I did not know how long that damned bird meant by his infernal "Stay!" It could be forever.

One foggy day as I stared out from my narrow leaded windows at the hurrying people passing in the London street, the carriages burning their lamps in spectral glimmers, each a little circular glow isolated from the others, with the moisture hanging on the trees and the railings, I made up my mind. One day, I said to myself, one day I would return to Kregen. I would take up the broken threads of my life. Why, then wouldn't it be a fine thing to learn all I could, here on this Earth, against the time of my return to all that I held dear?

I needed a purpose in life, here on Earth.

I would make that purpose a conscious effort to learn all I could. I would return a master of statecraft, of science, of engineering, of war. I would seek the answers to the questions on Kregen that had plagued me, and I would seek what I could here.

Foolish, pathetic, ludicrous even. Oh, yes, all of those. But it gave me back a semblance of sanity, for by studying I assured myself that I did have a future on Kregen to which to return one day.

So, rousing myself from my lethargy, I left London. On Magdalen Bridge in Oxford I stood and gazed up at the stars.

That upflung tail of the Scorpion was barely visible, but even if it was not, I could visualize it clearly. The red star that was Antares, the huge red star and the smaller green companion—I imagined I could see the constellation of Scorpio, and I would stand gazing up into the star-speckled night. I know the look on my face must have been one of infinite longing and infinite regret.

I am sure you can see that the idea of secrets on Kregen plaguing me was a fallacy, for I had long since felt that my life with Delia and my family far outweighed anything else on Kregen. But to bolster my resolve and to give a neat scientific and logical approach, I set down in tabular form the questions to which I would like answers.

The very first name was, of course, the Everoinye, the Star Lords.

Next the Savanti, those mortal but superhuman people of Aphrasöe.

Then the Todalpheme, the meteorologists and tide-watchers.

Then followed a list of various strange peoples, of whom I have introduced you so far to only a fraction. These included the volroks, the flying men of Havilfar.

Then the Wizards of Loh.

The secrets of the silver boxes of the fliers, of course, had to figure, for we in Valka were still only able to produce flying craft which could merely lift and must find their propulsion from the breeze like sailing ships.

As to unfinished business, well, there was indeed a formidable list of that, as you who have listened to these tapes must be aware.

Various religious cults were written down, and chief of these was the abominable practice of Lem the Silver Leem.

If I fail to mention anything in connection with the inner sea of the continent of Turismond, the Eye of the World, it was because I ached for that locale and for the Krozairs of Zy.

All the titles I had won on Kregen could be stripped from me and I would not care a jot. But I was a Krozair Brother, a Krozair of Zy, and that did mean something.

How often I had planned to revisit Zy, that magnificent island fortress of the Brotherhood, or Sanurkazz, the chief city of the Zairians of the red southern shore of the Eye of the World. Well, something or other had always cropped up to prevent me. Now, back on Earth, that something had turned out to be the biggest obstacle of all.

The list did not satisfy me. Nothing satisfied me. Oxford at this time appeared to me to be an intellectual desert, its ancient halls given over to mindless pursuits after false doctrines. The studies pursued here seemed to me to offer no help or guidance to the things a man needed to know in the real world, for all its products strutted the preeminent stages of this world here on Earth. Through my accrued wealth and the machinations of powerful friends on my bankers, doors were opened to me that would, had I remained simply Dray Prescot, lieutenant in the Royal Navy, have remained firmly closed in my face. I tried Cambridge with a similar result.

The best hope of education in these times lay with the Dissenting Academies, although my knowledge of the Greek Heroes was furbished up, for although, as I have said, I have always considered Achilles to be a poor show beside Hector, the sheer rage and panache and barbarity and honor of those times bears some pale reflection of times on Kregen that go on to this present hour.

The Star Lords had dumped me down on Earth after what has since come to be called the Year of Revolutions. For a time I was too nearly a madman to bother with the world and its doings. There had been a king come and gone on the throne of England and now we had a queen. I knew about queens. The one at this time, though, bore no possible connection with any of the queens I had known, and I thought longingly, of the fabled Queens of Pain of Loh. Queen Lilah, Queen Fahia and Queen Thyllis, she who was now the Empress Thyllis. By Vox! What a spectacular collection they were, and all up there on Kregen waiting, waiting . . .

As for the kings, because of my connection with the July days in Paris in 1830 and the dismissal of Charles X and the installation of Louis Phillipe, I sought as a change from universities and academies and as an anodyne to my agony some light action as Prince Louis Napoleon, President of the French Republic for three years, overturned that Republic and obtained election as President for ten years. I did not then think that I would still be on Earth when his term came up for renewal; I saw him made Emperor, Napoleon III, and I cursed the day I still remained on Earth.

The attempt of Russia to dismember the Sick Man of Europe and the involvement of France and England are well known. As they affected me, however, I let events take their course. The Crimean War, it seemed to me, a fighting man, might give me fresh opportunities to bash a few skulls and so in my sinful way find a trifle of surcease from the despair and anguish consuming me.

My part led me to action earlier than the Light Brigade on that fateful day of October 25. As a participant in the Heavy Brigade charge I believe we did a more thorough job than the more highly publicized Charge of the Lights. Three hundred British heavy cavalrymen charging uphill against three thousand Russian cavalrymen. It sounds as maniacal as events on Kregen. The Grays were in the thick of it. General Scarlett's second line came on, piecemeal, driving through and through the thick gray ranks. The Russians, incredible though it sounds, had enough and broke and scattered and fled.

The Light Brigade fiasco—however glorious—followed later. I fancied that even on Kregen soldiers would look askance at generals who had last fought forty years ago, or who had never fought, or who were often so old and doddery, without any clear understanding of what they were about, that they were as much a menace to their own men as to the enemy.

After that came the Indian Mutiny and I went to take a part. I have said that I do not intend to dwell on those portions of my life spent on this Earth. But on this occasion the years ticked by and I grew ever more morose and savage, bitter with the bitterness that eats the spirit, and it is right that you who listen to my story should understand.

My studies progressed by fits and starts. The marvels of steam and engineering and iron ships and the industrial changes that shook and transformed England were absorbed. I followed closely all the developments of science and philosophy and the arts of war I could. Agriculture also repaid study. But through all this I was aware that I was like a man asleep, merely walking through a part on a dimly lit stage.

As for the war in America—the American Civil War or the War between the States—I was there. I shall not say now what side I fought on, although that may appear more obvious than it truly was, and I did not enjoy it. By the end of May on that last dreadful year of war I was sailing back to England. A gentleman I had met and talked with in odd circumstances, a gentleman from Virginia, struck me as a man who would go to far places and, perhaps, hunger for a life akin to mine on Kregen. I wished him well as we parted.

Whenever the opportunity had offered I had made fresh inquiries about Alex Hunter. He had been a Savapim, an agent of the Savanti, recruited from Earth. I had seen him die on a beach in Valka and had buried him and said two prayers over his grave. As a shavetail in the old U.S. Army he had been subject to influences I fancied I could duplicate during my period in the U.S., but the armies of the war were very different from the armies both before and after. There was nothing, I thought, to be gained from the trail of Alex Hunter.

The idea that the Savanti—who labored to bring dignity to Kregen, they had told me—recruited people from this Earth to work for them led me on to a consideration that perhaps they maintained agents here. I had seen the Savapim Wolfgang fight to protect apims against diffs in the Scented Sylvie, a notorious drinking den of the Sacred Quarter of Ruathytu, the capital of Hamal, the Empire on the continent of Havilfar, which is on Kregen. Kregen! I do not think a single day of my life on Earth passed without a longing thought of Kregen under Antares. No, I am wrong. I do not think—I *know*.

In working out a scheme whereby I might put myself in contact with a terrestrial agent of the Savanti I had to discount the Everoinye completely from the calculations. The idea began to obsess me. Where hitherto, after that first destructive fit of lethargy, I had flung myself into violent action to blot cruel thoughts from my brain, I now positively dwelt on all I knew of Kregen as it affected the Savanti, the mortal but non-human people of Aphrasöe.

If newspaper advertisements would help I would deluge the daily sheets with advertisements. This was the time I became involved with some of the more dubious aspects of Victorian science.

As a trapped rat will turn and struggle against whatever opposes it so I struggled against invisible bonds. In the process I ran across weird people, ordinary human beings, and yet people possessed of some quirk of nature that led them to gather to themselves superior powers. Most of the time they were mere quacks, charlatans, impostors. Of Doctor Quinney I had my doubts.

A thin, snuffly individual, blessed with a quantity of lank brown hair—hair that grew, it seemed, from every part of his face except his eyes—Doctor Quinney dressed in shiny black clothes, much worn, and a stovepipe hat elegantly blocked out after whoever it was had sat on it. His snuff blew everywhere. His eyes watered and gleamed with fanaticism; he claimed to know the Secrets of the Spheres.

"And I assure you, my dear sir"—his steel-rimmed pince-nez flashed in time to the pendulum motion of his head, the dramatic gestures of his gleaming-knuckled hands—"in the Spheres like mystic gossamer balls lie the ultimate Secrets!"

I had taken chambers in a quiet London side street and the landlady, Mrs. Benton, was slowly growing accustomed to the procession of odd characters daily pulling the doorbell. As for my own clothes, they were unremarkable, simple English town clothes of sober cut and style. Doctor Quinney regarded me as a man who, also anxious to unravel the Secrets of the Spheres, happened most fortunately to be blessed with the wherewithal to satisfy that craving.

I tolerated him for what he might bring me, rather as a ponsho might be staked out for a leem.

"Listen to me, Doctor Quinney, and mark me well. I expect results from you. It might go very ill for you else." He started back and dropped his handkerchief. I know that he had seen in my face that awful mad glare marking a clansman of Segesthes, marking me, Dray Prescot, the Lord of Strombor.

Chapter Five

Madam Ivanovna

Now began a different period of my life on Earth. More and more I mixed with the learned men, the savants, the scientists and chemists, the philosophers and engineers. To speak the truth, many of the new discoveries daily amazing this Victorian world had been spoken of in Aphrasöe. Because of this I was able to hold my own in argument and debate.

When Charles Darwin and Alfred Wallace read their paper before the Linnean Society I had been in India charging about with a saber and uselessly trying either to blot out all thought of Kregen or to imagine myself there as we battled. Many of the ideas expressed in *The Origin of Species by Means of Natural Selection*, Darwin's book that appeared in the November of the following year, made me realize that people on Earth were capable of great things, despite their flaws, and that Aphrasöe was a place of logical human development.

One day, it seems to me, our selfish brawling Earth may turn into the paradise I still—despite all!—believe the Swinging City to be. As you must be aware, since I speak to you in the seventies of the twentieth century and much has transpired over the past one hundred years on Kregen, I know much more now than I knew then. At the time of which I speak, though, I knew practically nothing. Nothing. The Savanti had their purposes, and I had surmised these were for the good of Kregen and for the dignity of humanity. As to the purposes of the Star Lords, I held hazy ideas, nebulous theories, but all was embittered by their treatment of me and my resentment against them for their aloof high-handedness.

When the Savapim who called himself Wolfgang had

talked in Ruathytu of the problem of evolution changing the many different races set down on Kregen I had been able to talk with him and understand. Now Darwin, of Earth, was opening terrestrial eyes to this mutable genetic structure.

My advertisements in search of a Savapim, an agent of the Savanti, here on Earth, proved fruitless.

Doctor Quinney, filled with an excitable eagerness and blowing snuff everywhere, told me he had found a "wonderful and incredible new source of psychic powers."

Arrangements were made. I canceled a trip planned to take me to Vienna, for I found I had grown inordinately fond of the music of Johann Strauss, and thus thankfully missed the Seven Weeks War in which Prussia dealt with Austria and set herself on the course of German unification. There was another new emperor on Earth now, Kaiser Wilhelm I. The agonizing thought that my son was the grandson of an emperor, you may readily conceive, touched me with renewed longing. Every day, every single day, I longed for my Delia and for Kregen.

Before this meeting with the "new source of psychic powers" discovered by Doctor Quinney, I finally parted with Victorian scientists over many questions. They were working on the right lines, in many cases, for what they required. I had worked with chemists in stinking laboratories attempting to duplicate the gas used in the paol silver box, and had got nowhere. As to the minerals in the vaol box, simple nomenclature defeated even the first stumbling attempts. I made mental notes on rare earths and scarce minerals, trace elements as known at that time—a time of great expansion and, equally, a time of ludicrous conservatism among the ignorant—and came to the conclusion that Earth science held no help at all. I went ballooning and enjoyed it enormously, but a Kregen voller was out of any balloon's league. And, into the bargain, my own experience as a sailor meant I already knew enough to sail my driveless fliers by means of the wind alone, as I have told you.

The date of the meeting was set. Doctor Quinney, canny old Quinney, kept his new protégé secret. I could not blame him, for I knew of the intense professional jealousy animating the people of the mystic circles and their adherents. And then, out of nowhere, came a situation which presented me with a problem I felt a sense of humanity compelled me to solve.

In our little group, among a Grub Street scribbler, a civil servant connected with the sewers, I believe, and a prosperous leather merchant who had recently lost his wife, a certain lordling attended our meetings. This young lord—I do not give his name—seemed to me a revolting example of that chinless pop-eyed, insufferable scion of an ancient noble family gone to seed. He owed his title to the dubious bedtime antics of an ancestor who had been rewarded for her exertions by being created a countess, in the name of her complaisant husband, the first earl. The young lord possessed wealth, a vicious temper and a good eye with a gun. I spoke only the necessary civil words to him. For his part, it was quite clear that plain Mr. Prescot was mere dirt beneath his feet, like all the others who did not overshadow him in nobility. Without breeding, without a lineage, a man could never enter his world. I did not wish to. There were far more important things to be accomplished than spending idle days, vapidly admiring oneself among cronies, a parasite upon the nation.

One day my landlady's daughter, young Mary Benton, wore a red and tear-swollen face as she tidied my chambers. I chided her and soon the whole story came out. It was sickeningly familiar. As I looked at Mary, a sweet, innocent creature who worked hard from crack of dawn until well into the night, and heard her broken words, her shame, and contrasted her life with the elegant, luxurious, feckless life of this lord and his cronies, I fancied I might assist her. Money, of course, was immediately forthcoming.

Probably I would have left it at that. Mrs. Benton was grateful; I shushed her and Mary was packed off to reappear subsequently with a new sister or brother, niece or nephew. I would have done what I could and left it, but this young lord could not leave well alone. On a night before the meeting that, however much I considered Doctor Quinney to be a fraud, yet excited me with its possibilities, the young lord was boasting and laughing, elegantly waving his hand, his blue pop-eyes very bright, his pink tongue tip licking the spittle on his lips.

My chambers were filled with Victorian shadows, the oil lamps' casting their separated pools of light, the old furniture highly polished to mirror-gleams, the smell of cigar smoke and distant cooking in the air; through the curtained windows the clip-clop of passing horses and the grind of iron-rimmed wheels reminded me I was in London and not in Valkanium.

The hot words were spoken, words that might have been: "Damned impertinence! D'you forget who I *am*?" And: "I know what you are, and no gentleman would tolerate your presence." And: "I'll horsewhip you, you guttersnipe!" And: "You are perfectly at liberty to try." And the blows and the bleeding nose and the challenge, the hostility, brittle and bitter, and the hushed-up scandal.

It would have to be in Boulogne.

"I shall meet you at the place and time you choose."

"My seconds will call."

Well, as I recall it all went as the copybook said it should. The sobering aspect of this struck me as we waited for Doctor Quinney. Something had happened to stir the sluggish blood. I didn't give a damn if this puppy spitted me or shot me through the heart. I'd do it for him, if I could. He had brought his own downfall on his head, through his folly and his damned superior ways and his unthinking selfishness. Had he eyes in his head he could read—and see!—information on the state of the poor. There was no excuse for the rich to plead ignorance. Pure selfishness, allied to a grotesque assumption of superiority led the people of his class to act the way they did. I looked forward to Boulogne with grim and unpleasant relish, Zair forgive me. For wasn't I, Dray Prescot, acting in just such a selfish way?

Well, for those of you who have followed my story so far, perhaps you will understand what I only vaguely grasped of my character.

Of all the incidents of my stay on Earth, that evening in the oil lamps' glow, with the sounds of London muted through the windows and the circle sitting around the polished mahogany table, remains most vividly with me. Doctor Quinney arrived, his snuffbox under firm control, ushering in a tall cloaked figure. When the cloak's hood was thrown back everyone in the room sat up. We all felt the magnetic presence, the consciousness of power allied with understanding, the sheer authority of this lady.

"Madam Ivanovna!" cried Quinney, his voice near to cracking with pride and emotion.

The woman seated herself after a slight inclination of her head that embraced the company and seemed to take us all into her confidence. I saw a mass of gleaming dark hair and a face, white and unlined, of a purity of outline quite remarkable. Her eyes were brown, large, finely set, dominating. Her mouth puzzled me, being firm and yet softly full, suggesting a complex character. She wore long loose garments of somber black. This was quite usual, set she wore the garments in a way suggesting mystery and excitement and great peril—quite alarming and yet amusing, charming, and I sat forward, ready to take part in the evening's charade.

As I moved I observed that Quinney still stood there, an idiotic grin on his face, his hand outstretched. The others of the circle sat perfectly still. Sounds stretched and became muted. The ticking of the ormolu clock sounded like lead weights dropped slowly into a bottomless pool. I stared at Madam Ivanovna, feeling the tensions, the excitements, feeling that, perhaps, my staked ponsho had brought a leem. . . .

"Mr. Prescot," said this enigmatic Madam Ivanovna. "You will disregard the people here, well-meaning, even Doctor Quinney. You have been causing trouble and I am here because it seems meet to us that you should work again."

I remained mute. There was no doubt about it. The other people in the room remained silent, static, unmoving—*frozen.*

"Mr. Prescot, you do not appear surprised."

I had to speak. "I have been trying—"

"You have been successful."

I swallowed. Now that it had happened I could not believe it. I licked my lips. "Perhaps, then, I should not say, 'Good evening' to you, Madam Ivanovna. "Perhaps I should say 'Happy Swinging.' "

"You may say 'Happy Swinging' and you may say 'Lahal.' Neither would be correct."

Through the roar of blood in my head—for she had said "Lahal," which is the Kregish form for greeting new acquaintances—I wondered what on Kregen she could mean by saying neither would be correct.

"You are from the Savanti?"

"No."

"The Everoinye?"

"No."

If this was madness, a phantom conjured from my own sick longings, then I would press on. I recall every minute, every second, as we two sat and talked in a Victorian room stuffed with mummified people who saw and heard nothing.

"You know me, Madam Ivanovna. You know who I am. Why have you sought me out?"

"First, I use the name Ivanovna because it is exotic, foreign. It will soon be fashionable to have a Russian name in psychic matters. It helps belief when you found a society. But you may know my use-name. It is Zena Iztar."

I knew about use-names. My comrade Inch from Ng'groga was called Inch; his real name was different, secret, something, I then thought, he would share with no one.

"You are from Kregen?"

"Well, yes and no."

The blood in my head pained. I thumped the table. "Damn it!" I burst out. "You'll pardon my manner, Madam Ivanovna, or Madam Zena Iztar, but, by Zair! I wish you'd—"

She smiled.

That smile could have launched a million ships.

"Yes, Pur Dray."

I felt numb.

"You call me Pur Dray," I whispered. I swallowed. "You must know I hold only being a Krozair of Zy as of importance. Tell me, Madam Zena Iztar, tell me, for the sweet sake of Zair!"

She placed both white hands on the table. Her fingers were long and slender and white, as they should be, and she wore no rings. She wore no jewelry of any kind that I could see.

"Now," she said, and her voice in its hard practicality made me sit up. "The Savanti have set their hands to the work they consider proper for Kregen, for they are of that world and are a last faint remnant of a once mighty race. You have heard of them as the Sunset People or the Sunrise People. The Savanti have at heart the well-being of apims, Homo sapiens like yourself. As for the Star Lords, their plans are different, wider and more universe-embracing, and I shall tell you only that you will have to make a choice one day, and the choice will be the hardest thing you have ever done."

"Put me back on Kregen and I will choose!"

"Oh, yes, Pur Dray! You would promise anything now, just to return. I know."

"Can you—?"

Her look made me hold my foolish tongue.

"Am I not here? Do you require any other proof?"

"No, I meant only—"

"You have always been reckless, foolhardy, as that brash bird the Gdoinye says, an onker of onkers."

How it warmed my heart to hear the brave Kregish words, here in London, even if they were insults!

"Now," she went on, in that firm mellow voice. "If you will cast your mind back to your arrival in the inner sea at the Akhram, when you struggled to remain on Kregen?"

"Yes. They were going to banish me back to Earth, but I fought them and so returned—"

"That was a compromise. The Star Lords and the Savanti had different purposes, as the Gdoinye and the white dove of the Savanti showed. So you went to Magdag, along the Grodnim green northern shore. You became a Krozair of Zy, a fanatical believer in Zair, the red sun deity of Zim, and an opponent of Grodno, the green sun deity of Genodras; that was our doing."

"Your doing? Who—?"

Again she smiled and lifted one slender finger. I stopped.

"All in good time. The Star Lords have other instruments, as have the Savanti. They were not pleased. But there are checks and balances, and you lived. Mortal men may see only so far. It is a wearisome burden to see further. One day, I believe, you will be called on to see and to make your choice, and you will feel an outcast, a pariah, a traitor. Yet think back to this day and remember."

I could bottle up my screaming fears and questions no longer. This talk of the mysterious destiny of Kregen and the shadowy desires of powerful superhuman beings was all very fine. But I was Dray Prescot, and there were torments tearing at me far and away more important than the fate of worlds.

I said: "You are from Kregen. You have great powers. Tell me, Madam Zena Iztar, what of—?"

Her smile would have melted the blasphemous heart of a silver statue of Lem the Silver Leem.

"Fear not, Pur Dray. Your Chuktar Tom returned in good time. Your Delia and your son, Drak live."

"Thank Zair!" I could say no more for a while, just put a hand to my face, and so we sat in silence.

Then, quietly, she said, "Yes. Yes, you should thank Zair."

Slowly I looked up at her.

"Your son is a great man now. And your daughter has already refused five offers of marriage."

"Good God!" I said, dumbfounded.

"Time passes on Kregen as on this Earth, although not necessarily at the same rates, as you know. Reckoning in Earthly years you left—" As she said *"left"* I know my fierce old lips twisted up, for the word more appropriate was "banished." She put a hand to her cloak and felt some object beneath, under the curve of her shoulder. "In Earthly years your son Drak was near fourteen and he is nigh on thirty-two now."

At this I groaned. Aye, I, Dray Prescot, groaned. Thirty-two! Incredible and impossible and yet true. What years I had missed! As for Lela, in a life span of two hundred years or so, a maiden of thirty-two had no fears of the future or of being left on the shelf. I also knew this would make Segnik and Velia both twenty-one. My Delia had been twenty-one when we had first met, although it is a curious fact that on Kregen people appear to put little store by their ages or their birthdays. As to the latter, that is easily understood, I suppose, given the forty-year cycle, the absence of definite terrestrial years and the confusing mass of temporal measurements by the different moons. I became aware of Madam Zena Iztar looking at me with a quizzical gaze, almost a look of mockery.

"And you will send me back, Madam Iztar, now?"

"I stand here in a merely consultative capacity. You have been causing trouble and there is work for you to do. When the time comes you will know what the work is. To tell you now would invalidate your integrity." I guessed she spoke in these terms to conceal a blunter meaning.

"Eighteen years!" I said. If the words came out of my mouth as a plea, I do not think I can be blamed.

"The Savanti are a mere rump of a once proud people.

They may well find a use for you yet, despite your flouting of their principles. As for the Star Lords, certain events on Kregen have not turned out as they expected—"

"So they cannot see the future?"

"Oh, they can riddle a future or two, but the trick is guessing which one will eventuate. They will use you again, Pur Dray, I am quite sure."

"And can I resist them?"

"You must try, if that is your wish. Your will may then receive help from . . ." Here she paused and smoothed her cloak reflectively so the black material shone in the lamps' gleam. "I can say that the Star Lords are only partially to blame for some of your misfortunes; they are not omnipotent on Kregen—who is?—and intense effort of the will may deflect their hold."

"And you will tell me nothing more of their purposes?"

"There are many clues if you open your eyes." She spoke with an edge of testiness, very bracing. "But I will tell you no more. For one thing, even the Star Lords are divided among themselves. For another, to tell you what they think they plan to do will quite evidently, given their nature, cause them to do something else."

"Out of spite? The Star Lords . . . out of spite?"

"Not out of spite, you onker!"

Then it was my turn to smile. How familiar that was!

She looked around my room at the few belongings I had collected. "I must wake these poor famblys. Your Doctor Quinney proved a fine ponsho, Pur Dray."

I had the grace to nod my head without speaking.

"Now you have this tiresome business over the duel. After that—who knows? Even Grodno may play a part; stranger things than that have happened."

Chancing a venture that might prove disastrous, for I saw she was arranging her cloak and gown and preparing to wake up my guests, I said, "And Lem the Silver Leem? Do you . . . ?"

She flashed those large brown eyes at me, very fierce and commanding. "If you obliterate Lem completely," and she said it with a fair old temper, I can tell you, "Then you would do well in the eyes of the people of Kregen—and of Earth."

Before I could ask what she meant by that last alarming
statement Doctor Quinney was starting forward, grinning,
and the others were moving about and buzzing with the arrival of this formidable Madam Ivanovna in our midst.

The meeting which followed meant nothing, of course.
What ideas, what concepts, what conjectures flashed through
my aching head!

Eventually things were brought to a conclusion and an as-
tral voice came from Madam Ivanovna in her part as a psychic; the voice chilled the company and satisfactorily ensured
a fat check would pass from me to Doctor Quinney. Then we
were saying our farewells. No one cared to partake of the refreshment Mrs. Benton had provided. I shook hands and ushered them out. As she passed me Zena Iztar smiled, a quick
flash that was gone as soon as formed.

"Good night, Mr. Prescot." She was very close and she
bent a little forward, her words for me alone. "Remberee,
Dray Prescot, Krozair of Zy. Remberee."

I caught a flash from the black of her gown where the
cloak lapped open. A tiny gem gleamed there, hidden before.
I saw a jeweled representation of a cogwheel, a gearwheel,
and I found myself thinking that this was a strange device,
so mechanical, for one so psychic. Then she had gone and I
was alone with Doctor Quinney. The check was written, dried
and handed over. Quinney took it as a man accepts a flask of
water in the burning deserts far south of Sanurkazz.

"A pity," he said, folding the check, "that we were not
honored with our lordship tonight."

"A pity," I agreed two-facedly.

"I hear he has taken a trip to Boulogne."

"Has he? No doubt he has business there."

As Doctor Quinney took himself off I determined that no
one should know of my intention to catch the packet to
Boulogne the next day.

If you imagine I slept that night you could be right, for everything passed in a daze until I realized I was in Boulogne
and must meet this lecherous, dandified earl the following
morning at first light, when the air was cool and limpid and
no curious observers would be around. My second, a courageous, empty-headed army officer with whom I had had a
few skirmishes in India, was already in France. He met me

on the appointed day, a polished mahogany box under his arm, with the information that all was ready, a doctor was in attendance and the carriage waited. With blinds pulled down we wheeled out along the seashore.

Well, as with all my fights, this duel could mark the end of me. The weapons were to be pistols. I account myself a fine shot. I'd had plenty of experience in America. A pair of very fine London-made dueling pistols had come into my possession and I knew how they shot. The lordling would have his own, no doubt. I well remember a remarkable man in the Royal Navy who was the finest shot I have ever known. As he used to say, in his own tarpaulin way, "If I can see it I can hit it—if I know the gun."

He had been a captain when I knew him and we had got along, for he was a man who, like myself, had come up onto the quarterdeck through the hawse hole. I would have liked him at my side on Kregen. His middle name was Abe, but only his family called him that, of course. I missed him. He was ten years older than myself, so if he still lived he'd be one hundred and two years old. With a pang I recollected myself. He lived on Earth, not Kregen.

The petty formalities of the duel wended through their paces: the apology was asked for and refused, we took up our positions, the signal was given, we walked, turned, fired. Two flat smacks of evil hatred in the cool morning air. Two puffs of smoke. He hit me in the right shoulder, high. I shot the kleesh clean through the guts.

Turmoil followed and the doctor scurried. The seconds tried to hurry me away, but I had been keyed up. I acted as I might have acted on Kregen and not on Earth. I walked over to the lordling as he lay writhing, screaming in pain, choking. I bent over him. His second tried to drag me away and I pushed him and he staggered and fell. The doctor wadded a handful of white cloth that turned red in an instant. The lecher would most likely die. I did not think Earthly medical science at that time could save him.

I bent over him and he glared up at me, choking, screaming.

"You are going to die, you bastard," I said, quite calmly. "In your agony, think. Think if your pain was worth what you did to Mary Benton."

I did not spit in his face. I remembered I was on Earth and, anyway, that would give him greater importance than the rast deserved.

My second said in his gruff army way; "My God, Prescot! You're a devil!" And then, brushing his stiff mustache, "You won't be able to go back to England now."

"There will be other things to do. Thank you for your assistance."

We parted then, and I suppose he is buried somewhere on Earth, his gravestone moldering away over a corrupting coffin. Time has no mercy.

So it happened that, waiting for the summons of the Scorpion, I was in France for the pathetic business of the Franco-Prussian War, a most unhappy affair. I admired the brisk efficiency of the German Army and felt great sorrow for the shambles that overtook the French Army. I'd fought them at Waterloo, and fought with them in the Crimea, and I'd fought with the Germans in that old war and was to fight against them unhappily in wars to come. The nonsense of national identities when they destroy happiness had been laid plainly open to me in the disputes between Vallia and Pandahem and between Vallia and Hamal. I was learning all the time.

Although I now have a much clearer idea of what must have gone on in the three years between Zena Iztar's visit and the day I found myself helping in a bloody hospital in Paris as the guns thundered about our ears, I will refrain from a guess, for that would destroy the appreciation of many of my actions. Hindsight can destroy logic and truth. I am making the attempt, painful though it is, to be as truthful as I can possibly be in this record. If that record makes me out to be the prize fool I am, then I stand guilty of being an onker.

A balloon had just been inflated and sent off and the Prussians were firing at it. I stood a little apart, my hands and arms smothered in blood, looking. I looked up. The blueness stole in, or so it seemed to me, on the clouds of gun smoke. The noise of the cannon and rifles blended away and away and I was falling—heavenly, wonderful, superb, sublime!— falling and the Scorpion enfolded me in its arms and bore me away. Never did man more thankfully quit this Earth.

Chapter Six

Of slings and knives

Twenty-one years!

Twenty-one whole terrestrial years had now passed since I had set foot on Kregen. What might have happened in that long span of time? I admit to a tremulous feeling as I stood up and looked around, wonderfully conscious of the streaming mingled radiance of Zim and Genodras falling all about me and lighting up with glory all my new hopes for the future. I felt weak, like a newly born ponsho. I felt light-headed. My heart wanted to burst from my breast. I stamped my naked foot on the ground, on the short tufted grass, and deeply breathed in that indescribably bracing air of Kregen, air like wine, air that no man of Earth can possibly imagine. I was home!

And yet Kregen is a large world with a greater land mass than Earth. Home, for me, was Valka or Zenicce or Djanduin. I might be anywhere. I didn't give a damn where I was. Just so that I trod once more the same earth as my Delia, that when I had cleared up whatever mischief lay to my hand I could fly or sail or ride—walk or crawl—back to my Delia, that was all I craved. I would return to my Delia, my Delia of the Blue Mountains, my Delia of Delphond.

Many and many a time have I returned to Kregen and few times ever created in me more sheer joyful feelings of thankfulness as that occasion. I had thought myself abandoned and cast off. Now I was back.

These thoughts sped through my mind with the speed of a Lohvian longbow shaft. As I stood up the reason for my arrival and the problem confronting me revealed itself plainly and, as always, unpleasantly.

Naked as usual—for it had been a unique exception when the Star Lords had taken me back to Vilasca for the second time and given me my weapons—I would have to be the same old hasty, reckless, intemperate Dray Prescot. Maybe the Star Lords had gone down in my estimation for having provided me with weapons. I do not know.

A flung stone whistled past my ear.

The slinger, a small and agile fellow almost as naked as I was, had come springing out of the thick-leaved bushes. The sounds of combat beyond him told me where the action lay; those sounds combined in the light of Antares with the scream of frightened people and the shrill, shocking yells of vicious killers. I started toward the slinger.

He was apim. The next stone missed also, but only because I dodged sideways. This fellow might be one of the people I had been sent here to assist; he might be one of those I must fight. I did not know. This problem confronted me as of old, the difference on this occasion being that I had no guidelines at all. A second man now followed the first, swirling a sling about his head. His stone barely missed the first slinger, who turned, reloaded and swung. By the time I had reached him he had sent his missile full into his pursuer's face. The second man pitched to the ground, minus an eye and with blood flowing.

I grabbed the slinger as he swung back. I had run noiselessly and his face contorted with terror, shattered at thus being taken without warning.

"Now, dom," I said. "You can tell me all about it."

"The slavers!" he cried, wincing from my grip, trying to kick me, trying to bite, struggling to get his knife out. He wore a breechclout of decent fawn cloth, with a bag for his slingshots, a leather belt, the knife and dusty sandals.

"Slavers," I said.

"They are taking away the girls! I must save them, and yet . . ." Here he stopped struggling. He was very young. His voice fell. "And yet I ran away."

"Then we must run back and see what we can do."

If the Star Lords looked down on this comedy and were displeased with what they saw, I might find myself back on Earth for another twenty-one years. Even as I took a grip on the lad's arm and ran him back to the bushes, I considered that from what had happened to me on Earth it could well be that the Star Lords had had no hand in this return to Kregen. It could be the Savanti who had called on me. We ran into the bushes.

At my back the ground trended dustily away to mountains with no sign of human habitation. Beyond the bushes lay a well-trodden path. Further bushes and then a few scattered cultivated fields extended ahead. A house burned. Well, as I have said, sounds of strife and sights of burning houses are often my lot when I return to Kregen.

Along the path the girls in their fetters struggled, shrieking and wailing, terrified. The difficulty was in judging who was attempting to abduct the girls and who was trying to rescue them. At first glance there seemed very little difference between the two sides. Both wore the fawn-colored breechclouts, both used slings and knives. They were all apims, with a mixture of hair ranging from light to dark brown, so I must discard that as an identification. A stone almost took my eye out, and I moved away smartly, marking the man who had flung.

"Him," I said to my captive. "Is he friend or enemy?"

"That is Noki and he was always an onker! He couldn't hit the mark at twenty paces!"

A trifle local friction here, I decided. Noki saw what was going on and tried again, whereat my captive bellowed, "Hold, you get-onker! This man will help us!"

"I thought you were slain, Mako!" yelped this Noki. "Hurry! They are dragging the girls to their ship."

I perked up at this. So far this appeared to me to be a parody of the times I had fought for the Star Lords. The time was slipping away, for already most of the girls had vanished around a bend in the trail. They were all shackled to one another, stumbling on. While it was clear enough to see which of the men were trying to release them, it was not as easy to see who was slinging at the locals and bringing them down.

I made up my mind.

"Follow, Mako and you, Noki! You must fight!"

Then I was off, haring along the trail, dodging flung stones until, passing the struggling, shrieking girls, I reached the head of the column around the bend. The sea blazed before me, rippled with a breeze, glittering with the twin fires of the

Suns of Scorpio. A large open pulling boat was drawn up on the sand. There was going to be no mistake now.

I went straight in at the three fellows hauling on the shackles at the head of the procession, dragging the girls along. They all dropped the ropes and slung at me. I dodged. Three blows took care of them. Against knives a fist is a useful weapon, lacking anything better. The unarmed combat disciplines hammered into me by the Krozairs of Zy also ensured I could take out a man armed only with a knife. As for the slung stones, they could break an arm or crack a skull. Two more slavers went down, their faces abruptly bloody, as they tried to jump me. And all the time I was leaping around like a frenzied fire-dancer, trying to present so shifting and erratic a target that the slingers would be bound to miss.

It all struck me as remarkably fatuous, not real, as though I was being run through a slow-motion reprise of what had gone on long ago in much more gory detail. But the truth was there in the blood and the screams and the agony. This was real enough. The missing factor was twenty-one years away from scenes of Kregen, I was the one at fault.

What I had left, only moments before, still seemed more real to me. The Parisian hospital, the Prussian guns, the balloon, the blood there. Already, because one of the slavers twisted his knife as I struck him down and spitted himself, I had blood on my hands. Blood. Is blood, then, so inseparable from life?

"They climb into the boat!" screeched Mako.

"Don't just stand there shouting about it!" I bellowed at him, running down the beach. "Stop them!" I did not have the heart to use the great word *Jikai*, and I think I was right.

An older man ran across as I started. A knife slash had brought blood in a line across his side. He was panting. "Let them go," he said, his chest heaving. "They may kill more of us."

I ignored him. His was the word of wisdom, of course, for the girls had been saved and the last of the slavers were evidently only too anxious to push off and row away. But I had other ideas. It was through no bloodthirsty madness that I acted as I did; I simply needed that boat. I did not know where I was but, by Vox, it was a long way off the beaten track.

The younger element was anxious to follow my lead. In a last affray in the surf, where, I admit, I stood back at the end and let them get on with it, the last of the slavers were seen to. Up on the beach the people on whose side I had fought were going around carefully slitting every living slaver's throat.

The girls, their shackles torn off, played a lustful part in that butchery too.

Presently I was able to go back to the older man who was being seen to, his wound stanched by a pad of leaves. No one produced a kit of acupuncture needles. Truly, I was out in the boondocks. Something about the light at last demanded my full attention, and I looked up. Yes. Yes, up there the huge red sun preceded the smaller green sun across the sky. In the forty-year cycle, which is never really an exact forty years by virtue of Kregen's Keplerian orbit about Antares, the suns had met and eclipsed and parted again. I thought of Magdag. What did they get up to on that occasion in that infamous city, when the green sun passed in front of the red? Could the smaller sun even be seen against that massive somber red glow?

"We owe you our thanks," said the older man, who said his name was Mogo the Wise.

I still remained on Kregen so I must have done the right thing.

Looking at the people here, the girls hysterical in their relief, the men comforting them, and now a stream of other people, old men and women, youngsters, coming running along the path from the village, I wondered which of them the Star Lords had wanted preserved. They did not seem a likely lot of prospects for a great destiny on Kregen. That was not my concern. Exchanging polite greetings with the headman was not my concern. I wrapped a fawn breechclout around my nakedness and possessed myself of a knife, a poor thing with a bone handle and a bronze blade, indifferently made. These people were poor. I cut through all the chatter.

"Tell me where this place is," I said, then, quelling their inquiries, I added, "for I have been shipwrecked and am lost out of the sea."

The head-shaking at this, the lip-pursing, made me wonder what they ordinarily did to shipwrecked mariners.

"Why," said Mogo the Wise, screwing up his eyes. "This is Inama. Everyone knows that."

In my screaming desire to know, to return to Delia, I wondered what fool had ever called this fool wise.

"And where is Inama? What is the next island called? The nearest mainland?"

"The next island is where those devils of Yanimas come from. As to any other large island, there cannot be any as large as Inama or Yanima, although there are smaller. And, as for what you call mainland ..." Here he turned to his people and lifted his hands to his temples. Whereat everyone laughed. I kept my temper—just.

"Do any ships call here?"

"Of course. But they come to kill us or take us prisoner. They sail from the Ice Floes of Sicce. We run and hide. Sometimes they leave things behind." He held out his knife. It was of iron, with an ivory handle. "This is a great knife, left by a ship."

Of one fact I felt relief in my dangerous impatience: these poor people talked of the Ice Floes of Sicce. That particular version of a Kregan hell, perhaps the most famous, was not the only one. I took heart from this talk of hell.

I said: "I will take this boat."

The headman looked dubious at this, with much pulling of his lower lip. One or two of the young bloods fingered their knives. I said, "I have saved your girls. I would like you to place water and food in the boat." More head scratching and eyes turned to the sky. "By Vox!" I said. "And would you wish the Yanimas to find a boat of theirs here when next they call?"

That was a two-pronged argument, but Mogo the Wise took the point as I had intended.

"That would make them very angry."

"And they would kill many of you. Put food and water into the boat and I will leave you."

So it was settled.

The hideous anticlimax, the dread truth, the damnable situation in which I had been placed screamed at me, screeching with impending madness in my skull. Here I was, back on Kregen, and I had absolutely no idea where. I was lost. And all I had for transport was a mere rowing boat. Truly the

Star Lords—if they had pitched me back here—took their revenge harshly.

But lost or not, rowing boat or not, I would set off to find Valka and my Delia. To the Ice Floes of Sicce with the Everoinye!

Chapter Seven

Lost on Kregen

Some experiences in one's life one would wish to forget. Certainly I rate that little boating excursion as among that group of experiences I would do a very great deal never to repeat.

By the position and altitude of the suns I could make a fair stab at latitude; longitude remained as much a mystery as it used to be on Earth before John Harrison gave the deep-water mariner a chronometer that would keep time with incredible accuracy. I had two alternatives and neither appeared over-appealing.

Despite the fact that Kregen possesses a much greater land area than Earth, there is still a vast amount of water. Here I was, in a cranky, stubborn rowing boat, adrift somewhere on the waters of Kregen and with every direction on the compass to choose for my direction.

The other alternative, simply allowing the winds and currents to push me where they willed, in the anticipation that I would be cast up on a frequented shore, I dismissed. By more bargaining as the food and water were brought down I obtained a sheet of cloth—that fawn material the women made up from the fibers of a cottony plant—and cut down a tree to make a mast and spar. Fashioning a crude dipping lug and stepping the mast as well as I could, I determined to sail where I was going under my own power.

The little dipping lug reminded me of the muldavy of the Eye of the World. This boat was a rough and ready affair, split logs being bent to shape, secured with trenails and with quantities of hair packed in with clay. It was more of a raft than a boat, but it would serve. It would have to serve.

With clumsy pottery crocks filled with water, a supply of cooked chickens and strips of bosk, dried in salt, and piles of various fruits of which palines formed a sizable proportion, I set off.

No doubt the islanders thought me mad. This island of Inama was clearly situated dwaburs off the shipping lanes, and my task was to find either a ship or land as speedily as possible. It would not be easy.

I could go east or west and be sure of striking land eventually. But if I was to the east of Havilfar and sailed east I'd be voyaging into an empty sea until I struck the lands of the other continental grouping from which came the shanks. And if I was to the west of Turismond and sailed the boat west, the same thing would result.

The problem was a knotty one.

If I sailed north I fancied I'd stand the best chance. Southward would take me toward the equator and therefore away from Vallia.

In a similar situation on Earth there would be a strong possibility that a sailor would feel the ocean he sailed: the blue of the Pacific, the raw gray of the Atlantic, the sense of the Mediterranean. I had had no experience of these far outer oceans of Kregen, so I sailed north. The breeze veered toward the east and, accepting this as the kind of fate that had dogged me, bore away toward the northwest. The lug sail pouted, the boat more forced its way through the water than glided along, and I maintained a most strict rationing of the meager supplies.

The day came when I could not prolong the supplies by any artifice whatsoever; I had none. I do not intend to labor overlong on the rigors of that voyage; suffice it to say I caught fish and slit them open for their small quantities of fresh water. I drank a few handfuls of seawater per day for the moisture, knowing I could tolerate that small amount of salt, and I ate fish, which I detest, not only because of the damned fishheads from around the curve of the horizon.

Whether or not I could have survived without that immersion in the Pool of Baptism in Aphrasöe I do not know. But the day came when, almost out of my head and scarcely believing what I saw to be true, an argenter appeared, backed her maintopsail and so picked me up.

The hands that lifted me from the boat, the faces that stared down on me, were all a shining lustrous black. I knew I had fallen into the hands of apims from Xuntal, people of the same race as Balass. I had always found the Xuntalese to be firm, thoughtful, generous, fierce when they had to be. It seemed wise to appear in worse case than I was. So they carried me below decks and I flopped in a peculiar bunk built into the side of the ship and went to sleep. Water, food, everything I needed of bodily comfort was provided when I awoke.

There is little else to say about the argenter. She was *Scepter of Xurrhuk*, much after the style of those broad argenters of Pandahem, although, I fancied, not quite so wide and stubby and with another knot of speed in a fair breeze. She was painted in brilliant colors of many tones and shades and her sails were all of purest white, which delighted and amazed me, an old salt accustomed to the drab tawny sails long exposed to the elements of my own vessels.

Her master, a tall, imposing man wearing dyed blue garments of the finest ponsho wool, invited me to his cabin. The sweep of the aft windows brought back memories. I sat and drank a very fair Maxanian, straw-colored, light on the palate, and the master introduced himself as Captain Swixonon.

"You are a lucky man, dom."

"Aye, Captain. Xurrhuk of the Curved Sword smiled."

His craggy face regarded me gravely. "You are not of Xuntal."

"No. But I count at least one Xuntalese as a good friend. Tell me, Captain, where are we bound?"

"We sail from Mehzta to Xuntal."

"I know a good friend from Mehzta also."

"You are a much traveled man?"

I did not laugh but I said, "No. I met them far from their homes. I cannot pay you now for a passage, but I know ships. I can work. Later, when I am home, I will remit payment through the Lamnias."

"Very well." He was a captain, a man who made his mind up rapidly.

"Thank you."

"And your name? And your country?"

"I am Dray Prescot, of Vallia."

He raised his eyebrows. I did not think he had heard of me. After all, Kregen is a large place and my doings, although making a stir in the countries I had been, would mean little elsewhere.

"I am pleased to make a connection with Vallia. Maybe we can arrange something later."

He was shrewd. Trading over the oceans is a chancy business. There are fliers on Kregen, as you know, but most of that marvelous world's commerce is carried on by ship or canal or animal transport. Fliers—as I well knew—are often rare and precious objects, completely unknown over many and many a highly civilized land. Havilfar holds her secrets well.

With that in mind, I said, "I would like to hire or charter a flier in Xuntal. The Vallian embassy is still open?"

He looked puzzled. "Why should it not be, dom?"

"I have been away ... politics. I shall be glad to be back, by Vox!"

In his shrewdness I fancy he read more into me than I intended to give away. He asked no questions about my arrival in a small boat, but he must have seen her and noted her lines. The rest of the journey I acted as a simple seaman and, I swear by Zair, despite the pressing urgency forcing me on, I recognized that the argenter could go no faster so I took some pleasure from the tasks of shipboard life again.

To pass very rapidly over the next few weeks is to bring me to the Vallian ambassador in Xuntal, that island off the southern promontory of Balintol, the large subcontinent of Segesthes. Mehzta, from which came my good comrade Gloag, lay off the northeast coast of Segesthes. Here in Xuntal I was about the same distance southeast of Valka as I was of Zenicce, where Gloag ran my House of Strombor. Yet, because of Delia, it was to the Vallian ambassador I went and not the Stromborian. Between Xuntal and Mehzta lie the Chulik Islands. Between Xuntal and Vallia lie the islands of Undurkor. At least I knew where I was on Kregen.

There was a little trouble in my seeing the Vallian ambassador. The embassy, a splendid and imposing building as befitted the Empire, lay along a shady avenue of other magnificent buildings housing various embassies and consulates. I barged right in and told the flunky I wanted to see the ambassador and to jump. I realize now that I was at fault. But I'd been away for twenty-one miserable years and I was in a hurry. They offered to throw me out.

Eventually, carrying one guard under an arm, four or five others holding aching heads in a trail on the floor in my wake and the last and most gorgeous of them, in golden robes, thrust along ahead with my hand around his neck, I presented myself before the Vallian ambassador.

The room was ornate, filled with light, expensive. I heeded none of it. The ambassador rose to his feet from the chair behind his desk. He had been talking to a shifty-looking Rapa who still sat, lifting his vulturine head to observe the proceedings.

"What do you want? Get out! Rast, out!"

I pitched the golden-robed flunky to one side.

This ambassador was one of your red-cheeked, pouchy-eyed individuals, all choler and bile. He wore decent Vallian buff-leathers, but a fancy decoration of black and white looped around his collar. I knew those colors in Vallia. He was a member of the Racter party, the most powerful political party of Vallia, and a gang who had given me trouble before and were to give me trouble again—aye, so much trouble I wonder any of them are still alive, by Vox!

I said; "Cramph! Your name! Instantly!"

He saw my face. I did not know him. I do not think he had ever seen me in Vallia before. But he saw my face and some of the color fled from his cheeks.

"Guards!" he screamed, waving his arms.

I picked up one of the flunkies' rapiers. I swished it around. I said, "I shall not ask you your name again."

Maybe there is something in me, in that stupid, thick-headed Dray Prescot, which guarantees that the yrium—the charismatic power that I detest and yet cold-bloodedly use when I have to—can shine through despite my lumpen ways.

"I am Vektor Ulanor, the Trylon of Frant! You rast, you will rue the day you—"

"I am Dray Prescot, the Prince Majister. You need not abuse yourself or show fear, for you could not know me. I need a flier at once. Let there be no delay. *Jump!*" He gaped at me.

I said: "I shall not ask you again. A Trylon? As ambassador to Xuntal? Very proper, for we value the Xuntalese. But you may well not be a Trylon for very much longer, Ulanor. You might not even be a noble at all, not even a Koter. You might be allowed to sweep the road of zorca and totrix droppings, in the great Kyro of Drak the Victorious in Vondium—if I am minded to be merciful."

Well, it was all most unpleasant and distasteful; in the end I secured the flier and supplies and bid a much shaken Trylon Vektor remberee.

Even then, as I sped through the clean air of Kregen, I wondered what this ambassador Ulanor had been up to with a Rapa in Xuntal. The Rapas, those diffs with the strong vulture-heads and fiercely curved beaks, are not often found in the guise of merchants. If plots were being hatched I would have to attend to them the moment I had assured myself everything was shipshape at home. Trylon Vektor had given me a brief rundown on the situation in Vallia. I gathered little had changed in my absence: the Emperor still ruled with his iron, despotic sway partially tempered by his Presidio, the Racters were still in strong opposition to his plans—this I had gathered by what Vektor Ulanor did not say and by his facial tic—and Valka, as far as he knew, had not sunk into the sea.

He conveyed the impression that he would be particularly pleased had my island done so.

After that first heated exchange he would have done as I commanded him; only afterward would he doubt his sanity and believe me an impostor. Luckily for him—I didn't care—one of the grooms in the embassy had been in Vondium with another employer and had seen me there. He was able to assuage the Trylon's fears as to my identity.

I gave them no explanation whatsoever of my presence in Xuntal or of my absence, about which they were well informed. I did give instructions that a fair passage money with a bonus should be paid in broad golden talens to Captain Swixonon, with my thanks. I also advised him, privately, to go for business to the Stromborian embassy and to say the Lord of Strombor had sent him. I added I did not think the Vallian ambassador would be of any use to a friend of mine.

Now I sent the little airboat racing over the surface of Kregen under the Suns of Scorpio.

She was an unhandy little craft and not overly fast, being capable of little more than eight dbs.* So as I urged her on and we passed over the sea dropping Xuntal astern I settled down to the long haul ahead—if the flier did not break down. The flying furs wrapped me against the slipstream. At last the dim and faraway blue and brown flicker of islands to starboard told me I was passing the Undurkors. Northwest I went, over the suns-glittering sea, northwest as the suns sank and Kregen's primary moon, the Maiden with the Many Smiles, shone forth in pink and golden glory. A few clouds wafted against that glowing orb, for the moon was almost full, and I expectantly looked back to the east to see a sight I had never seen on Earth. Soon the fourth moon, She of the Veils, rose and the two moons rolled along above me, casting down their fuzzy pinkish light, most wonderful, most gorgeous, most comforting. Two of the lesser moons hurtled across, as though in welcome to see me again.

I am an Earthman, a terrestrial, and yet on Earth I had found having only one moon in the sky a most unsettling experience. How quickly we adapt and change, how quickly we grow accustomed to the bizarre . . . and yet isn't just one moon as bizarre as seven? My Delia would have thought so.

At this speed it would take me over a day and a half to reach Valka.

That journey proceeded with nightmare slowness. As I journeyed nearer and nearer to Valka and all the place meant to me, I grew more and more irritable, more agitated, more apprehensive. The closer I came the more I feared. All manner of phantasms rose to torture me. Anything could have happened, anything could have gone wrong. Twenty-one years! The idea of invisible, near-omnipotent Star Lords directing me and controlling my destiny sickened me. My own estimation of myself, my own foolish achievements, all meant nothing beside the enormity of their power.

Dbs: dwaburs per bur. A dwabur is five miles and a bur is forty minutes. Dbs is the usual measurement for fliers. Land or sea transport speed is more often given in ubs, ulms per bur. An ulm is about 1,500 yards.

A.B.A.

My Delia! She must be there, waiting for me, smiling, running to greet me with outstretched arms!

Close to dawn I knew I must be entering the areas of my former life on Kregen. Below me, as the first ruby fires flickered over the eastern horizon, must lie the dark outlines of islands I knew. First rose Zim, that great crimson sun that is called Far in Havilfar, and has many and many a name over other parts of Kregen. I roused myself and stared ahead in that rosy dawn. The sea sparkled empty before me. I cursed. When the vivid emerald fires of Genodras, the smaller green sun that in Havilfar is called Havil and likewise has many other names, rose to drench the bloodlit sky I saw a faint smear on the northwestern horizon. I was gripping the wooden rail of the flier like a drowning man. My head jutted above the little windshield and the breeze roared in my face, streaming my shaggy mop of brown hair, bringing water to my eyes.

I wore an old red-and-white checked shirt and a pair of breeches that barely fitted. Around my waist in a cheap leather scabbard and belt hung a rapier and main-gauche I had borrowed from Trylon Vektor. I stared ahead and I could feel my heart thumping. This—this homecoming was what I had craved for twenty-one unendurable years on Earth.

Islands flashed past below. I saw the cream of surf, the windblown trees, here and there the orderly signs of cultivation. Villages and towns flashed past and then more open sea. Ships sailed down there, toy models with swelling sails. I looked ahead. Valka! Yes—there rose the high battlements of of the Heart Heights, those inner mountains where the freedom-fighters had rallied to oppose oppression. Now I could see the coastline, the whole fantastic sweep of the Bay, with Valkanium dotting the bright slopes with white and multicolored buildings. The high fortress of Esser Rarioch atop its hill, the banners and streamers, the brave red and white of Valka, the suns streaming their glorious mingled rays upon all that vivid scene, it was a fusion of color and movement, and brightness as the voller swept in a lancing curve to land on that high terraced platform.

I stepped out.

I looked around.

By Zair!

Home—home after twenty-one years and four hundred light-years. I felt dizzy, dizzied with the sheer ache of longings fulfilled.

People came running.

Many I knew. Many I did not know. There rose a babblement of voices. I laughed. I, Dray Prescot, laughed. Up above my head a patrol of flutduins curved, those famous saddle birds of Djanduin with my riders of Valka perched on them. A voller swung away, assured by the people below that all was well.

Panshi came forward, smiling, holding his great staff of office, full well understanding the importance of this occasion.

"Master!" he said. He looked at me and I saw the expression on his face and I clasped him by the hand, mightily shocking him and yet perfectly conveying the impression of welcome and homecoming we both experienced.

"The Princess Majestrix! Prince Drak and Princess Lela! Prince Segnik and Princess Velia! Where are they?"

"My Prince!" he said.

And I chilled.

"Prince Drak is in Vondium with his grandfather, the Emperor. Princess Lela and Princess Velia stay with the sisters of the Rose. Prince Zeg is gone to a far-off place that must exist, for he has been there and returned, but it is beyond all men's knowledge."

My hands were gripped together. I was aware of the throng pressing, the shouts as the word passed: "The old Strom is back!"

I hardly understood what they said. The *old* Strom.

"And the Princess Majestrix?"

I did not like the look on old Panshi's face. But he was a good and loyal man. He straightened up.

"She too is gone, my Prince."

"Gone!" I was shouting. "Gone where?"

He waved his hand before his face. The great staff of office shook against the flagstones.

"I do not know, my Prince, I do not know. But she is gone."

Chapter Eight

"And so the Princess Majestrix went alone?"

My private rooms, my inner sanctum, were smothered in dust. Dust and decay harbored here. I smashed the rapier flat against a chair and the dust flew. Sitting, I stared at Panshi, who had followed me here. All others I had waved away.

"Fetch me food and drink, Panshi. Send for it. You must tell me all that has passed."

"Yes, master."

A Fristle fifi I did not know scurried in with refreshment, looking frightened. When she had gone I said: "You said Prince Zeg?"

"Yes, Prince. He is no longer Prince Segnik." Then Panshi revealed he was still the same old retainer, for he added in a more sprightly voice: "He said he would not have the *nik* added to his name any longer, and he fought Prince Vanden, whose father visited here, and gave the brat—I beg your pardon, my Prince—gave the young lord a bloody nose."

That sounded likely. This young Prince Vanden's father was that same Varden Wanek, Prince of the House of Eward of Zenicce, a good comrade to Dray Prescot, so something at least of the old alliances continued.

"Go on, Panshi." I spoke more calmly now. This was not the homecoming I had expected, hungered for. The emptiness in me rang hollow with mockery of my hope. But, after so long, how could I expect everyone to be home waiting for me?

"Prince Segnik went away—to a place—and when he returned he called himself Prince Zeg."

I fancied I knew where Segnik had been, and you who listen to these tapes will have no difficulty in understanding just where he had been and what he had been about.

"And the Princess Majestrix has gone there too?"

"I believe so, my Prince. But I cannot be sure."

"Tell me."

"Men came. Strange men. They were closeted privately with the Princess, and Turko the Shield had to be told by me most stringently that she was not to be disturbed. We waited and fretted and when the Princess bade the men remberee she looked—I crave your indulgence, master—she looked sad and tired. We wanted to help; but she would not confide in us."

"Didn't Prince Drak have anything to say?"

"He was in Vandayha over a matter of a silversmith who had adulterated his metal. There was a scandal and Prince Drak—"

"Yes, yes." I saw then that young Drak had been carrying on my government while I had been away. Well, wasn't that the proper function for a dutiful son?

"The young Prince and Princess—" began Panshi, but in my impatience I interrupted.

"And Turko and Balass and Naghan, Melow the Supple—they are all with the Princess?"

He looked thoughtful and adjusted the upper hem of his robe, for he had somehow managed to find the time to dress himself in his full regalia so that he looked at once imposing and faintly ridiculous, an eminently practical appearance for the Chief Chamberlain. "I do not know for sure, my Prince. They were called away with the Elten of Avanar to—ah—attend to the disturbances of the Strom of Vilandeul. He conceived the idea that he was entitled to the lands west of the Varamin Mountains and led an expedition—"

I felt not so much the shock of that as the annoyance. The Elten of Avanar was my old blade comrade Tom Tomor ti Vulheim. He was my Chuktar in command of the army of Valka. If the Strom of Vilandeul, a Strom governing his Stromnate on the mainland of Vallia, conceived that land in my island of Can Thirda belonged to him, there was going to be trouble. The shock, when I thought about it, was the wonder that the trouble should occur at all in the Empire of Vallia. Surely the Emperor was not so decayed as to be unable to maintain law and order? This was a matter that must be looked into. But not now; now I only desired to find my Delia. The children were quite clearly making their own lives. It was my Delia I must concern myself with.

"In this trouble, the young Prince would have been—" started Panshi.

"And so the Princess Majestrix went alone?"

He did like my tone. He lifted his thin shoulders. "She would not listen, my Prince. We tried—she left when the Strom of Vilandeul played a false tune. I think, if I may be permitted to say this, my Prince, that when the Princess went the Strom fancied his chances."

"But Tom will fix him," I said. With Vangar and the air fleet, the cavalry and aerial cavalry and the superb Archers of Valka, my Stromnate should be able to resist this upstart Strom's plans for conquest and occupation.

"Master, men did go with the Princess, a small bodyguard she agreed to take, and Melow the Supple—"

"Ah!" I said. At once I felt more reassured.

Staring about the dusty room with the furnishings so carefully chosen, I wondered. As Panshi poured a fresh cup of tea—that superb Kregen tea on which I dote—I prowled around the familiar room, seeing that the weapons adorning the walls had all been most carefully greased, noting the books in their serried ranks, the pictures, the banners, marking all the old items, domestic and flamboyant, that made this room and these chambers a place to feel at home, to relax, to laugh and enjoy life.

"Why is the room dusty, Panshi?"

"The Princess would not allow anyone here after you—ah—went away, my Prince. There were some who whispered you were dead. But we who know you knew better. The young Prince, of course, did not—"

"Was a message entrusted to you?"

"Only that when you returned you were to be told what I have told you. I think, Majister, another message may have been left."

I thought so too. So I prowled, going to the writing desks and the bookshelves and all those peculiarly Kregan furnishings that make a Kregan home a place of color as well as comfort. I did not find a message from Delia. Well, I knew enough. There remained one item to learn, one remaining fact. I hesitated to ask, dreading the answer. But one must accept the needle, as they say on Kregen.

"When did the Princess leave?"

"Seven months of the Maiden with the Many Smiles."

Over a year ago, in terrestrial reckoning! The Kregans' measurements of time are a vastly complicated affair, with their seasons and their months calculated to the phases of the three major sets of moons and the passages of the suns. I felt again that heaviness at my heart, that hollowness within me.

"You will have messages sent to Prince Drak and the Princesses, Panshi," I said, with as firm a voice as I could muster. "I have no time to write. Say I am returned and gone to seek their mother." I began to strip off the old red-and-white checked shirt. "And I will have a fleet voller readied, well provisioned and weaponed. I will select the weapons myself."

"I will do all you command, master. And the young Prince?"

"Since he is probably where I am now going I shall be able to speak with him myself."

I saw Panshi's eyebrows lift a tiny fraction, then he nodded and bustled off to prepare what was necessary.

There was no time to take the Baths of the Nine, for though Delia might have left over a year ago, I did not wish to waste a mur. As for weapons, I plundered the armory and took a fine selection. For clothes I had a whole wardrobe in a wicker basket placed in the chosen flier and made sure a quantity of scarlet cloth was included. I was traveling where men fought in different fashion from men in Vallia and Zenicce and Pandahem. And, to be truthful, in a way that was both advantageous and disadvantageous.

The state of Valka and my other lands was sketched by Panshi: the army as I had seen was in fine fettle; the shipyards prospered; we were recovering from a poor samphron-oil crop; the Princess Majestrix had trouble in Delphond, but the leader of the high assembly of Valka, grim old Tharu ti Valkanium, continued to shoulder the burdens of office. I remembered him with affection.

As always my mind turned towards my comrades, men and women of Kregen I counted as friends. Seg Segutorio, for whom young Segnik had been named—and how had he taken this changing of his given name, I wondered—knew where I would be going. I felt I could count on him to assist me. And Inch too would assuredly come. I must make time to write them. The pen squealed over the paper, for there was no time for the fine Kregan brushwork, and I stated to them both very simply that I was back and needed their help; I added that Inch should first contact Seg and they should journey together.

Then I crossed out the Kregish word for *should* and substituted a euphemistic expression that conveyed the idea of a request and a gracious permission on their part. After this lapse of time they would be deeply immersed in their own affairs. How could I expect them to drop everything and go flying across Kregen after a harebrained onker like me, rushing headlong into adventures again, as we had in the old days?

For I knew as surely as Zim and Genodras ruled the daytime sky that fearsome adventures loomed ahead. This was no picnic on which I embarked. And my Delia had gone—alone!

Well, not quite alone. I was marvelously cheered at the thought of a ferocious jikla, a Manhound of Faol, pacing at her side with slavering fangs ready to rend any who would harm her.

When I saw the flier Panshi had provided I could not prevent a tiny droop to my lips. She was not one of the best. He saw my face and hurriedly said, "Master, all the fliers save a very few have been taken, as I have told you. Even the sailers. San Evold and San Khe-Hi are with Prince Drak."

I knew what he meant. Nothing more had been done about deciphering the secrets of the silver boxes that powered vollers.

It was necessary for me to observe the fantamyrrh with great care as I stepped aboard the voller. This I did.

A young Hikdar of the Valkan Archers looked up at me. He bashed his red-and-white banded sleeve across his chest.

"My Prince! I would like to go with you. I and a choice band from my pastang."

I looked at him. Yes, I knew him. He had been a waso-Deldar when last I'd been in Valka. Now he wore the insignia of a shebov-Hikdar of the Fourth Regiment of Valkan

Archers. In twenty years he had gone from the fifth rank in the Dedlar structure to the seventh rank in the Hikdar. Even when men live for two hundred years there is still promotion when there is fighting to be done.

"I am sure your pastang is a credit to the Fourth, and to the Valkan Army, Hikdar Naghan ti Ovoinach. But your duty lies here, to protect Valka, as you have been detailed."

His face lit up at my remembrance of him, and showed sadness at my words. But he bashed me another salute and stepped back to where his pastang, a full eighty superb bowmen, lined up. I saw that a strong hand had been running the army, at least, while I had been away. As the voller soared up into the limpid light of the suns I guessed that strong and guiding hand to belong to my son Drak. How odd to think that, even though I was chronologically over ninety years of age, my son at thirty-two was an older man than I. I had been thirty when I'd taken that dip in the Pool of Baptism.

Although no one had mentioned it, I knew well enough that he was regarded as the Strom of Valka, that when I was mentioned it would be as the *old* Strom of Valka. Oh, yes, I knew.

I set the controls at due west and thrust the speed lever hard over. The persistent habit of driving vollers at their top speed had been growing on me. This was no time to make an exception.

Rising into the air, the voller swung west. I looked down over the rim where the lacing of leather to the wooden rib had frayed and threatened to rip apart in the slipstream. This was an example of the more common form of voller which, while being able to move of its own volition by reason of the two silver boxes, was yet susceptible to wind pressure. If this craft failed me somewhere over the sea . . . Well, that would be an end to Dray Prescot, onker of onkers.

Unless of course, the Star Lords still needed me for their inscrutable purposes. The veil that had been partially lifted on the Everoinye, allowing me a dim glimpse of secrets to be discovered, had shown me potentialities for conflict that staggered me, courses of disaster I did not wish to steer.

Below me Valkanium vanished aft, with the peak of Esser Rarioch lofting, its pinnacles and towers ablaze with flags and banners, the wink and gleam of weapons very comforting as

Hikdar Naghan ti Ovoinach and his pastang saluted my departure.

The voller whisked into the clouds and I was alone.

Once more I was set full on a fresh course for adventure and headlong action, hurtling across the surface of Kregen. The thought came to plague me that perhaps I was no longer the Dray Prescot who had first been transported here by the Savanti. Maybe I had lost my cutting edge. Well, as Zair was my witness, I would do all that I could for my Delia, and not reckon the consequences. No matter what perils I might encounter I would not surrender the fight until they shipped me out to the Ice Floes of Sicce.

Chapter Nine

Into the Eye of the World

I, Dray Prescot, Lord of Strombor and Krozair of Zy, flew for the inner sea of Kregen, the Eye of the World.

Since I had left the enclosed world of the inner sea with Delia, Seg and Thelda, much had happened to me and much time had passed. I had become all manner of fine fancy nobility, Strom of Valka, Prince Majister of Vallia, King of Djanduin and other titles in addition. I had become a father. I had been to Earth and back to Kregen. How could I, who still took real and genuine pride in belonging to the mystic Order of Krozairs of Zy, expect to recapture the sensations and excitements of my life on the inner sea?

As I flew through the clear and bracing air of Kregen I felt no doubts about what must be done. For I flew to find my Delia, my Delia of the Blue Mountains, my Delia of Delphond.

For her sake I would dare anything, anyone. I do not boast. I state a plain fact. I know too that she would dare all for me, and it is at that thought that I tremble.

At an average speed of approximately ten dbs the flier would take roughly two and three-quarter days to cover the distance from Valka to Sanurkazz. Despite all the urgency I felt and the maddening impatience that tore at me, there was nothing I could do but wait for the time to pass as the voller soared across Kregen. Vondium, the capital of Vallia, passed away over the southern horizon. The ocean that is called the Sunset Sea all the way from Vallia to Segesthes flowed beneath the petal-shape of the voller. By the time the shoreline of the continent of Turismond appeared ahead I was almost sunk in an apathy induced by frustration, fretting and concern.

My Delia had passed this way over a year before. What had happened to her? Then, as Port Tavetus, one of Vallia's colonial cities of the eastern Turismond coast, passed astern, I found a few remnants of sanity returning. Now I was headed for the Klackadrin. The earth had moved here at some time in the past, opening up a long narrow rift from which noxious gases poured, vapors carrying with them hallucinogenic substances that ripped away a man's sanity. I had traveled here on foot. The experience is one I seldom dwell on. The Phokaym, those coldly hostile risslaca men, riding risslaca steeds, gripped the land on the western edge of the Klackadrin in a fist of iron. The experiences through which I had been dragged there must have left deep scars, for I know I held on to the voller and prayed it would not break down over that hellish place.

The enormous rent in the earth's surface stretched for dwabur after dwabur north and south. I could see steam and vapors lifting and I drove the voller higher. The ground stank with barrenness. Remnants of the proud roads once driven across from east to west by the imperial powers of the old Empire of Loh glittered in the dying light of the suns. Now the Klackadrin on the east and the stupendous mountain bulk of the Stratemsk on the west effectively closed off the land between, land men called the hostile territories.

Believe me when I say that however inimical the hostile territories are, I heaved a sigh of relief when I passed safely over the Klackadrin.

As for the hostile territories, somewhere down there Delia, Seg, Thelda and I had marched and sang as we fought our way on foot from the Stratemsk eastward. Looking back, I could be thankful about what happened, that my friends were spared the horrors of the Phokaym and the Klackadrin.*

At the time, mind you, I was a very angry man.

Down there Queen Lilah might still be lording it over Hiclantung, aping the ancient ways of the Queens of Pain of

---

*See *Warrior of Scorpio*, Dray Prescot #3. Prescot's account of how he escaped the Phokaym and crossed the Klackadrin on foot is, unfortunately, lost.

A.B.A.

Loh. Without any feeling that the emotion was grotesque, I found myself wishing her well. She was merely what she was. At the least and for all its faults, Hiclantung was an oasis of culture in a sea of barbarism.

The changing face of the land below as it sped past gave no real indication of what was going on down there. One day, when safe means of crossing the Klackadrin had been found, the onward-pressing frontier forces of Vallia and the various nations of Pandahem would spill out into the hostile territories. The use of vollers alone would not be enough. I consigned these interesting prospects for the future to the Black Spider Caves of Gratz as before me rose the impossible bulk of the Stratemsk.

I have already spoken of the Stratemsk, the ranges of mountains extending north and south, defying reason, sprawling into the sky, cloaked eternally in ice and snow, cleft by deep humid jungle valleys, demanding everything of spirit and valor to dare. They shut off the eastern portions of the lands of the inner sea. I must cross them. My Delia had done so—three times. I had crossed them only once, and then we had crashed.

This was where I had first encountered flying animals and birds on Kregen of a size large enough to carry a passenger. Out in the hostile territories I had seen a few distant dots in the air and the speed of the voller had taken me past. Now I faced gigantic birds and animals in their natural state, untamed, ferocious, vicious, forever seeking food.

I fancied they'd find Dray Prescot a tough and sinewy mouthful, still, it behooved me to keep my old carcass out of their fangs and jaws.

The voller took me through the first of the foothills. Ahead the high peaks waited. Wending a way through the passes and gradually flying higher and higher, I skirted those ice-bound precipices, sped beneath the pinnacles of glistening rock and drove hard through watever open spaces vallies offered. The air cut to the quick. Flying silks and furs were heaped over me.

I crouched in the voller with only my eyes and nose showing and my fist gripped around the hilt of a longsword. If a flight of impiters caught me, those coal-black demons of the air would rip the voller to pieces. I could not hope to be saved once again by a gorgeous myriad of tiny pink and yellow birds.

Straight on past two mountain flanks that seemed ready to topple inward and grind together, I sent the voller hurtling down over the saddle. The long valley ahead swarmed with birds swooping from the rocks. I held to the center Mists coiled below. The farther end of the valley showed its V-notch and chill white-blue sky beyond. Due west, always due west. . . .

The voller fluttered and dived.

Useless to bash the controls, to rave and curse. Down swooped the voller, down and down, plunging into the mists. I ripped open the panel which in this small craft covered the two silver boxes in their sturm-wood orbits. A single glance told me the mechanism was functioning correctly, the orbits moving one with the other on their bronze and balass gearing. So the trouble lay within the vaol box. If there was trouble with the paol box there was nothing I could do. To open that would release the cayferm and that box would never function again.

The idea that this voller's power source had reached the end of its useful life, when the silver boxes dulled, had given me a nasty turn; now I must land and dismantle the vaol box.

The mists coiled more thinly. Huge bloated tree trunks passed. I had the speed down now and felt confident of making a respectable landing. The muggy heat rose. Here in these deep valleys the air hung heavy and humid, ground heat and the greenhouse effect combining to make jungle miniatures within the mountain mass.

A confused jumble of orange-speckled yellow, of leprous growths with medusa-arms, of black and glistening trunks, swished away. The voller roared past a lichened rock outcrop, clipped yellow powder from hanging clusters of puffballs, making me sneeze, and came to a shaky stop amid tendrilous yellow ferns. All about me the spectral trees rose like a wall. Bloated, whiplike, fern-fanned, the variety of forms displayed a massive and frenzied struggle for life. Lianas draped everywhere. The smells were fetid and yet not overly unpleasant and I guessed the busy scavengers were at work breaking down every last fragment of refuse.

A bulky something moved ponderously among the trees. A glimmering white outline, immense, inhuman, something like a giant slug with orange horns, slid past between the trees. The longsword lifted, but the monster glided on, tearing at the branches.

Putting the longsword down close by, I ripped out the vaol box and carefully opened it. How often I had done this! Inside the box the minerals were clumped, packed mostly at one end with only a scattering of powder moving freely. I used a dagger to stir the powder free, to break up the clumps, to return the mix to its original loose condition. By the time the lid was back on the sweat poured from me; the humidity was murderous.

The vaol box was slicked with moisture and I knew that enough had been trapped inside to make the box unusable again before too long. It would have to get me through the Stratemsk. I reseated it within its orbit and reconnected the gearing train.

It was at that moment, straightening up, ready to hit the controls, that the xi lunged.

There was barely time to scoop up the sword and parry that first vicious thrust.

The xi whirred its diaphanous wings and backed off, chirring in frenzy. Its iridescent scales glimmered in the diffused light. The xi was something like a dragonfly, with four glistening wings behind a head that was a nightmare cross between a bird's beak and a snake's wedge. But all likeness to a dragonfly was lost when the xi whipped its sinuous snakelike body from side to side and coiled it for a stinging blow from beneath. Besides, the xi was ten feet long—a flying monster, aiming to skewer me and then devour me at leisure for lunch.

A single dominant thought obsessed me: I must dispose of this fellow before the rest of the swarm found me.

It darted in again and I ducked the lethal lunge of the tail, the longsword slashing down at his forward antennae. The keen blade sheared through the black furry feelers, surged on to gouge into the bright and staring eye on the left of that wedge-shaped head. The xi's wings fluttered madly. It whirred away, spinning, flying clumsily. From the longsword a green ichor dropped.

The voller went up cleanly. Up and up, past the tumbling,

pathetic shape of the xi, up to burst through the mist and so
bring me into the chill upper air.

"By Vox!" I said explosively. "I was lucky there!"

In those last few murs before the mist enfolded me I had
seen the glittering swarm approaching, flying fast, a blurring
mass of shining wings and iridescent scales, the lizards of the
air, swarming to devour me!

There is a considerable variety of xi, and I had just met a
type whose body had nearly evolved into a whiplike snake
form, away from the original, bulkier lizard form. Whatever
family they belong to, the xi are bad news.

And my Delia had flown this way!

Straight on I forced the voller. Like the end of a nightmare
the last valley opened out and all before me stretched the
downward trending slopes of the westward face of the
Stratemsk. Here fresh dangers lurked. The flying furies of the
mountains might all be behind of me, the impiters and corths,
the zizils and bisbis, the yellow eagles of Wyndhai and the
iridescent-scaled xi; now I must fly over the lands of the crofermen.

Savage, untamed, cruel and suspicious, the crofermen inhabit the outer reaches of the Stratemsk. They live an ardu-
ous life filled with peril, defending their ponsho flocks against
the demons of the air, continually fighting among themselves,
man-beasts of lowering aspect and formidable ferocity.

I, Dray Prescot, say this with all truth: I was lucky to be
able to fly over them and not have to come to ground.

As you know I had been well informed that it was against
policy to take an airboat into the lands of the inner sea. Delia
had landed her flier some way off the eastern edge of the sea
and had taken local transport when she had come searching
for me before. The people of the Eye of the World had little
if any knowledge that it was possible for a man to fly
through the air.

Now I knew that interdiction must have come from the
Empire of Hamal, which made and sold vollers, and the law
had been implemented by the Presidio of Vallia because they
did not wish to lose their franchise. Hamal would not sell
vollers to Pandahem or Loh, and their lack had proved disastrous in the past.

I consigned Hamal and Empress Thyllis, with whom I had

an outstanding debt, to the Ice Floes of Sicce as I bored on through the bright air of Kregen, angling to fetch up in Sanurkazz itself.

How often I had promised myself I would return to the Eye of the World! And how often fate had destroyed my intentions, one way or another, every time. I had planned to return on a joyous holiday, to take my Delia and the family, to revisit the haunts of my existence there as a Krozair captain and see my friends once again. Now I came in urgency and haste, desperate that Delia might be in peril.

My plans were very simple. I would go first to Sanurkazz, the chief city of the Zairians, and seek information. If I found nothing I would fly on to Zy, the island fortress of the Krozair Brotherhood, that order of which I was proud to account myself a member and which, I truly think, meant more to me, for all the tiny scope of its activities on Kregen, than anything else except Delia and my family.

The journey had taken the best part of three days. I had flown in as straight a line by the compass as I could contrive, a great-circle route that wasted not a dwabur of distance. The distance would have taken months to travel by land and sea. It had taken me month after weary month to travel in the opposite direction. As the land opened out below and signs of cultivation appeared, I felt those irritable, apprehensive, fearful sensations attack me once more as I neared my goal.

It seemed to me that Delia had come here because she had had bad news of Segnik—he who was now Zeg. I had pushed all that from my mind. But what other explanation could there be? I had discussed with Delia the education of our children many times. She knew that I intended Drak and, in his time, Segnik to go to the Krozairs of Zy. I believe the most profound education was possible with them. I had intended to take a hand to soften the teachings that emphasized the hatred for the Grodnims of the green northern shore. Oh, yes, as you know, I hated the overlords of Magdag and all the other Grodnims of the northern shore. But I felt mature enough to hold that feeling in its proper perspective. I had worn green clothes of late and I had met in friendship those to whom green and religions associated with the color were good and fine. It was the inner strength the Krozairs of Zy give, the spiritual teachings, the skill at arms, the knowledge of self, all those mystic disciplines that make a Krozair a man among men that I wanted for my sons.

Dealing with the religious beliefs of Kregen, it was in the pure and life-enhancing teachings of Opaz, the embodiment of the Invisible Twins, that I wished my family to be brought up. But nowhere else could the skill, the powers, the self-control, the mystic self-knowledge of the Krozairs be found than here, in the Eye of the World. To be a Krzy is a great and precious gift.

Then a twitch afflicted my grim old lips. Among all this high-level occupation of my brain the tickling thought emerged that I would see friends here who would bring me down to earth—or Kregen—with a bump.

I would again see Nath and Zolta, my two favorite rascals, my two oar comrades. By Zair! We'd roister all night in Sanurkazz! We'd have the fat and jolly mobiles falling over their feet as they tried to arrest us, dancing through the streets, a flagon of drink in one hand and a pretty tavern wench in the other! What a fool I had been not to return here sooner!

And there would be Pur Zenkiren to see, that upright, grim, but scrupulously fair Krozair who had been a good friend to me and who must by now be the Grand Archbold of the Krozairs of Zy, for Pur Zazz, who had then held that exalted post, had clearly almost run his long life on Kregen when I had last spoken with him.

Then, too, there was Mayfwy. All my pleasant thoughts of anticipation clouded as I remembered with great affection and pride my oar comrade Zorg of Felteraz. He had died under the lashes of the whip-deldars of Magdag. His widow Mayfwy, her son Zorg and daughter Fwymay had made Nath and Zolta and myself very welcome at the estate of Felteraz. Yes, I would like to see Mayfwy again.

So there were many places and people I must visit. But first I must assure myself that Delia was safe. To look back was agony. Twenty-one infernal years!

Because people of Kregen live to two hundred years or so, once they reach maturity they change only slowly. I held a vision of my Delia in my brain that could not have altered in any great particular. Our thousand-year promise of life meant a great deal to me, quite apart from the obvious, for twenty-one years' separation on Earth would destroy in time's remorseless flow the joys we knew. How I hated the Star Lords when I allowed myself to brood on their high-handed usage of me!

That, along with all the rest of the nonprofitable pining, had to be thrust aside. I would go on in my old way. I knew what I was about. If Zair was with me—and Opaz and Djan too, to be sure—I must succeed.

Chapter Ten
I am cruel to Mayfwy of Felteraz

Brilliant, glittering, filled with color, the waters of the Eye of the World rolled before me.

The twin Suns of Scorpio hung in the western sky, drenching the world in color and radiance. The air smelled sweet, sweet with the fragrance of Kregen. Below, the tended fields passed in neat checkerboards of cultivation. Here there could be habitation close to the shore of the inner sea, for ahead the massive frowning fortress guarding the careless city of Sanurkazz offered sure protection. As I looked ahead over the windshield, I saw that smaller but no less dominating fortress of Felteraz rise into view.

Felteraz, with its lush estates and its town and its fortress, was built into the sheer rock over the sea. Memories of the view from the high terrace there swam into my mind. How alike and yet how vastly different was the view in Felteraz from that dizzy prospect over the Bay and Valkanium from Esser Rarioch! Yet I loved this place. As my course took me over the gray battlements with their freight of banners, a sudden shaft of cunning pierced me through so that I trembled with my own deceit and struck the levers that sent the voller swirling down through the bright air.

There was no impediment to an aerial landing in the lands of the inner sea, for they knew nothing in their daily lives of aerial armadas and saddle flyers. The cities of the hostile territories were festooned with anti-flyer defenses. I was able to make a swooping landing, still the voller and step out onto a broad platform just below the highest terrace. People came running, astonished at the apparition of a man falling from heaven. I dare say, many of them took the commonsense view that I was a visitor from Zim.

Bronzed faces surrounded me. I saw again the mesh link mail of the men of Zair, the white surcoats blazing with a device I knew. That symbol, stitched in red and gold, with a lenk-leaf border, represented a pair of galley oars, crossed, divided upright by a longsword. Oh, yes, I knew that symbol. Hadn't I proudly worn it myself as a Krozair captain of a swifter of the Eye of the World, that device of Felteraz?

I knew none of the faces.

A longsword's point hovered a knuckle before my breastbone.

"Your name and your business, dom."

"My name is Dray Prescot. My business is with the Lady Mayfwy of Felteraz."

Only after I had spoken did it occur to me that Mayfwy might be dead, another here in her place as chatelaine of Felteraz.

The few murs of hesitation before the guard Hikdar spoke caused me great uneasiness, which vanished in a flood of relief as he said: "The Lady Mayfwy is at home. I think I have heard of you, Jernu,* from my father."

He looked at me doubtfully and did not lower the longsword. I would have faulted him in his duties had he done so. And from his father! Well, it had been a half-century by Earthly reckoning since I had been here last. I do not smile easily, as you know, so I looked at him and said, "Probably, Hikdar. If you will inform the Lady Mayfwy—"

"At once, Jernu."

He dispatched a swod of the guard and remained on the alert, watching me. The ring of people, joined now by women and girls, kept respectfully back and none offered to go anywhere near the voller. That was a marvel. I saw a movement in the pressing ring of people, in the direction opposite that taken by the guard swod, and I looked, seeing men and women moving quickly aside. A woman stepped out before

---

Jernu. This word for *lord* belongs to the Zairians and is not often used by Prescot. It equates with the Vallian *Jen* and the Hamalian *Notor*. Its correct use is clear in this context.

A.B.A.

"A woman stepped out before them."

them, holding a long silver wand in her hand with which she had no need to touch anyone who lagged in moving. I did not know her. I stared at the girl—the woman—who followed through the opened path.

She did not look quite the same. There was about her sweet face a graver air, a shadowed resignation to life that greatly pained me. In all else, though, she was the same lively, spritely, elfin girl who had first welcomed Zolta and Nath and me as we drove rattling up in our ass cart. Her dark, curly hair gleamed in the slanting rays of the suns, her pert nose uptilted and that small, soft sensuous mouth trembled and opened on a gasp. Her eyes widened and fastened on me a look that thrilled me through, a look compounded of pain and gladness, of joy and abiding sorrow.

With not the slightest holding back, with not a heartbeat of hesitation, she ran forward, lifting her arms.

"Dray! Oh, Dray! You have come back!"

And then she was in my arms and clasping me close and I looked over her shoulder with the scent of her in my nostrils and I felt the weight of Kregen crush in on me and knew myself for the most evil of devils imaginable—as I truly was.

She would not cry. Even with the emotions filling her she would not break down before her people. She stood back and held my hands and looked at me. I saw the brightness of her eyes, the tremble of that soft mouth.

"You have not changed, my Lord of Strombor!"

"And you," I said. "Mayfwy, you are the same dear Mayfwy."

"Oh, no. No, I know better than that." She glanced at the robed woman with the wand. "We will go to the terrace, Sheena, and be alone. Bring refreshments, Zond wine, for Pur Dray, the Lord of Strombor."

"At once, my lady."

And so there we were, Mayfwy and I, alone on the terrace as the sinking suns painted opaline radiance in the air and drowned the cliff face in color. I saw and I ached. How long it had been, how foolish I was! Fifty years—and then some of the iron returned, for twenty-one of those damned years had been wrenched away from my power by the Everoinye. Mayfwy took up a goblet of wine, laughing, handing it to me, and yet I saw the deep pain in her eyes. I gravely drank to her.

"Dray, there is so much to tell."

"Aye, so much."

"But first there is news that will gladden your heart . . . strange news to come from us here. . . ."

So I knew.

"Delia! She has visited here? You have seen her?"

A shadow flicked across Mayfwy's elfin face and passed, then she lifted her chin proudly and smiled.

"Yes. Delia has been here. She sought you."

I looked at her. My relief was obvious, for Mayfwy went on: "Yes, she crossed the Stratemsk in safety. There was a beast, a horrific beast, with her, that I swear would tear a leem to pieces. My men were uneasy until your Delia reassured them.

"Melow the Supple."

"That was the name."

"She will not harm you, Mayfwy. But tell me of Delia!"

How cruel that was, those words of mine, my whole demeanor, to this girl!

"You treat women harshly, my Lord of Strombor." She paused and lifted her goblet. Its ruby decoration in chains around the gold caught the light and blazed blood-red. "You say you love them and you leave them, for seasons on end. And should I call you Prince Majister now? Or even King?"

"You call me Dray Prescot, as you always have. It is not of my will that I left Delia—or you—without saying remberee. There are dark and evil forces in my life—but enough of this. Is Delia well? Did she speak of the children? Where did she go? Tell me, Mayfwy, for the sake of my dear friend and oar comrade, Zorg."

"Zorg." She drank then, and it was a benediction. "She is well and she says the children are well, although wild—well, we all know how wild our children are."

"Forgive me," I said quickly—me, that Dray Prescot who never apologized except to Delia. "Young Zorg and Fwymay. They are well?"

"Yes. They are well. Zorg is now a Krozair of Zy, which is as it should be, I suppose. He captains a swifter. He has much of his start to thank you for, Dray."

"Nonsense! A lad like that will forge his own way on Kregen."

She looked at me oddly. Well, not so long ago I had been standing in a Parisian hospital with the Prussian guns thundering and Kregen was four hundred light-years away. So I said: "The Zairians will always need men like young Zorg. And Fwymay?"

"She has made me a grandmother twice, the minx. She married Zarga na Rozilloi, who is a Krozair Brother, and a very pleasant young man."

I knew that this Zarga na Rozilloi must be of importance to warrant the *na* as his connective term, but he was not a Krzy. Had he been, Mayfwy would have said.

"He is a Krozair of Zimuzz." She was looking at me.

"A fine order," I said. But we both knew there was no other order as fine as the Krozairs of Zy.

Now the suns were almost gone. The purple shadows dropped across the terrace. Soon the Twins would be up, eternally revolving one about the other, to cast their mingled pinkish light down on Kregen. We moved into the inner room where we had often sat and talked and listened to the music provided by the citadel singers. The room looked just the same, except that a full-length portrait of a splendid-looking man had been added to the other portraits. This must be Zarga, for he wore the symbols of the Krozairs of Zimuzz. I ignored this new son-in-law and walked across, planted my feet on the thick rug and stood firmly looking up at the portrait of Zorg of Felteraz. Mayfwy moved silently away and left me. I looked at this painting of Zorg and I remembered, I remembered the warrens of Magdag and the rowing benches of the Magdaggian swifters, with Zolta and Nath, and I remembered our shared agonies and perils, the onions we had divided up, the lashes we had taken and, finally, Zorg's death, there in the stench and filth of a Magdaggian swifter. I remembered. And when I turned back to Mayfwy she put a hand to her mouth and did not speak for a moment. I suppose a great deal of what I felt showed on that ugly old face of mine.

Then, as though what she said had been jolted out of her by this reunion, by my abstraction, she said: "I used to hope I could place your portrait there, my Lord of Strombor."

I shook my head.

Then she cried.

Afterward I gave her another cup of wine and wiped her eyes with a clean cloth—she wore no makeup and had need of none—and said: "I must press on to find Delia. You know that. It is a fate I cannot—would not—deny. Until I know she is safe I cannot rest."

"I do understand. But please forgive me for saying . . . and for crying." She tossed her head back so that the clustered dark curls glistened in the samphron-oil lamp's gleam. "What young Zorg would say I do not know. No Krozair's mother cries!"

"I do not believe that. And Zorg, if he is a true Krozair as I know him to be, does not believe it either."

"If only he would get himself married and have children, they would be a comfort to me here."

There was more talk after that, and a fine meal which I knew had been especially prepared for me, and more wine—that smooth splendid Zord wine that Nath was so fond of—and Chremson if a difference in the tickle of the palate was needed. But Mayfwy could see the impatience burning in me. Truth to tell, I felt that Delia would understand when I told her that I had broken my journey to see Mayfwy, more so now that these two had met. How I had both welcomed and dreaded that encounter, for I desperately wished for them to be friends. But sober reality would seem to indicate the opposite. I would have to see what my Delia had to say.

I stood up.

Mayfwy rose, lithe as a neemu, her gaze wide on me, a hand to her breast. She wore what I remembered as being her favorite costume, a sheer gown of shimmering silk, white, simple, deeply cut, fastened at her shoulders by golden pins encrusted with rubies. They must be the same fibulae. They would be the same when we were all rotting in our graves or shivering in the Ice Floes of Sicce.

"You must go? So soon?"

"When I find my Delia we will return, Mayfwy I shall not again be such an onker. Do you forgive me?"

As I said the word that must have cut her, that simple "my" Delia, I cursed myself again. It seemed I could bring nothing but pain into the life of this girl. And girl she seemed to me still, despite all the lonely length of time she had lived, for she kept up her appearance out of her pride in being the widow of Zorg of Felteraz, a Krozair of Zy.

Luckily I did not ask her why she had never married again. That would have been the action of a clod; while I am a fine full-bloomed specimen of a clod, I did see clearly enough that the question would have been a slap in her face.

We stepped out onto that paved square high on the flank of the cliff where my voller waited. A guard had been posted around the craft, but no one had ventured near. Perhaps this was the very first airboat ever seen in these parts. I didn't care if it was or not, and I didn't care for the Hamalians and their dictates either. There was no remorse whatsoever in me for stopping here. Mayfwy told me that Delia had said she would fly direct to the fortress of Zy to find me. She had not confided in Mayfwy why, after a space of twenty years, she had thus come flying into the Eye of the World. But Mayfwy told me that Delia appeared sad, confirming Panshi's story.

I would brook no longer delay.

"Delia came riding a sectrix," said Mayfwy. She put a hand out tentatively and touched the leather and canvas of the voller. Her hand trembled. "You will use this marvelous thing?"

"If Delia went by here a year ago and then took ship for Zy, I can catch her all the quicker by voller."

"Voller? Ah, the flying boat."

"Yes."

"There are many of these ... vollers, in the outer world? In the world of Vallia and Valka, of Djanduin and Strombor?"

"Yes."

"It must be a marvelous place."

"It is, but in many things it is not as marvelous as the Eye of the World."

"We have our troubles. I fear for Zorg and for Zarga, my son-in-law. Those horrible greens of Grodno bear down our defenses. We are in parlous case, these latter days, my Lord of Strombor."

She went on to tell me in a small voice that the Grodnims pressed hard on the Zairians, that many battles had been lost; the Grodnim swifters might still be kept at bay; but the

Grodnim armies swept on, irresistibly, it seemed, from victory to victory. Her son Zorg scoured the seas and gained success in single-ship actions—how my blood fired up at the thought!—but Holy Sanurkazz lay sunk in apathy, awaiting the stroke of doom. I could scarcely credit this. When I had left here the Zairians, under the command of my friend Pur Zenkiren of Sanurkazz, had been pressing on to victory along the eastern shore in alliance with the Proconians, a people distinct from the red and green.

"Proconia?" I said.

She made a little moue. "They keep themselves aloof. They resist any attack on their territory. They no longer wish to ally with us in the fight."

"Then Zair will see they do not ally themselves with the damned Grodnims."

"That is what we all pray."

I did not tell her that with the politics of this region—politics I had previously regarded as simple and straightforward—if the Grodnims gained an upper hand the Proconians, aye, and all the other uncommitted peoples, would jump in to be on the winning side. Once the slide began it would gain speed with frightful force.

"Perhaps I will call in at Sanurkazz," I said as I stepped up into the voller, observing the fantamyrrh. "On our way back. There has to be an explanation for what you say."

"King Zo still rules, Dray. He will be pleased to see you."

I put my hand over the levers. The Twins rolled along above among a myriad of stars. The Maiden with the Many Smiles would soon be up and then She of the Veils. This would not be a night of Notor Zan, the Tenth Lord, the Lord of Darkness.

Felteraz lies about three dwaburs to the east of Sanurkazz and the distance in a flier's straight line to the island fortress of Zy from there is roughly a hundred and sixty dwaburs. At my voller's best pushed speed of ten dbs I ought to sight the island cone well before daylight. So I looked down on Mayfwy and she looked up. The fuzzy pinkish light played tricks with her features; but I knew she was not crying.

"Rembaree, Mayfwy."

"Rembaree, Pur Dray."

I thrust the levers home and the voller shot skyward.

To relate the events that now befell me is to relive a time of scarlet horror, a time when reason itself vanished from Kregen, a time when my reason for a while deserted me. My recollections tumble all confused and distorted, as the massive russet bodies of the chunkrah swim and haze when seen in the heat of the campfires of the Great Plains of Segesthes.

The voller did not fail me and I came at last in sight of the extinct volcanic cone that is the heart of the fortress of Zy. On the journey I had eaten and drunk of the supplies so liberally provided by Mayfwy, and I had slept. As I stared eagerly forward with the slipstream blustering in my face and saw that grim black pile harshly upthrust against the moons-glowing sea I rejoiced. Soon, soon, I would clasp my Delia in my arms again and she would clasp me. . . .

I sent the voller straight for the tall rock arch leading to the inner harbor. Only a few dim lights burned where I had been accustomed to seeing many lights blazing from the rock and the pharos lantern, swung from chains in the arch of the rock, casting its friendly greeting on the waters below. In a penumbrous circle of indistinct forms I dived for the entrance.

It is a commonplace experience, universally observed, that when a person returns to a place of his former abode everything in building and architecture and scale appears to him much smaller than the memories he had carried over the years. I had not experienced that in Valka. To a certain extent in Felteraz, yes, I had noticed, but then, it is the very smallness of Felteraz that enjoins so much of its beauty. Here, as I swooped the voller under the immense rock arch of Zy I felt only renewed awe at the grandeur about me. The water rippled gently below, pitch-black and runneled with the reflected lights of torches. Lights clustered on the dock. I touched down on the stones and stood up, stretched and cocked a leg over the side of the voller.

"Stand still! Declare yourself or you will be feathered."

That seemed perfectly proper to me.

"I am Dray Prescot, Krozair of Zy."

To say those words again, here in the very heart of all that made the Krozairs of Zy so formidable, so much a part of my life, in the very sanctum of the order, gave me a sweet, dizzied feeling of homecoming that marched with those other feelings of homecoming I had experienced in Valka.

"Climb down from your flying contraption, Dray Prescot. Do not touch your weapons as you value your life."

This was carrying precaution to an extreme. Still, I accepted. After all, eternal vigilance was part of the Krozair creed. I stepped from the voller to face the party of men who accosted me.

They wore the white surcoats over their mesh mail. The old familiar device glittered from the breasts of the surcoats, bravely shining in the light of the torches, the scarlet circle enclosing the hubless spoked wheel embroidered in silks of blue and orange and yellow. I saw the faces enclosed in the mail hoods, hard, fierce, dedicated faces, all a strong mahogany brown from the suns and the winds, with those arrogant upthrust black mustaches bristling. Yes, these were my Krozair Brothers.

I felt strange, outré, a stranger, in my decent Vallian buff. I wore a longsword, true, but it was not a real Krozair longsword, crafted by master smiths in the workshops here. Out of habit I still swung a rapier and main-gauche from my belt. I took a step forward, and a dozen longswords were whipped from scabbards and leveled at my breast.

"Lahal, my Brothers," I cried. "Lahal and lahal, in the name of Zair."

"There is no lahal for you here, Dray Prescot," said a Krozair Brother, a Bold, one of those dedicated to the most intense efforts within the fraternity, a man whose whole life was bound up in daily service to the order. "Forsworn! No longer are you Pur Dray, Krozair of Zy."

I gaped at him. I did not understand.

"Forsworn, Dray Prescot, less than nothing, Apushniad, ingrate, traitor, leemshead. You are no longer a Krozair of Zy."

Chapter Eleven

Apushniad

Apushniad!

That was a terrible word to a Krozair. Traitor, ingrate, leemshead, outlaw.

A man cast off from the order.

A man denied fellowship, a man despised by those who had once been his fellows.

And I, Dray Prescot, had been dubbed Apushniad!

I stood within the Hall of Judgment. The room was small, holding only a double hundred of Krozairs, ranked in their pews along the walls, the banners hanging in the lamplight above, a dusky, glittering mass of gold and scarlet. Small, that Hall of Judgment was, hewn from the living heart of the Rock of Zy. Small, because it was so seldom used. Once, long ago, I had witnessed the ritual trial and banishment of a Krozair Brother, accused of a crime no Krozair could own to and remain a member of the order. The ceremony had created a deep and lasting impression. So I knew what I faced.

They had clad me in a white surcoat and on my breast blazed the great symbol of the order. They had hung a scabbarded longsword about my waist. It was my own sword, not a Krozair longsword, but a good workmanlike blade fashioned in the armory of Valka at Esser Rarioch by Naghan the Gnat and myself. It had served me well before. Now I stood in the Hall of Judgment, robed and armed like a Krozair, and I had no memory of how I had come there, how I had been dressed, what had happened after those terrible words had suddenly fallen on my uncomprehending ears.

If I say that in the days and sennights, aye, and months that followed I do not clearly recall all that happened, I think

it no marvel. I was gripped in a stasis of horror that seemed
to me impossible and that must vanish in the next heartbeat,
yet it never left me as day succeeded day. So I stood there,
facing my accusers. In the high throne sat the adjudicator, a
Bold, a man in whose heart no mercy for the Grodnims
could exist and therefore a man in whose heart no mercy for
those who did not fully support Zair could exist either.

To one side, in a throne with a hooded carapace fashioned
after the likeness of that mythical bird, the Ombor—for
whose name my House of Strombor in Zenicce was named—
sat the Grand Archbold.

I had thrown him a single despairing look, expecting to see
my old friend Pur Zenkiren, expecting to receive some ac-
knowledgment, some sign of understanding.

Pur Zenkiren did not sit in the Ombor Throne.

I knew the man who sat there.

He sat with bitter down-curved lips, this man, the Archbold. This man who had succeeded Pur Zazz held the destiny
of the Krozairs of Zy in his hands. I remembered him as a
bold, free, ruthless Krozair captain, a man who would ram
his swifter into the very jaws of the Overlords of Magdag.
This was Pur Kazz of Tremzo, but different. A ghastly
wound puckered the whole left side of his face, taking out an
eye so that only the socket glared forth, rawly red. His bitter
mouth twisted in the tail of that terrible scar. He sat hunched
forward, his scarlet robes drawn about him, and I saw his
hands shaking.

A Krozair Brother lifted a scroll.

"Step forth, oh man who is called Dray Prescot, Lord of
Strombor."

A longsword point in the small of my back emphasized the
demand. I stepped forward, onto the round raised pulpit
where cunningly arranged lamps shed a concentrated light. I
felt dizzy. I forced my head up and stood straight, bracing
those wide shoulders of mine back with a conscious effort.

"I am here!" I cried. "And I do not understand! What—?"

The Brother with the scroll began to read, drowning my
words.

As I listened I felt my spirit tremble and shrink. I, Dray
Prescot, felt the awful weight of what he said crush down on
me and rend my ib so that I had to grip the lenken rail and

hold on while all of Kregen rocked about me like a swifter in a rashoon.

I heard his words—vague snatches of them recur in times of nightmare. I feel that neither my walk from the Phokaym across the Klackadrin nor the coronation parade of Queen Thyllis in Ruathytu, when I stumbled along at the tail of a calsany, scarcely moved me more, could have been more terrible. There have been other awful experiences through which I have gone on Kregen; perhaps this being out of the Krozairs of Zy affected me more powerfully than any of them although, when I think back, I now understand that I did not really believe what was taking place before my eyes.

The Call had been sent. The great Call had been sent out, the Azhurad, the Call to Arms which would bring every Krozair of Zy to fight for his order against enormous perils. Every Krozair of Zy had answered the Azhurad, as was his sworn duty, every Brother had come joyously to fight for Zair against the evil of Grodno, every single Brother—except one.

All except Dray Prescot had answered the Call.

I shouted: "But I did not know!"

The adjudicator leaned forward.

"That is a lie! You live, therefore you must know."

A Brother stood up at my right. He was a young man. He did not relish his task. But the Krozairs point a path of justice in their dealings; they do not punish without trial and reason. This man, this Pur Ikraz, had been appointed to speak for me in my defense.

He said: "It is true that any living Krozair must hear the Azhurad when the Call is sent. But is it not possible that, in this one instance, Pur Dray, somehow, in a manner we cannot guess, did not receive the Call?"

The Adjudicator said, "It is impossible."

Through the mazy sounds of that chamber I recalled speaking to Pur Zenkiren and to Pur Zazz, promising them that wherever I might be in Kregen I would answer the Azhurad. It had been explained to me. As part of the initiation ceremony I had been escorted down into the heart of the Rock of Zy and in a great cavern scooped from the living rock I had been shown the Horn of Azhurad. I knew nothing then of radio waves and of telepathy; I did know that when the Archbold set the giant bellows into action, pumping air through the myriad holes in the rock, the Horn would sound. The Azhurad would tingle with powers that could fling a note around the world, resonating in the skulls of every member of the Krozairs of Zy. Only through mystic disciplines of which I do not speak could a Krozair Brother hear the Azhurad, only one trained in the arts could understand. Hearing and understanding, he would joyfully don his surcoat with the hubless spoked wheel blazing within the scarlet circle, belt on his longsword and so go up with his Krozair Brethren against the foe.

I gripped the rail. I shouted over their noise: "And if I did hear the Call, am I not here? Have I not answered? I was in the world of Kregen outside the Eye of the World. It has taken me many months of travel to reach you here."

I was prepared to plead anything to avert the horror.

The Adjudicator placed a forefinger to his lips as he spoke. "So you did hear the Call?"

I would not lie.

"No. I did not hear the Azhurad. But I am here now!"

"It is known that it is impossible for a living Brother not to hear the Call. You stand condemned on two counts: if you did hear and did not come, you are condemned, if you did not hear that can only mean you were never properly a Krozair of Zy. You were not pure enough of spirit, your ib remained befouled with the dross of everyday life, so you stand condemned on that count, also, to be banished, Apushniad."

A thought so despicable I winced at my own vileness occurred to me. I lifted my head again and jutted my jaw out like the rostrum of a swifter.

"My son Drak! Prince of Vallia! He was to join the Krozairs of Zy! And my second son Segnik, he who is now Zeg, he was also to join the Krozairs of Zy!"

I could not go on. Not for myself could I use my sons.

The Adjudicator hissed between his teeth.

"Your sons answered the Call! They came with great gallantry and they fought with joy for Zair! But you—"

"They are safe?"

"They live still. It was they who told us you were not dead, as we had believed. They did not know where you were. Had you been dead it would have been better for you."

Now Pur Kazz, the Grand Archbold, lifted his golden rod. Everyone fell silent and turned to the Ombor Throne.

"When you did not answer the Azhurad, cramph, you were tried and condemned in your absence. Now you have the effrontery to arrive, here crying and mewling. The sentence of that trial will be carried out. We stage this trial now in order to show you, who deserve nothing, that the Krozairs of Zy do not punish vengefully, out of spite, but out of law and order and love of Zair."

I stared at him. His voice slurred. His hands trembled. I remembered him as arrogant and brash and filled with vigor. The disfiguring scar must have addled his brains. Besides, he had called me cramph, which is a term of abuse. Not one other of the Brethren had descended to insults.

I shouted at him. "And my Delia! The Princess Majestrix of Vallia! She is here! I demand to see her!"

"You demand nothing!"

The Adjudicator's quick words were chopped by the bellow of rage from Pur Kazz. I could not understand what he said, and I do not think anyone else could either. But we were all fully aware of the passions of anger and enmity blazing in him.

"Let the sentence be carried out."

Pur Ikraz, the man to speak in my defense, started to plead in mitigation, but Pur Kazz waved his golden rod and brought it down with a crash and bellowed. My defense withered away.

I do not fully recall what happened next. I have memories, lurid, black, lightning-shot, of men coming forward and speaking ritually above me. Of others ripping the bright insignia from the white surcoat. A dull realization of why they had clothed me in the emblems of the Krozairs of Zy shook me then. I had been clothed so that I might be stripped, in humiliation and shame.

My longsword was lifted from the scabbard. I could see three different reflections of myself in tall mirrors, the Three Mirrors of the Ib, positioned to reinforce what went on in the mind of the accused, to make him see himself in all his shame.

As the sword whispered from the scabbard I swung back. I saw Pur Kazz leaning over the golden rail of the Ombor

Throne. I saw the torches and the lamps, the massed faces of
the Brethren; I heard the chanting as they exorcised the evil;
I heard and I saw and I do not remember anything else until
I found myself standing in that cleared space below my pulpit, the sword grasped in my fists in that cunning Krozair
grip, cocked. I heard myself yelling—wild, strange, mad
words, tumbling out pell-mell—and saw the ring of watchful
Krozairs, bearing their swords in grips like mine, waiting, circling, ready to destroy me.

I saw my reflection in the Three Mirrors of the Ib.

I saw a madman. I saw the huge rent in the breast of my
white surcoat. I saw the face: that devil's face with the fur-
rowed brow and the snarling ugly mouth, the eyes like leems',
glittering, maniacal, mad. I saw a man I did not recognize.

But I knew the truth.

The maniac brandishing a sword here in the Hall of Judgment, who would not accept the dictates of his onetime fellows in the Krozairs of Zy, that man who had reverted to all
the old intemperate ruthlessness I had tried so hard to overcome, that devil incarnate here in the seat of wisdom and
learning and great devotion—that madman was me, plain
Dray Prescot.

I threw the sword down with a clang.

"You cannot understand why I could not answer the Call!
If I said I was in a place where the Call did not reach, you
would not believe! If I say I prize being a Krozair of Zy
above all else on Kregen, you would sneer! I have failed you
in your terms! But I have always kept the faith, I have not
failed! It is you, who do not believe in Krozair Brother . . ."

But I could not go on. How could they believe my wild
stories about living on another world? How could they
conceive of a world with only one sun, a world with only one
moon, a world with only apims?

Then, truly, my reason left me.

Only vague and rending impressions remain.

Someone must have picked up my sword. It hung before
me in the air, the lamplight striking a star from the tip, the
blade gleaming straight and true. A crazy thought afflicted
me: how would Naghan the Gnat relish what was being done
to his handiwork?

For the sword was placed across the twin Stones of Repudiation. Basaltic blocks, hard and bleak and unforgiving, they hunkered like extensions of the very earth itself. The sword glimmered. I saw the Hammer of Retribution lifted. It rose high, poised in the muscular hands of a Krozair Brother whose title I will not repeat. I saw his naked arms flex. They bunched. I wanted to look away. I could not. The Hammer of Retribution smashed down. My longsword rang once, with a gong note, twisted, echoing, lost in the crash of sundering metal and the hammerblow against the rock.

In shapeless shreds my sword lay on the floor.

I cannot tell what happened next. I can only piece together those earlier memories of seeing a Krozair of Zy receive the Apushniad. It is painful. It is so painful I will leave that scene of desolation and horror. I was finally led away, head hanging, and although chains were placed on me they were unnecessary.

I do remember the hissing and vindictive voice of Pur Kazz, Grand Archbold of the Krozairs of Zy, shouting at my back.

"So goes he who once was Pur Dray, Krozair of Zy. Apushniad! Let no Krozair Brother's hand be lifted to help him. He is accursed. He is banished from our midst, as his sword is broken and his banner burned, and all the goodness of our hearts and faces is turned from him. Apushniad!"

It was finished.

Chapter Twelve

Conversation in a fish cell on the Island of Zy

No, I do not wish to dwell on those moments in the Hall of Judgment, nor on the days that followed. You who have listened to my story know how I would willingly, gladly, have given up all the tawdry, tinselly titles I had accumulated, every one, to remain a Krozair of Zy.

Apushniad!

Outcast, leemshead, I was thrust from the warm circle of the order, and yet there was still work I might perform, still a use to be found for my unworthy body.

I was not to be executed.

Oh, make no mistake, the Krzy would think no more of executing an Apushniad than they would of lopping the head off an Overlord of Magdag.

They knew my strength. Many in that small Hall of Judgment had fought with me in the long-gone past. They knew I had slaved as an oarsman in the galleys of Magdag. Now one of the minor points of the Zairians I had been forced to slide away from and overlook and condone was brought home: the men of Zair also employed slaves in their swifters.

So I knew my fate.

Down and down we went, the guard surrounding me with ready swords. They were expert swordsmen, as indeed they must be to become Krozairs at all. It would have been a great and bonny fight. It would have been a fight to warm a man.

But I knew as we went down the stairs with the water dropping milkily about us and the torches hurling black-bat

111

shadows ahead, that I could not fight those who had been my Brothers merely because they would not understand my wild talk of an earth with one sun, one moon and only apims. No, I had found, as I caught that dramatic reflection of the devil-figure who was me in the Three Mirrors in the Ib, that I could not strike out in hatred at a man who was a Krozair Brother, who wore the hubless spoked wheel within the circle as his emblem. Maybe there were other reasons. Perhaps, after all I had grown weak and flabby, lacking the will and the old cutting edge. I do not think I felt fear. If anything my feelings had been the reverse and I would have joyed to leap forward to my death.

Even then, though, even then I knew that I was still the old Dray Prescot, a stubborn onker who would never give up the fight but would always struggle on against despair and defeat.

They thrust me into a narrow cell whose walls glistened wetly and the iron bars clanged with that soul-destroying sound of finality.

Then they went away and left me to the darkness and the emptiness of self.

How long did I spend in that cell? It is of no consequence.

I was fed at intervals, washed, shaved, given a gray slave breechclout. My chains were checked and I was at last led out and up those long slippery stairs in the heart of the rocky Island of Zy beneath the gracious living areas of the extinct volcanic throat. Straight to the small harbor within the immense rocky arch I was led. It was night. The stars shone in spattering reflections on the water. There were no moons in the sky.

Among the guards I heard a muttering, as of a low-voiced discussion that could not easily be resolved.

Ahead I could see against the quay a long, low, impressive shape of power. There had been no swifters when I had flown in. There was no sign of my voller. Perhaps I would still not have made a break for it even if I had seen the airboat. I was down, beaten, face-first in the muck of life.

The moored swifter possessed two banks of oars and was lean and powerful. Despite everything, I found myself noticing that she was bereft of much of the ornate panoply to which I had become accustomed in the swifters of the Eye of the World. She had been stripped for action with a vengeance.

I heard one of the guards, a tough old bird with a scarred face, speaking hotly.

"To the Ice Floes of Sicce with him! He is Apushniad!"

And another, younger, with a strong determined face, spoke out.

"And yet she is very beautiful."

I reeled. I gripped the nearest Krozair and he grunted and shifted his sword hilt out of the way.

Mercy is a commodity in relatively short supply on Kregen. Zair does not teach mercy to a Grodnim. And Grodno teaches only implacable hatred for all Zairians. Even in my kingdom of Djanduin the pantheon of warrior gods led by the divine Djan must have the case for mercy argued and won before they deign to nod their heads in merciful acquiescence. For the religion of Opaz, the Invisible Twins, mercy is a guiding light, but that too is a mercy tempered with forethought for the welfare of those of Opaz. As for Lem the Silver Leem—they should receive the same mercy they show and they would all be extinct. For old Mog, the high priestess of the religion of Migshaanu, away there in Migladrin, mercy was a known and valued component of the religion, used with care as a precious unction.

I could expect no mercy from these men who had been my Krozair Brothers, men for whom I would have fought and men who would have given their lives for me in like manner, before I had been tried and judged and condemned.

I would not plead.

But through all the agony of spirit I felt the fire in my blood. The agony refreshed itself at the wellspring of a new agony.

I knew.

We hustled toward the rock of the side wall. The guards spoke in harsh whispers. "Keep quiet," and "Careful with the light," and "He should be thrown to the chanks." I stumbled along. A lenken door opened and closed, silently. An iron bolt dropped into place, silently.

A pitchy darkness confronted my groping fingers. My chains clanked. I heard a panel squeal and a voice, hoarse, say, "One bur only, my lady. Not a mur more."

A form moved. A soft pearly light shone across a littered floor of discarded impedimenta, fishing gear, a broken trident, crumbling floats, a scattering of canvas, wooden tubs and withy baskets. The light wavered.

I looked up.

It is a long time ago, I was in torment, I do not recall—I remember her soft arms, her lips, the touch of her hair, the thrilling whisper of her voice. Oh, I felt as poor and downtrodden and useless there as ever I have felt. That it should come to this! A beaten man, chained, thrown out of all he held dear, yet daring to clasp in his arms the most wonderful woman in two worlds!

"Dray, oh, my heart . . ."

No, I cannot tell more.

Delia—my Delia of Delphond, my Delia of the Blue Mountains.

Of all we babbled I remember little. She said these terrible Krozairs of Zy were incapable of being bribed. Nothing would move them to deny their duty. I could have told her that. There was no easy escape through gold here. She was well. She held a great pride in her sons and daughters. Krozairs, Sisters of the Rose, Princes and Princesses of Vallia. I could hardly talk. She wanted to talk of the youngsters, but I kissed her and we clung together, warm, warm, and again she wailed that there was no way of contriving my escape.

I do remember, in a pale pathetic reflection of my old arrogance: "I will win free, my Delia. I will. And I will tell you why sometimes I go away even if you do not believe."

"If you tell me I will believe."

I was charged afresh with a ludicrous determination. "I will win free. I will prove I am a true Krozair."

She held me. "Yes, yes, that is what you will do. I know. They are wrong. . . ."

"It is a thing I must do. I must."

How different this, from all my grandiose expectations! I had waited twenty-one dreary years, and all for this! My Delia, the most perfect woman of two worlds, how cruel that she should thus be tormented on my account. I held her close and my thoughts were clouded. I remember . . . I remember little then.

No, I cannot tell more.

The panel scraped and the pearly light strengthened. I held her close, but she was gone, gone, and the panel closed and the light darkened and I was alone.

The outer lenken door was flung back and rough hands grasped me and, with my chains clanking about me, I was led down to the stone quay and up the gangplank. So once more I entered on the life of a galley slave of the Eye of the World, which is the inner sea of the continent of Turismond on Kregen, spinning beneath the Suns of Scorpio.

A galley slave may survive if he can last out the first week.

My memory of that time remains hazy. I recall that the work came as a shock; I had grown slothful. My strength remained, but it was not as easy as I might have been forgiven for thinking. It took me some time to regain all my old toughness and hardness, to endure the incessant toil, and all that time I remained sunk in a spiritless slough. I cared little for anything. I even came to regard that dark meeting with my Delia as an hallucination. Had I really once more clasped Delia of Delphond in my arms? Could it truly have been my Delia of the Blue Mountains? Or was I gripped by the Drig-driven phantasms of the madness I know claimed me?

Reason had fled. I pulled my oar. I lived like a vosk sunk in swill. I endured.

Even thoughts of Zorg of Felteraz, and Nath and Zolta, my two oar comrades still living, penetrated like a nightmare, so that often and often I would call their names, thinking them laboring at the loom at my side.

As for the five other wights on the loom with me, I knew nothing of them nor cared how they regarded me. I was the madman of the benches. I shouted for Zorg when the swifter went into action, yelling for Nath and Zolta, cursing the Overlords of Magdag, pulling with frenzy so that I could drown out the blackness of a despair I had forgotten tormented me, or why, or how, sunk in the blazing mania of madness.

When I had been a slave in the Magdaggian swifters I had gradually surfaced from near-insanity. I had taken an interest in what went on, noting the galleys, their construction, their methods of working and sailing and fighting. Now I cared for nothing. I pulled. When the lash fell on me I yelled out in abandon, uncaring, all pride forgotten.

It is all a fragmentary scattering of scarlet memories.

One time we were rammed and the apostis crumpled in deadly splinters and the side caved in and three of the poor devils chained with me were crushed to red pulp. One time arrows sought down into the slave benches, for this craft was rigged anaphract, and I saw a shaft sprout suddenly from the back of the slave in front of me. I saw with perplexity and no sensations of pain an arrow pinning my foot to the deck. I wrenched the thing out with a jerk of my leg, seeing blood, feeling nothing, pulling, pulling, pulling. I must have been sent down to the sickbay and recovered of the wound. I remember nothing of that.

There was a space when I felt the rain and the wind on my face, and the heat of the suns, and then a space when I did not. Now I realize I must have been transferred from the upper bank to the lower; it made no difference to my madness.

Once, I dimly recall, I awoke to look up and see the immense arch of the rock harbor of the Island of Zy above my head and I cried out "Krozair!" in a terrible voice. I strove to rise and could not, for I was chained and manacled and the chains were stapled to the deck.

Now, later, I know it was after that experience that I was vaguely aware of people bending over me, of shadowy forms, of a shielded light, of whispers.

I recalled these fragments of the night as I labored at the oar by day. The suns scorched my back, my hair grew wild, I fined off the excess weight that being a prince and king brings. I know I was as hard and tough and enduring as ever I had been.

In the full circle of vaol-paol all things must come to pass.

One night I felt my chains shaking, and I cursed and turned over irritably, for sleep was a precious boon to a slave. I heard a whisper and a curse, and someone said, "Sleep, you Grodno-gasta!" and the soggy sound of a blow. Another voice hailed, it seemed from a distance. Closer at hand the first voice said with great viciousness: "May Makki-Grodno devour his intestines!"

The chains shook again, I heard a clink of metal, and then all was silent. I turned over and found a softer patch on the ponsho-fleece covered sack of straw and slipped back to slumber.

No use to ask me where the swifter in which I slaved sailed. I had no idea. I had no desire to know. I believe I did not even understand quite what this all meant, somehow regarding all the toil and agony as a part of a dream in which Zorg, Nath, Zolta and I slaved and labored through all eternity.

During the periods when the breeze blew fair and the square sails on the two masts could be set, the slaves might rest. On one evening when the suns sank into a metallic sea and sheened from horizon to keel in a single sheet of burnished bronze, I realized we were at sea. I thought Zorg must have the better share of our onion. Nath and Zolta would share theirs. We were down to half rations. As for water, a mere mouthful and no more must last us.

We pulled ourselves up on the benches as the sails were furled and we settled to the looms. The drum-deldar beat out his rhythm and, all as one, like beating wings, the oars dipped and rose to dip again. Silently we stole into the coast.

Nothing meant anything. When the final beat from the drum and the oar-master's whistle signaled a cessation to our labors, every slave drooped over his loom. I squirmed about for a softer spot on the ponsho-fleece, for without these sacks and the fleeces a man could never last at the rowing benches. I prepared for sleep and knew I would dream my nightmares.

I dreamed that Zorg was telling me how he had secreted a piece of cheese; he wanted to divide it between all four of us, but we must do it when the Rapas on the next oar could not see, for it had once been theirs and they could not understand where it had gone. Nath and Zolta had chingled their chains in one of the many signals we oarslaves used to pass messages.

The thing must be done furtively. Not only must we not alert the Rapas, but the whip-deldars walking the narrow deck would delight in any excuse to lash us with old snake at a time when we should be resting.

"Hold still, Stylor!"

That was Nath, breathing in my ear.

We spoke in whispers.

"Split it fairly, Zorg," I said, and instantly Nath said: "Quiet, Stylor! For the love of Zair! Quiet!"

And Zolta, strangely near for his apostis seat, whispered: "Hurry it up, you great fambly!"

And Nath, breathing hard: "It takes a man to do this, you nit of nits."

Well, they would always argue and insult each other, and each ready to hurl himself to death to save the other.

"Is the Grakki-thing free yet?"

"In a mur—in a mur—"

And I said, sleepily, "Make the cheese a nice juicy Loguetter, Zorg. In the name of Diproo the Nimble-Fingered, we've earned it."

"Quiet, numbskull!" And: "Clap a fist over his wine-spout, Zolta, while I"—grunt of effort—"finish this."

And, oddly, I felt a hand over my mouth. How, I wondered in my dream, could it be Zolta's? He sat at the apostis seat, almost fully over the water. But it was a dream; anything could happen in a dream.

The night breathed about us, a night of Notor Zan, when no moon shines in the sky of Kregen. In the darkness I dreamed that Zorg partitioned up his cheese and the Rapas had not seen. I reached out for my portion. I felt a fist under my fingers, a fist that spread into a hand that grasped my hand.

"Where—" I began, and the other hand clapped back over my face. I squirmed. My chains did not rattle.

I was being lifted up.

This was indeed a most miraculous dream. Was I astride a fluttrell or a mirvol or even a flutduin? I rose into the air and I felt hands grasping me and movement. I tried to turn over to find another comfortable place on the ponsho-fleece, but the hands gripped me so I could not move.

The strange swaying persisted. Then I was being passed down like a sack from a freighter. I felt a bump and something hard struck into my backbone. Before I could do anything or cry out a great evil-smelling canvas was thrown over me. I lay there, wondering when I would wake up and, however nightmarish the dream, preferring it to the reality of slaving on the rowing benches.

The softly swaying movement beneath me told me I lay in a small boat. Well, they might not ask me to pull an oar then.

I heard a voice, somewhere high overhead.

"Weng da!* Speak up, speak up!"

From close by my head Nath bellowed back: "Provision party, sir!"

"Carry on then, Palinter."

I heard a low chuckle in the boat. Why should the officer of the watch call Nath Palinter? Palinter was the title for the fat and jovially wicked fellows who were the pursers in—but no matter. This dream intrigued me through my madness.

The boat pushed off. There were two oars, I could hear.

The stroke was steady, the kind of rhythm that only two old comrades who had slaved together could row. I moved beneath the odiferous canvas.

"Lie still, Stylor. Only a few strokes more."

I lay still. I wanted to go to sleep and sleep dreamlessly. But this dream persisted, it pursued me, it would not let me go. The boat grounded. The canvas cover was thrown back. The night sky blazed above. I stood up. Nath and Zolta gripped my arms and helped me from the boat.

"All very nice, Nath, Zolta," I said. "But where is Zorg?"

They looked at me.

"I need my sleep. Let me go back to sleep."

Nath took my arm. "This way."

"Grace of Grodno." I stumbled along after Nath, with Zolta supporting me from the side. My legs felt like smashed bananas. "Zorg will row." The dream began to coil in my head. I panted. I felt the pains in my chest, in my head. My legs weren't there. "Zorg! Nath! Zolta! We must row—must pull—pull—"

"Nearly there, Stylor, nearly there."

I tried to haul up but they pulled me on.

"Nearly where, you two rascals? Is it wine and a wench you are after? I know you two, tow oar comrades, two great rogues. . . ."

We passed through a screen of trees, dark, massive and mysterious lumps in the star-flecked blackness. A clearing showed, with an arm of water curving into it hidden from the sea. A rickety hut of leaves and branches leaned over the water. I stopped, thunderstruck by a thought.

Weng da: Who goes there?

"Why do you call me Stylor? You know my name is Dray—"

"Yes, Dray, but we knew you first as Stylor. Now you are Dray Prescot . . ." Then, in a lower tone, Nath said, "Into the hut with him before he wakes the whole damned crew."

"Where is Zorg?" I said again. And then the thought finally rooted. "Zorg is dead! We have roistered in Sanurkazz, many and many a time, with Nath and his wine and Zolta and his wenches—and Zorg is dead!"

"Aye, Dray, Zorg is dead—and so will we all be if you don't stop yowling like a chunkrah in calf and get a move on!"

I felt my legs then. I felt the ground beneath my feet.

I trembled.

I touched Nath. I touched Zolta.

They were real!

I wrenched away from them. I pawed my eyes. The trees, the hut, the stars, remained. I hit myself in the chest. I did not wake up.

They were staring at me, there in the starlight.

"Yes, Dray, who we called Stylor. You do not dream." Nath smiled in the old reckless way.

"By Zair, Dray Stylor! We've rescued you from the Krozairs of Zy and they'll have all our heads if they catch us!" And Zolta seized my arm and ran me into the hut.

Rescued? Rescued? *Rescued!*

Chapter Thirteen

Two rascals of Sanurkazz

The succulent palines dropped one by one into my mouth: luscious cherrylike fruits, palines, sovereign remedies for the black dog.

I lay back on the rough pallet of the hut and marveled.

I was alone. Nath and Zolta, giving me no time to express my wonder, my fierce pride in them, my joy, had whispered ferociously that I was to stay hidden in the hut and they would be back as soon as they could.

For the first time I noticed they were clad as Zimen, the lay brothers of the Krozairs of Zy. Their dull red tunics bore the Krzy emblem decorously on the breast and back. Thick belts cinctured their waists and they swung seamens' knives there. They did not carry swords. They looked just the same as I remembered them—and then they were gone, melting back into the starlight.

"If all goes well on *Zulfirian Avenger*," were Zolta's last words.

And Nath's were: "By Zantristar the Merciful! Zair would not will it otherwise!"

So I was learning. The name of the swifter was *Zulfirian Avenger*. Nath and Zolta were still alive, were Zimen, a fact which before my downfall I would have gloried to know, and were acting against all their vows to the Krzy in thus helping me, who was Apushniad.

The penalties they faced were real and dreadful.

The mere fact of freedom, for however short a duration, began in me a process of drawing back from that frightening and bottomless black pool of madness. I began to think again. Of course those two dearly beloved rascals had called

me Stylor. That had been my name when we'd met, a name
bestowed on me by the Overlords of Magdag in those fester-
ing warrens. But how had they come here? I knew it could
not be by chance.

I began to think of that tragic meeting with Delia. I *had*
met her. I *had* spoken to her there in that dark cell in the
rock wall with its trash of litter on the floor. Yes, yes, I had!
I began to think of things she had said, items of information
spoken quickly, in whispers, while I held her in my arms and
tried to blot out the grim prospect of the future.

The thought of her presence dizzied me. By Zair but she
was marvelous!

Yes, yes, she had said Drak and Zeg had written that the
Call was out. As Krozairs of Zy they had responded. She had
been engaged in a legal struggle over encroachments on Delphond, Dayra had received a bad report from the Sisters of
the Rose—who the hell was Dayra?—the trouble with the
scheming leem the Strom of Vilandeul, the samphron crop
had been particularly bad in Valka and she had had to arrange to buy supplies from Vallia, her father the Emperor
had been complaining bitterly that she neglected him—a
myriad things of importance had been claiming her attention.
She had cast them all to the winds.

She had taken the fleetest voller to Esser Rarioch. There
she had arranged as much as she could and, on the very night
she was due to leave, she had been visited by Krozairs. They
had sailed in a ship of Vallia all the way through the Grand
Canal and the Dam of Days, around the west coast of Turismond and past Donengil, and so up the Cyphren Sea past
Erthyrdrin and on to Vallia. From there they had flown to
Valka. From this record of a perfectly ordinary sea passage
of one of our galleons I knew the letters of my sons had been
delayed. So now with two purposes, Delia had set out for Zy.

First, she knew in her heart of hearts I was not dead, so
she knew I would answer the Azhurad. She would meet me
in Zy.

Second, until I came she would plead my cause with the
Grand Archbold.

I quelled all hatred for Pur Kazz. He had acted as his instincts, his vows, his duties prompted. I wondered if Pur Zenkiren, had he become Grand Archbold as I had expected,

would have acted any differently. I would find out why Pur Zenkiren had been passed over. Could he be dead? No, I would have been told by someone in Zy.

The peripatetic Krozairs who had visited Delia knew where I was supposed to be found, of course, from my sons. They had wanted to know why I had not answered. Had I been dead, they would have known. That is a small part of the mysticism of the Krozairs. At that news my Delia had known so great a happiness that all else mattered little. Only the dire truth as she was told of my condemnation could penetrate, and even then she had scarcely been able to believe.

I was not dead. I would answer the summons to Zy.

By Zair! I had not done so in all ignorance and, in all truth, according to my vows, deserved to be condemned to Apushniad.

The suns declined over the trees. Nath and Zolta had warned me to lie close.

Rising, I went swiftly from the hut with many a careful scrutiny of the foliage and secreted myself among the trees. If Nath and Zolta were discovered and men came for me, I would be ready. Aye! And if my two oar comrades did not return I would go back to *Zulfirian Avenger* and seek those who constrained them.

They panted up, jog-trotting, bearing provisions and weapons. They saw I was almost back to the knave they had known, and we were able to greet one another in a seemly way, with much hugging and belly-punching, quite like my Djangs, and to drink hugely, eat and talk. They told me much which I will relate at its proper time in this chronicle of my life on Kregen. Suffice it to say the passage of fifty terrestrial years seemed to pass in that first starlit meeting.

They were Zimen, and proud of that, and I sensed that much of their pride came in remembrance of Zorg of Felteraz, who was a Krozair of Zy. I mumbled my lame excuses for not returning and then said; "I did not receive the Call. This is true. I have been banished from the order and I cannot tell you where I have been, or how. And yet you put yourselves in the path of peril for me. I am not worthy."

Nath chewed reflectively on a chicken bone. He belched. "You may not be worthy, Dray. I will not pretend the decision was easy."

Zolta frowned. "No, Dray. We have served the Krozairs of Zy long and faithfully. And we have not seen your face for many seasons."

Then they both chuckled and drank wine. Spluttering, Nath said: "But we hold you in our ibs and, anyway, you are an oar comrade. That is what counts."

"Also," said Zolta, and I glanced swiftly at him. He had the grace to smile as he spoke. "Also, we spoke to your lady."

"Ah!" said Nath.

My heart leaped. I made them tell me everything. I licked every honey drop I could as they spoke to me of Delia. She had waited in the fortress of Zy, quartered in the lay apartments on the outer face of the rock, unwelcome in many senses, yet in a peculiar and delicate position. When my two odd comrades had discovered what had happened they had seen her at once; without anything definite being said, the compact had been made.

"Now, Dray," said Zolta, "I understand why you left the Eye of the World. I would stride the Stratemsk for such a lady."

Nath belched again. "I would never touch another drop."

When we turned to other matters, after a time, I discovered we were on a small island near the western end of the Eye of the World in an area I had seldom visited previously. This was a small and secret watering place used by the Zairians. The Grodnims had at last achieved a significant ascendancy over the red southern shore. They had actually established outposts and brought troops across. They had won battles. Now they were pushing along the southern shore, from west to east. Nothing could stop them.

"That is when the Call went out. The Krozairs fought but they lost. The Zair-forsaken Grodnims strut on our southern shore and advance steadily eastward. Soon immortal Zy will be besieged."

"Aye! And then it will be the turn of Holy Sanurkazz."

We remained silent for a while, contemplating the impossible.

Nath took up a jug and upended it. The glugging did not stop until the jug was empty. He wiped the back of his hand across his lips.

"By Mother Zinzu the Blessed! I needed that!"

I chilled at his words. The lightheartedness had gone. The euphoria of my escape was fled.

I roused myself as Nath said they would have to be leaving.

"No suspicion attaches to you over the escape?"

Zolta shook his head. They were a pair of ruffians, with the black curly hair of Zairians, with the mahogany brown faces of sailors, with the merry eyes and reckless ways of those of Sanurkazz. But I marked them. The defeats were wearing them down.

"No, Dray. I am a chief varterist, and Nath, for his potbelly, is in charge of stores. We have a certain leeway."

"And a missing slave?"

Nath made a face and Zolta looked fierce.

"Slaves die. Slaves are replaced. We brought up a spare from below. They are mostly Magdaggians, criminals—"

"Criminals—like me!"

"Aye," they both said equably and went out. I saw them off. Their plans might work. They bid me remberee, but they would be back later on, either the next day or the following night. A boat was hidden in that curve of water. They had brought provisions. We would sail out and carve a fresh life for ourselves. I knew that my future, for all its darkness and somber brooding, could go only two ways.

There was much to brood on the following day and I took the same precautions when Nath and Zolta reappeared. They carried further provisions. This time I had taken a longsword into the trees with me.

"The swifter is due to sail tomorrow night, Dray. There are four of them and they plan a descent on a Grodnim convoy. News was brought in by a scout, a dinky little three-twenty swifter. It will be a notable blow."

They were still caught up in the struggle against the green here in the inner sea.

We sat and drank companionably. If they came with me my course seemed marked out. I welcomed them. I would shake off the whole world of the inner sea, forget it, drive from my mind any remembrance that once I had been a Krozair of Zy.

I said: "Did Delia tell you anything of what I've been up to in the outer world since I left here?"

They looked at me oddly.

Nath drank and wiped his mouth and declared roundly: "The Lady Delia is a princess! By Buzro's Magic Staff! She is a princess from the top of her head to the tips of her feet, and she says you are a prince——the Prince Majister of Vallia, no less."

"For my sins, Nath, old comrade."

"Aye," said Zolta, putting a finger to his beak of a nose. "And she says you are a king of some place called Djanduin. If that is to be believed."

"What, you great onker!" roared Nath. "Do you doubt the word of Lady Delia?"

"No, no, you great oaf of a chunkrah! I doubt that this poor fellow here, this Stylor, could ever be a king!"

Nath subsided, rumbling. By Vox! How I needed their fierce heartwarming clowning, but how hollow it all struck me as I insisted on contemplating the future I beheld.

"Yes. Yes, I am a prince and a king. They mean nothing."

I did not go on. They stared at me keenly, and then Nath slowly said: "Lady Delia told us to tell you." He stopped and glared at Zolta. "Well, you nit that crawls on a calsany's back! You are the lady-killer, you tell Dray what's what!"

Zolta put his jug of wine on the dirt floor. His fierce bold eyes sized me up. We did not know the history of Zolta, yet he carried the proud *Z* not only just in his name, but as the initial letter of his name. Much was to be known of Zolta. As for Nath, as the son of an illiterate ponsho-farmer from Zullia, which is a village to the south of Sanurkazz, his whole history was writ in his large and powerful frame, his weather-beaten face, his addiction to drink, his jovial roughnecking and his loyalty. Now both of them stared at me as though they pondered the wisdom of their deeds.

"Tell me, by Vox!"

"Vox?" said Zolta. "You have been away a long time."

I said nothing, only waited.

Zolta heaved up a sigh and fixed me with an eye like that of a fish on a slab. "Very well, then, but how you come to be married to so divine a creature . . ." Here Nath nudged him and he went on. Despite his inclinations the seriousness crept in to shadow his words. "Lady Delia has said that, in view of certain impending developments, she feels it her duty to return to—where was it?—Ester Rarok?"

"Esser Rarioch. It is my home in Valka."

"Valka. Oh, aye."

"Return home? Impending developments? Tell me, in the sweet name of Zair!"

Nath shuffled his feet. Zolta picked up his wine jug and put it down. "You saw her in some stinking fish cell in Zy?"

"Yes—yes!"

"So that's why she is going home."

I felt stunned.

Then Zolta said, "She is so well aware of you, Dray, knows you so well. You told her you wished to reinstate yourself as a Krozair of Zy."

"Did I? I scarcely remember. And I find I do not overmuch care now—"

"That's a lie!"

"Aye."

"So she wants you to do what you can. She believes in you. By Zair, you great fambly! If I had a wife like that . . ." And here Nath swelled his massive chest. "I'd be pretty damn careful about how I upset her, I can tell you, Makki-Grodno take me else!"

"Did I upset her?"

"It would take a very great deal," said Zolta, at last picking up his jug, "to upset Lady Delia. She wants you to regain your rightful place as a Krozair of Zy."

"Yes, she was very particular about that. 'Tell him,' she said, 'tell him I wear the Krozair badge still and will not unpin it until he returns home to Valka and tells me to take it off with his own lips.' That's what she said, aye, and she meant it too!"

They both nodded like those balancing birds dipping their beaks in liquid.

"Fight back! Fight for what you believe is the right of it!"

How well I could picture my Delia saying those words, proud, chin lifted, her eyes sparkling with a dangerous light that the uncouth might construe as unshed tears. How my Delia knew me! And yet was it so strange? I had made no secret to her of my attachment to the Krozairs of Zy, and she had sent her two sons there, without question, joying in seeing them go through the same stringent disciplines as their father had endured. She must see the good in the Krozairs. She must regard my Apushniad as a mere interruption, to be cleared up, a passing shadow.

My Delia is seldom wrong in matters of this kind.

I felt that no dramatic gesture was necessary. So I simply said, "It will not be easy. There are things I cannot explain. Things that no sane man would believe. But I will try! I will fight back."

They both beamed at me.

Nath slapped his knee and Zolta twirled his arrogant mustaches.

"Lady Delia said—well, no matter. She knew. She told us what you would say, almost word for word. You see, Dray Prescot, Lady Delia loves you as you love her."

Chapter Fourteen

The fight in the clearing

Soon the Zairian swifter *Zulfirian Avenger* would weigh and make for the sea in company with three others of her kind, long, low sea-leems of the Eye of the World, ready to fall on a Grodnim convoy and joy in battle and slaughter and destruction. As responsible Zimen, men devoted as lay brothers to the care and comfort of the Krozairs of Zy, my two oar comrades Nath and Zolta should sail in her.

They had aided me to escape from the rowing benches. So far they were above suspicion, or so they claimed.

One of the courses that had been open to me before they told me of Delia's words had been to take them back with me to the outer oceans, back to Valka, where I would heap honors on them and shower them with chunkrah herds and mineral wealth and broad kools of land and drown them in gold.

As Zair is my witness I did not then really know if that kind of life would suit them well or ill. They were rough, tough sailors, accustomed to the hardships of life afloat in swifters in the inner sea. How would they take to the ways of life of Vallia and Valka, of Djanduin and Strombor?

Then I reassured myself. They were adaptable. They would do more than survive. And with some of the pretty girls out there Zolta could be very happy, and Nath, I felt sure, would pronounce a good Jholaix as fine as his best Zond.

Well?

The truth was I did not intend to leave the Eye of the World until I was once more dubbed a Krozair of Zy.

The issue was perfectly plain.

I could not ask them to come with me on a mission of so

129

much peril and of importance only to me. They would throw everything for which they had worked away, abandon their careers, which I now knew had brought them to the ranks of zan-Deldars, ready to make the all-important leap across to ob-Hikdars. One was a chief varterist, the other a Palinter, a purser of the lower rank. No. No, it would be foully cruel of me to snatch them away from their own lives into lives filled with cruelty and danger and death, merely to serve my own selfish ends.

I valued them far too much to do that to them.

So I thought then, as I sat in the miserable hut and planned what I would do.

They had told me that Pur Zenkiren, who had known them too well for their own comfort, had been passed over when old Pur Zazz had at last died and gone to sit in glory on the right hand of Zair in the paradise of Zim. The battles he had fought up along the eastern shores had slid and slipped away so that gradually Proconia had been lost to the allies of Magdag. Nath had said, with a round Makki-Grodno oath, that the Grodnims he called Yoggur-cramphs had rolled down from the north with huge armies of diffs. Chuliks, Rapas, Katakis—at which my eyebrows had lifted—Ochs and Naor'vils like clouds driven before the winds of heaven, rampaging down with their mercenary ibs uplifted by the gold promised by the Overlords of Yoggur, following the green banners.

"We stopped 'em, in the end. The place was a defile, a good defensive position." Zolta licked his lips. "I was told by a Deldar who lost an eye. The place was called Appar, from which the battle takes its name. This Deldar did not relish the telling. But Pur Zenkiren marshalled his forces and we fought and we stopped them, the rasts of Grodno and their Zair-forsaken beast-men allies."

This was a thing I had long noted, how the men of the red southern shore seldom employed diffs, and how very few of the myriads of marvelous halfling races of Kregen made their homes along the southern shore of the inner sea of Turismond. How important a factor in my life—aye! and the destiny of Kregen—this proved to be you shall hear.

Appar is situated south of Pattelonia, which is the capital of Proconia. We had lost much ground then. And because of this, with no thought given to his final heroic stand, Pur Zenkiren had not been elected to be Grand Archbold of the Krzy.

His presence in the Ombor Throne in the Hall of Judgment would have made no difference to the sentence passed on me. I had been tried in my absence and found guilty; the Krzy merely gave me the outward show, as my right as a Krozair, to witness my own condemnation. Zenkiren could scarcely have subverted justice. So I must see him. There were one or two plans I had in that direction. When I say the Krozairs have no mercy I must qualify the bald statement as, clearly, you will already have realized is necessary. I had been granted the boon of a short meeting with my wife. For this the Krozairs showed the compassion which made them human. Without this Zair-inspired gift I doubt if my allegiance to the Krzy and my willingness to place the education of my sons in their care could have existed.

The day passed slowly. I drank sparingly and ate well and sharpened up the best of the longswords my rogues had brought. They were not Krozair longswords, being of that pattern issued to the men who fought in the swifters. For all that they were fine weapons. Naghan the Gnat would have sniffed at them, no doubt, as would Wil of the Bellows in far Djanduin, but they would serve.

As I had done before I slipped out before the last of the glow of the Suns of Scorpio faded from the sky. From my leafy point of observation I awaited either Nath and Zolta, a party from the swifters intent on retaking me or simply no one at all.

I saw the leaves moving alongside the trail and I frowned. Whoever approached the hut was coming up from the other direction. I took a grip on the sword. This looked promising.

The last of that glorious streaming mingled light of Antares fell on the edge of the little clearing past the corner of the hut. It sparkled on the strip of water curving in and shone on the loose camouflaging cover of the boat hidden there.

A warrior stepped out onto the path, tensed, head high, his weapons ready.

He was a Chulik.

I did not need the green badges, the embroideries and studding of his uniform to know him. A mercenary Chulik in the employ of Grodnim yetches, he stood there alertly while he was joined by two of his fellows. I marked them well.

All wore their heads shaved beneath the helmets, with the long tails dangling down their backs, all dyed green, bright and ominous in the last emerald fires of Genodras.

Chuliks are born with two arms and two legs and possess faces which, apart from the three-inch, upward-reaching tusks, might have been human, except that they know nothing of humanity. Their skin is oily yellow and their black eyes are small, round and habitually fixed in gazes of hypnotic rigidity. They are strong, with bodies well-fleshed with fat, and they are quick. They are superb weapon-masters.

These three quite clearly were a scout party, sniffing out the secrets of the Zairians on this small island. Once they saw the four swifters they would report back. The projected attack by the men of Zair would be betrayed—betrayed and doomed.

No doubt the swifter from which they had come lurked on the opposite shore, ready to race back to the main fleet with news.

Well, I had been dishonored and condemned by the men of Zair. I had been rejected, considered fit for the fight only to pull an oar. I was a Valkan, a Vallian, Lord of Strombor, King of Djanduin. What were the petty squabbles of red and green to such a mighty man as I? These sarcastic thoughts passed through my head and were gone like swallows at evening. Surely this was a test, sent by Zair himself.

Slowly, comfortably, I stood up and stepped out into the clearing. The last shards of emerald light fell across the trees, turning them into jeweled marvels. The air sang with the sound of evening insects. The grass glittered with dew.

The Chuliks saw me.

I was still hairy although washed clean. I wore a brave old scarlet breechclout. They knew, as I knew, that we could not allow a survivor. They must slay me or I must slay them. The destinies of Grodno and Zair demanded nothing less.

With an absolute confidence that might have shaken less of a maniac than I am they advanced, their longswords ready.

The first Chulik surprised me.

"The Chuliks saw me."

"Cramph! Lay down your sword and yield, lest we slay you."

I overcame my surprise. This was not mercy. This was a mere device to take a prisoner and extract information.

I said: "You three are dead men."

Chuliks and I, we do not laugh often. A diff of another race might have thrown his head back and guffawed his scorn and merriment. These three spread out and came on, silently.

The green light would soon be all gone. The sword glimmered like ice in my fists. I did not use the cunning Krozair grip. I have spoken a little of this Krozair longsword grip, but there is much more to it than the mere spacing out of the hands on the handle, much more, including the angle of the hands, the placing of the thumbs, the delicate and yet brutal over- and underhand play—yes, much more. The Chuliks would know about Krozairs. They came on with sure purpose. After that first exchange it was all silent and deadly there beneath the dying green sun.

I leaped.

I did not wait for them.

The sword chirred. In the moment of leaping, before I landed and gripped the bulk of Kregen beneath my feet and struck, I had shifted grips. The full force of the longsword flung by the cunning, twisting motion of the Krozair grip ripped the head from the first Chulik's shoulders.

Stupid! Wasteful! This was not the professional fighting man-killer Dray Prescot; this was the old savage and barbaric Dray Prescot of bygone years.

The second Chulik bored in, his sword thrusting for my belly; the third circled and slashed down at my head.

I parried the one and slid the other and whirled the sword back. The Chulik leaped clear, but I had aimed short and so was able to carry the blow around, low and dirty, and cut the ankles from number three. As I leaped back, the longsword snapping up into position again, I cursed. I was fighting with power and fury and letting my muscles do the work. I, who had been a hyr-kaidur of the Jikhorkdun! Passion and senseless ferocity marked me during that fight. I needed to bash a few skulls, the black blood in me seething to run foaming and free.

The second Chulik—now so dreadfully the last—did not

back off. He was a fighter—well, all Chuliks are fighters—but he fancied his chances, seeing the massive anger I had put into my strokes. He would feint with me a while and then use his skill to slay me. So he thought.

The blades touched and rang and then shirred in that shivery sound of war-metal striking war-metal. He lopped and aimed to slash, shortened and thrust. I parried and then bashed him back. From the tail of my eye I could see the footless one crawling along leaving a trail of red. If I trod near him he'd reach up and spit me. I angled away.

The swords blurred. The shadows dropped down. It was all very quick in the nature of a fight and yet all the hallmarks of the slow, mail-crushing longsword fighting held us both. This Chulik might have done better with his shortsword against me, an unarmored man. He most likely would not have though, I think, looking back.

He fought well and then I had him. A neat parade and hand-rolling movement dazzled him long enough for me to clear space to swing backhanded at his neck. The mail hood erupted. This time I struck with force sufficient only to strike through to his neckbone. His head lolled off, most grotesquely, with the blood spouting onto his mail, fouling all the bright green insignia.

The crawler knew he was finished and slit his own throat.

I felt a tiny whisper of surprise at this; it was known, but rare among Chuliks.

I dragged the three of them back off the trail, out of the clearing. When I straightened up the stars glittered in their hosts and She of the Veils floated serenely above, a new sharp crescent among the stars.

Removing their armor was not difficult and relieving them of their weapons was likewise easy. I would have to cobble the rents in the mail together. I took everything and the supplies from the hut down to the boat—a muldavy with a dipping lug—and threw them all in and covered them with a flap of canvas. I did not know if Nath and Zolta would return this night or not. If they did not come my relief would be genuine. If they did I would have to make sure they got back to their ship in time.

They did arrive, puffing, swearing, calling on Mother Zinzu the Blessed, and searched around. I had moved the muldavy.

They found nothing. I heard them arguing and insulting each other. I had to restrain myself, hold myself back from leaping up and embracing them and pummeling them to once more recapture our old comradeship.

But my life held no joys for them.

Eventually, with many a Makki-Grodno curse and a wonderment at my intentions, they wandered off back to the swifter. I waited on the island until the four swifters and the small scout vanished into the darkness. One day, I vowed, and this time I meant to hew to the resolution with great tenacity, I would see them again and explain my ingratitude, so that once more we might go carousing in Sanurkazz and roll into the Fleeced Ponsho, roaring for wenches and drink, skylarking, merrymaking, creating havoc until the fat and jolly mobiles with their rusty swords came waddling up, wreathed in smiles.

But all that could only happen if the evil green of Magdag was banished, sent recoiling back to its foul warrens. If the Grodnims overcame the Zairians in the Eye of the World there would be no more lighthearted roistering in Sanurkazz for Nath and Zolta and me—or for any other who followed the red of Zair

It is at this point that the last cassette finishes those making up the Rio de Janeiro tapes. Prior to this point, an event I had come somewhat to dread as denying us anything more of the fascinating and incredible story of Dray Prescot on the planet of Kregen under Antares, a further supply reached me. They were transmitted in the same way as previously, namely, in a packaged box addressed to Mr. Dan Fraser, sent by the executors of his estate to Geoffrey Dean and so to me. They had been dispatched originally from Sydney, Australia. This time there was no covering letter to explain their existence.

As usual with Prescot at the controls, the opening of the Sydney tapes is fuzzed with a fair amount of wordage completely lost or so distorted as to be indecipherable. It is possible to make out Prescot talking at some length on the tangled political situation of the inner sea. It seems clear he took the little muldavy and sailed her to the western part of the southern shore in pursuance of his plan to reinstate himself as a Krozair of Zy.

He also speaks—and here his deep voice rolls out—of a name which appears to affect him profoundly. The name is Pakkad.

We are supremely fortunate to be blessed with further cassettes from Dray Prescot and the manner of their arrival here together with the maps he appends is of less moment than their content. Now we may look forward to further adventures on Kregen beneath the red and green suns, and share with Dray Prescot the barbaric color and headlong action of his life under the Suns of Scorpio.

Chapter Fifteen

Duhrra

"Step up! Step up! All comers! Duhrra the Mighty Mangler challenges all comers! A golden piece against one fall! Step up, my fine Jernus!"

Torchlights threw lurid splashes of color across the scene. The soldiers and sailors and workmen crowded close among the tents and bales and packing crates, all the impedimenta of an army stores base. The streaming radiance of the Twins threw fuzzy pink shadows into the corners, but the flaring torchlights dominated the shifting, erratic patterns, throwing greedy reflections on lips and anticipatory gleams in crafty eyes. Here was where an army disported itself when out of the line.

"Come on, doms! Come on, Jernus! Duhrra the Mighty Mangler welcomes all challenges. Clean wrestling, with the first fall to count against a gold piece! Where's your pride?"

The speaker—or, rather, the shouter—was a thin weasely individual with the face of a wersting, all fangs and ferociousness. His thin body, incongruously clad in a flowing scarlet robe, cinctured by a trashy brassy-gold belt, looked scarcely capable of lifting a longsword. He wore a tall white and red mitered cap streaming with arbora feathers, and he kept tossing a gold piece up and down in the clawed palm of one hand. With the other hand he pointed with great meaning to Duhrra the Mighty Mangler.

"There stands Duhrra! Undisputed champion of Crazmoz! Any swod of the army who can best him takes away a gold piece! Step up, Jernus, step up!"

The half-mocking tone in which this barker addressed the clustered crowd, calling them Jernus, lords, made them laugh.

"There stands Duhrra, the Mighty Mangler!"

But they eyed the massive bulk of the wrestler, shuffled their feet and averted their eyes. No one seemed anxious to step forward into the marked circle.

I studied this Duhrra. A magnificent body, yet bulky, probably not as slow as he looked, with immense corded thighs and plated muscle over his chest—and a belly that would do well to accept a few flagons less of Zond or Chremson.

I was here on the tail of the army with a purpose.

Somewhere further west, engaged in fighting the Grodnims, was Pur Zenkiren. I had to talk to him. Yet I needed a mount, I needed food and drink—shelter could be found under the stars—and for all this I needed money.

Money was the one thing Nath and Zolta had failed to bring.

All kinds of coins circulated among the Zairians. There were the Zo-pieces, minted by King Zo in Sanurkazz. There were many other mints of other free cities of the southern shore. There were the coins of great mercantile houses, banks, lords of the southern shore. And there were the gold and silver oars of Magdag.

The price to engage in combat with Duhrra the Mighty Mangler was a bronze so. That is, a three-piece. I did not possess even an ob, a one-piece.

About to make my move, for I felt confident that I could take this man despite his massive body, I checked. A bulky dwa-Deldar of the varters stepped forward, flinging off his red cloak, baring his hairy chest, bulging his muscles. He tossed a so to the barker with a confident shout of: "I'll show this hunk of vosk-steak how to fight!"

"Hai!" they shouted. "Hai for Nath the Biceps!"

I studied the ensuing instructive combat.

This Duhrra knew his business. His head was shaved bald, with a small peak and a descending pigtail, somewhat after the manner of an Algonquian or a Chulik, but far less flamboyant. His face bore a blank, expressionless flatness, with a smudge of a nose, upturned upper lip, and a general air of idiocy I felt belied the keenness he would show in hand-to-hand combat. He uttered a low gurgling cry of pleasure as the dwa-Deldar surged forward to come to hand grips.

The dwa-Deldar circled, lunged, gripped, tried to hoist Duhrra and throw him, as doubtless he had done many times to unruly swods in his outfit. Duhrra grunted. He scarcely moved. His corded thighs ridged as he grasped this Nath the Biceps. I saw the smooth heavy face abruptly blaze with power, the small dark eyes suddenly filled with great joy. Then, with a mighty heave, the dwa-Deldar, Nath the Biceps, flew into the air to land with a dust-billowing crash on his back.

The crowd yelled. There were a few boos. But the gold coin continued to flick up and down in the clawed palm of the barker and he chuckled his mirth.

"Undefeated! Duhrra the Mighty Mangler, champion still, winner by a fall!" And then: "Step up, doms! Step up! A gold piece to be taken this night!"

The crowd began to drift away.

I sidled quickly to the barker and said, "You are losing their interest, dom. Your man wins too easily."

He flicked me a liquid glance.

"Aye, dom. I know. But Duhrra is a real champion."

Across the aisle between tents a brilliant concentration of torches lit a crude stage upon which half a dozen girls danced. They wore beads and feathers and they writhed enticingly. The soldiers gaped up, licking their lips. Further along a man kept swallowing balls and snakes of fire, helping them down with daggers. His barker bellowed louder than the one before me.

"I will wrestle with Duhrra," I said.

"Where is your so?"

"If I lose you shall have your so."

One swod with the patches of a sectrixman heard and swung back, calling to his comrades. I stared at this barker who let the gold piece fall to lie in his palm.

"If my old father could see me now!" he cried. "Me, Naghan the Show! Reduced to shilling for nothing!"

"Hurry!"

"He gonna fight or ain't he gonna fight?" demanded the cavalryman. The crowd hovered.

I made up this Naghan the Show's mind for him.

"I will fight," I declared and threw off my old red cloak. The belt with the longsword and the sailor's knife followed. Clad only in the old scarlet breechclout I walked into the

marked space. Duhrra the Mighty Mangler eyed me. I
saluted him.

"You are a man, my friend," I said. "I bear you no ill
will."

His dull eyes sized me up. He said: "Uh ... no, dom ...
uh ... no ill will."

Somewhere a woman screamed, "Duhrra'll kill him!" And
another, shriller still, joying: "No! Lookit him!"

I fancy my good comrade Turko the Shield, who is a very
hagh kham indeed in the syples of the Khamorros, would
have disposed of this Duhrra with no less difficulty than I.
The Khamorros are mightily dangerous men in the disciplines
of unarmed combat, able to kill or maim with a blow. Yet I
had proved my own disciplines of the Krozairs of Zy were
superior even to the khamster skills of the Khamorros. Could
this Duhrra have benefited from Krozair training? I did not
think so.

That, as you well know, made me a cheat, for Duhrra
stood little chance. Yet he was a massive man, ridged in
muscle, iron-hard, with that bald domed head like a battering
ram. I would have to be very careful indeed and imagine the
mocking bantering eyes of Turko upon me all the time.

The fight is scarcely worth the chronicling, for I was
minded to be merciful to Duhrra. He attempted to seize me
as I advanced and I drew him on. Then, as we had done so
many times in the unarmed combat drills in the fortress of
Zy, and later as I had with Turko in our little practice area in
Esser Rarioch, I took him and turned and twisted and for all
his enormous bulk he rotated about the grip and flopped
back, toppling, to fall ponderously on the flat of that massive
back.

I could not stop myself from saying "Hai Jikai!"

But that was a saying from other places and times.

The crowd stood silently and then, suddenly, burst into
roaring applause. I merited no applause. I reached down and
took Duhrra's hand and hoisted him to his feet. I stared into
his dark dull eyes and saw an expression there I recognized; I
did not know whether to be joyful or shiver with the apprehension of a new responsibility.

Naghan the Show waxed highly indignant.

"The gold piece, Naghan!"

In the end he handed it over.

I had the thing, warm from his claw, in my hand, and was bending to don my cloak and belt when the first shrieks and screams laced the air with panic.

Everyone was running. Pandemonium broke out further along where the bulk of the piled stores cut against the stars. I heard the fierce warlike yells, the battle cries, and I heard again that hated shrilling of: "Magdag! Magdag! Grodno! Green! Green!"

The longsword shivered in my grip.

Naghan the Show was screaming. He ran. Duhrra scooped up a red cloak and ran with him. I followed. They ought to know their way about this showground outside the base store camp. The devils of Grodnim were raiding from the sea. They aimed to destroy the stores here, in the rear of the army. These civilians, the tail of the army, the camp followers, were mere meat to be butchered. They must flee for their lives. I was not minded to flee, but I wished to fight where I felt success would attend my efforts. To be killed now in a stupid affray would nullify all I fought for in the wider realities. I had to quell that perfectly natural feeling that I ran like a nulsh from a fight. A fighting man who does not pick his field usually does not last long. But I admit I felt the shame and the indignity of running before those hated cries of "Magdag! Grodno! Magdag!"

I owed the Overlords of Magdag. Once I had nearly defeated them with my old slave phalanx of vosk-skulls. Now I must find the guard detail here and form with them to bash these green sea-leems back to their ship and burn them there.

So you see I had changed from the old Dray Prescot who had once roamed and fought over the Eye of the World.

Or so I thought in my folly.

Naghan the Show panted out, "Into the ruins! There we may hide from these cramphs of Magdag."

Duhrra gave a low grunting cry, unintelligible. When Naghan stumbled he caught the slight body up and carried him as one would carry a feather pillow.

Behind us the sky began to light up as the Grodnims started their fires among the stores. Away to our right along the shore the dark masses of tents and the long sectrix lines remained silent. If the guards did not counterattack soon they might as well shut up shop. The crazed mobs of people were running every which way. Ahead up a slight incline, sandy and scattered with thorn-ivy under the light of the moons, lay the sere gray skeletal arms of the ruins.

"Careful of that damned thorn-ivy, Duhrra," I said.

"I will ... uh ... take care, master."

"I am not your master."

He did not reply but ran on, carrying the complaining form of Naghan the Show over one brawny shoulder.

Still no sign of the necessary counterattack. We had broken clear of a mass of people. There were soldiers in that mass. I stopped running.

"Damn it!" I burst out. "This won't do! By Zair, I'm not running from some kleesh of a Magdaggian!"

Duhrra stopped also. His smooth massive head turned and that blank, heavy-lidded idiot-face gave me no inkling of what he thought or felt. Then:

"I shall fight with you, master."

"There is no call. You are not a soldier."

"Yet I can fight."

"Aye. Aye, by Zair, you can fight, Duhrra."

He put Naghan the Show back on his feet. He patted the fancy clothes into place, perched the tall miter cap squarely on the narrow head. Naghan squealed.

"What are you trying to do, Duhrra? Ruin me!"

"Zair needs all our arms this night, master."

Turning back, I spread my arms and yelled, as I was wont to yell hailing the foretop in a gale of Ushant or bellowing at my Djangs in the arrow-storm, halting the running mob. Quickly I roared a dozen or so soldiers back to a semblance of their duty. One, stricken with fear, insisted on running. Him I struck senseless with my fist and gave his sword to Duhrra. Then, with little hope but with hard determination, we went back to face the leems of Grodno.

Fortunately, for the fight would have gone ill for us, the guard eventually turned out and we smashed and bashed our way against the hated green. In among tall piles of lumber, massive lenken logs needed in fortress construction by the army engineers, we fought and chased the raiders of Magdag, as they fought and slew us.

The erratic light from the Twins cast pinkish reflections

from burnished armor, caught rosy stars in the twinkling weapons that withdrew darker red, made seeing difficult. Pursuing a group of Magdaggian swods—they were apims like me—up an alleyway between stacked lumber I sprawled headlong over a corpse whose dark red blanket-cloak completely deceived me in the rosy glow. I cursed and stumbled up. Ahead of me and backed against the lumber a young man in red fought two Chuliks in green.

The young man was yelling—screaming—as his sword blurred this way and that. He would not last long.

He screamed in high desperation: "Dak! Dak! Aid me now! For the sweet sake of Zair, Dak, to me! To me!"

Past the Chuliks were three other Chuliks and two Rapas, their vulturine beaks gaping with the passions of battle. Ringed by these five stood a man whose white hair blazed with pink highlights and roseate shadows, an old man, a man past two hundred years old. Yet, as I staggered about feeling the effect of that sprawling fall, I saw this white-haired man surge against the nearest Chulik, duck the blow, strike the Chulik's legs, cut back against the nearest Rapa, screech his blade along the diff's side. The longsword whirled underhand. The white-haired man shouted, a high full voice that drew every ounce of effort from him.

"Hold, Jernu! Hold! I am with you!"

And then—it was wonderful, courageous, bold; it was the true Jikai—this man, this old white-haired man called Dak smashed his way past the two Chuliks, ripped the guts from the last Rapa and so hurled himself at the two opposing his lord.

He had no chance. He exposed his back as he struck shrewdly at the first. The blow was parried. I saw the slowness of this Dak's reactions, saw that the strength had been drained from him. He knew his end was come and he flashed his longsword before his eyes and so drank for the last time of a foeman's blood.

As he fell beneath the slashing blows he shouted for the last time.

"Zair! Jikmarz! Jikmarz!"

He fell.

The whole incident took practically no time at all, less time than it took me to scrabble up from the corpse and shake the infernal ringing of those famous Bells of Beng Kishi from my skull, take a fresh grip on my sword and leap forward.

The young man screamed now, screamed high and shrill like a dying leem with the long lances of my clansmen transfixing its lean and evil body.

"Dak! Dak! Sweet Jikmarz! *Dak!*"

"Hold!" I bellowed, surging forward. "I am coming!"

As I smashed into the Chuliks and the group of apims I had been pursuing Duhrra came to my side. Together we fought against the foemen, seeking to save the young man. We slew until our arms ran red with Magdaggian blood, until the last Chulik fell with his body hacked and butchered before he would drop, but when we reached that young man, that Brother of the Red Brethren of Jikmarz, he was dead.

Duhrra, his plated chest expanding and contracting evenly as he drew in enormous lungfuls of air, regarded me somberly.

"You fight well, Dak. Yet is this boy slain."

That he called me Dak was a mere mistake of the moment, a chance that he understood the Red Brother of Jikmarz to be calling on me when he screamed for Dak. The amazement was in his way of speaking, with no hesitation, no idiot's repetition of the opening "duh" to every sentence, no slurring of speech. Was this only the result of battle?

"Yes. It is the will of Zair."

I looked up. The mass of lumber moved. A beam toppled, twisting, falling.

"Stand clear, Duhrra!"

I leaped back. Duhrra braced to spring and the side of the stack of timbers bulged as a grain sack bulges in the moment it is slit open. The enormous weight of the logs rolled smashing down on Duhrra. In the leaping dust I caught a single glimpse of his left arm outflung toward me with the moon-oval of his face glimmering pinkly through the shadows. I grapsed his hand and pulled. His mouth opened, but in the rolling noise of toppling logs I did not hear him. He would not budge. A beam struck my legs away from me and I cursed and surged back, then, mercifully, the logs lay still. The dust plumed in the air and drifted down. There was a sickly smell of rotting vegetation puffing from the lumber. I looked at Duhrra.

He was trapped.

His body lay on the ground, with his right hand caught between two squared beams of timber. I knew, looking, that his hand would be squashed flat, ironed out, ground into a flat and useless pulp.

"I cannot move, master."

Bending to look closely, I was aware that I could see very well. A quick glance back showed me that the loose timber among the stacks was on fire, burning fiercely. The beams, thick and massive though they were, were tinder-dry. They would burn.

And Duhrra lay trapped in the path of the flames.

"It is finished for me, Dak. You had best leave—"

"Shut up Duhrra! I will not leave you."

"Then you too will burn."

Down past the spouts of flame shooting horizontally from the crevices in the stacks a shimmer of movement came closer, the wink of firelight on steel. I peered. In the red firelight the colors down there looked black. Green.

Turning his heavy round head Duhrra saw too. He licked his lips.

"Put my sword into my left hand, Dak, my master. I would die well."

"You are an onker, Duhrra! There is no need to die. I cannot move the beams—"

"Aye. I could not move one. Together we could not move one. And they are piled up on my hand."

"Yet is there a way, if you will take it."

His heavy-lidded eyes regarded me with the shock of a new idea forcing its way into closed and resigned determination.

"Another way? Besides striking until I can strike no more and so go down to the Ice Floes of Sicce?"

"Aye. If you will take it. Many men would prefer to die . . ."

"I see, Dak, my master. It is clear now."

"Well?"

He regarded me with a maddening slowness, almost complacency.

"It is for you to choose, Dak, my master."

"I'm not your damn master! And there is a saying where I come from: Where there's life there's hope. So that's settled."

Don't think I was unaware of what the decision meant to a man like Duhrra, a superb physical specimen—somewhat on the heavy and bulky side, to be sure—who had lived by wrestling. To any man the decision would be hard. But I had seen the way Duhrra had used his longsword in his right hand, all heavy swishings and smashings as though he cut down trees. With his great physical strength that method of using a longsword would serve, at least in the yelling confusion of a battle. He would not have lasted long against just one of the Chuliks with space to display technique and bladesmanship.

"The green sea-leems come on," said Duhrra. "I am no calsany in these matters. Why do you hesitate?"

"I would like to know you are resolved first."

"I am resolved."

The fires spurted closer; the green cramphs from Magdag approached with hungry weapons. Perhaps the choice was not as difficult as I had imagined.

From one of the corpses I ripped a strip of humespack and tore the cloth with vicious fingers. As I had seen the skilled doctors of Valka do so I bound a strip around Duhrra's arm and knotted it until I brought a dinting furrow between his eyebrows, all the signs of pain this man-mountain would condescend to show.

I stepped back and took up my longsword.

He said, "Do not tarry, Dak. The rasts of Magdag are almost here, and the fire burns."

The longsword slashed down.

I dragged Duhrra to his feet, leaving his squashed hand and a tiny portion of his wrist to burn away between the logs. The blow had been good, the aim true. Blood spurted, of course, but he would survive until I could have a doctor treat his stump.

The fires roared and crackled and the smoke beat down as the breeze blew. I held Duhrra. More figures appeared, men wearing the red. Now I deliberately moved away from a fight. A Hikdar shouted, high, triumphant: "We have the cramphs on the run!"

I did not grunt sourly at him that the Grodnim-gastas had done the work for which they came.

Together Duhrra and I went from that scene of carnage

and fire and blood to seek a needleman to tend Duhrra's pain and stump.

He breathed a harsh intake of breath. "I do not think, Dak, that I would like men to call me Duhrra the Ob-Handed."

"If you insist they do not, they will not," I said peacefully.

"That is true."

So we walked away, and I ruminated that I had had the best of the bargain that night.

For Duhrra had lost a hand and I had gained a name.

Chapter Sixteen

I come to my senses

I, Dray Prescot, Lord of Strombor and Krozair of— No! No! I was no longer a Brother of the Krozairs of Zy. I must not forget that. I could not forget that. It was branded on my brain with a searing iron.

I, that same plain Dray Prescot who had born many names on Kregen under Antares, no longer a Krozair Brother, had to assume a fresh alias.

The reasons were plain and pressing: should a man calling himself Prescot be encountered among the army here in the west, where there were many Krozair Brothers, then the word would pass, the retribution would be swift.

I obviously had to have an alias, and one had been given into my keeping. I would honor the name of Dak. The old white-haired man had proved a true Jikai. In my misery and determination I keenly felt the task of keeping the name of Dak unsullied.

The conceit must have moved me that I had used the name Drak many times before; it was the name of the mythical hero of Vallia, part-god, part-man, and it was the name of my eldest son. Drak and Dak. Yes, the conceit moved me.

The next day the wreckage of the base could be surveyed.

The Grodnims had wreaked great destruction, yet there was much left they had not touched. This had been a pin-prick which, of itself, would not materially harm the armies of Zairians fighting in the west, but which, added to many other similar pinpricks, could place all that strenuous effort in jeopardy.

Still, no longer a Krozair, what business was this of mine? I held warm affections for Mayfwy and for Felteraz. I could

150

see the patterns of warfare out here plainly enough. But I held to my own destiny. My Delia had given me my orders, fully understanding my own agony of spirit, the tearing torture I must have experienced in leaving the Eye of the World with all I had held dear there in the Brotherhood of Zy blackened and ruined. And yet ... and yet. Was being a Krozair Brother so marvelously vital and important a part of my life when set against all that waited for me in the Outer Oceans? No. No, I was a fool, as usual.

For twenty-one miserable years I had not beheld my Delia. I had seen her for a mere bur, there in the fish cell of the fortress of Zy. Looking around at the ruined camp, seeing workers and soldiers hard at repairing, restacking and carrying away burned and ruined stores, I seemed to feel the scales drop from my eyes.

Pride.

That was all it had been. Mere stupid pride.

I had felt my idiot self-esteem hurt, because the single body of men I held in most regard on Kregen had turned me out, disgraced me. And I even understood why they had done it, why they had acted as they did. As the Savanti had thrown me out of the paradise of Aphrasöe and I had felt no real animosity toward them, knowing I had transgressed against their laws, so this time I held no animosity for, in the understanding of Kregen I had again transgressed. No amount of arguing or pleading could possibly change a single Krozair's mind, let alone that of Pur Kazz, the Grand Archbold.

No. The answer was simple.

I had come to my senses.

I would not deny myself or Delia what rightfully belonged to us.

And that, by Krun, was that!

How vicious and cruel those damned Star Lords were! They had banished me to Earth for twenty-one years. And in all that dolorous length of time my Delia had waited for me. When I had previously been banished from Delia—as when I fought in the arena of the Jikhordkun in Huringa, or when I made myself King of Djanduin—she had spent only a fraction of time in waiting. The Star Lords had created a time loop by some alchemy of their own, so that, when, for instance, I fought in Valka and cleared my island of the slavers and aragorn, I had been acting in the past, and my Delia had not even known.

Because of that feeling that Delia was not at home pining for me—and the marvel of why so perfect a woman should ever bother her head over a hulk like me always escapes me—I had acted as I would have acted in a time loop. Then the agony of waiting had been for me alone.

Now my Delia shared that agony.

I was worse than a mere fool, an onker of onkers. I was an ingrate, a tormentor, a prideful villain, and I deserved all I got.

The decision was made.

I went to say goodbye to Duhrra.

His stump had been cauterized and bound up and he was cheerful enough, considering.

"It is remberee, Duhrra."

"I found Naghan the Show. His head had been cleft in twain."

"It grieves me to hear it."

"I cannot wrestle with one hand—"

"Come now! You could lay most two-handed men flat on their backs without blinking. And think of the billing! The famous wrestler fights with one hand tied behind his back. You would make a fortune."

"It no longer appeals to me."

"So what will you do?"

"You say you are going to the west? That is where the army fights."

"Yes. But I do not go to fight."

He regarded me with a lift of one heavy eyebrow. His thick shoulders rolled as he eased his arm, favoring the stump.

"They are going to fix me up with a hook."

"Is it Duhrra the Hook, then?"

"No!"

I said, "I go to find a ship. Maybe I will have to go as far as the Akhram."

"I have been there."

"It is on the green northern shore."

"True. But the Grand Canal and the Todalpheme of the Akhram stand aloof. As they must."

He still looked the same, still with that same heavy, doughy, expressionless idiot-face. His dark eyes looked at me with meaning. He could be highly useful.

I said, "The Todalpheme are very wise."

He said, "I think I will go with you. It will be strange not to stand with folded arms and a stupid expression and listen to Naghan the Show extolling my prowess. It will be strange to walk the world again. I am not a clever man, Dak. I know that. But, just perhaps, I am not quite as stupid as I once thought I was."

You couldn't say fairer than that.

The lightness of my spirit astounded me.

Now that I had made the decision the whole world of Kregen appeared to me in new colors. I did not laugh, of course, and I cracked but the one smile for Duhrra—and that pained—but I felt liberated, free, all that weight of despond sloughed from me. I had made up my mind. The very Suns of Scorpio blazed the brighter.

"I have but twenty-nine silver zinzers left, for I spent this morning on breakfast, and ate like a king."

How incredibly humorous that statement was. I *was* a king!

"Yes, Naghan always managed to welsh. He slipped you a smaller gold piece than the one he tossed up, I'll bet."

"A nikzo."

Half a gold Zo-piece. Only thirty instead of the sixty silver zinzers I had won by hurling Duhrra flat on his back. He surprised me. He reached into the flat leather wallet on its strap over his shoulder and I heard the clink of coins. His left hand brought out, with a wink and a flash, another nikzo, brother to that one I had broken in the refreshment tent, paying a whole silver zinzer for tea and vosk-steaks, followed by palines, that would never cost a dhem in Pandahem or a sinver in Hamal. Still, silver coins varied in weights, just as did gold and copper ones. At sixty zinzers to a full gold Zo-piece, you were bound to get less than for the fatter sinvers.

Duhrra saw my expression and misinterpreted it. I was thinking that the damn war was sending prices skyward, the bogey of inflation as much a specter on Kregen in areas where men were stupid enough to fight wars, whereas Duhrra took it for a reaction of pride to his generosity.

He held the nikzo out.

"This is rightfully yours. You floored me."

I wanted to be canny. "More by luck than judgment." I hoped that would pass. "Still, a bet is a bet, and I need the cash." I took the money. Pride and I had fallen out.

The truth of the matter was that I held for this big man the same admiration I held for a zhantil: the wild, untamed savagery on the zhantil's part matched by the controlled docility of the savagery on Duhrra's. The apparent dichotomy is only apparent. The idea that he would accompany me pleased me. But that was all.

Duhrra lifted his stump swathed in bandages and stared at it critically. "I must wait for my hook. Tell me what you think best. There is Shazmoz ahead, but it is besieged. They could fix my hook there."

My mind was made up in the time a zhyan strikes.

"We go to Shazmoz. There is a man there I must see. After that it will be the Akhram."

Chapter Seventeen

Of a Pachak hyr-Paktun
and a Krozair

Making our way into Shazmoz was not going to be easy.

We eased our sectrixes on the rise and let them blow gently while we looked down the long slope toward the army of Zairians encamped below. The sea glittered blue to our right. Not a speck of sail broke that wide expanse. The sky lifted high, high above, blue and distant, and the radiance of opaline light streamed mingled down about us.

"I hear there are thirty thousand," said Duhrra.

"And how many have the Zair-forgotten Grodnims?"

He waved his stump, still wadded in bandages. "No one knows. Men talk. Uh . . . sixty thousand."

"But they must lay siege to Shazmoz and at the same time front our field army. It is not easy for them."

"May Zair rot their bones and turn their livers green."

Shazmoz itself was distantly visible at the end of an inlet, a vision of white cupolas and towers, long white walls baking under the suns. Over there the bestial scenes of siege were being enacted; below us the camp seemed to slumber in the light.

I had heard that the general in command here was a certain Roz Nath Lorft.* Men spoke well of him. He was not a Krozair. His task, relieving Shazmoz, appeared daunting and I held the shrewdest suspicion that this Nath Lorft would keep his army in touch, feeling the enemy, keeping them in play for as long as he could. Then, when Shazmoz fell, he

---

*Roz: title of nobility similar to outer oceans' Kov. Duke.

would fall back. It seemed the Zairians had lost the ability to meet the Grodnims in the open field with any hope of success.

Scattered parties of men were about the eternal tasks of soldiers. Very few people chose to live close to the shore of the Eye of the World; from time immemorial raids have devastated the inland coasts. If there was no secure fortress very close at hand, the coastline would lie empty and deserted under the suns, so these men were totally dependent on the supply trains. They might try to send forage parties inland, but the hated green ruled there by virtue of its greater numbers and this devil-inspired confidence of winning any open encounter.

Duhrra waited my commands. His assumption of my mastery irked me. I found him dour and taciturn as a rule, which suited me as I was alike in the matter. But I wanted him to feel and act the part of a companion. This he was either unable or unwilling to do. I shook the reins.

"Let's go down and make a start."

The camp merits no detailed description, being an army camp, except for the one particular that it was a camp of men of the red southern shore of the inner sea, and therefore a camp of highly individualistic Zairians. I doubt there was one single straight row of tents. Higgledy-piggledy, set down in the best site available, to the Ice Floes of Sicce with regimentation—this was the attitude of the Zairians. Oh, they were formed up in formations as to title and number and function, and no doubt in some dusty office of the Pallan responsible papers were to be found with the details scribbled down. But the Zairians fought as they lived, sprawling, rambunctious, riotous, each man anxious to get to hand grips with his opponent. The cavalry would lower lances and charge the instant anything approached they considered chargeable. The footmen would rave and yell and boil over in their efforts to keep up. Only the varterists held some discipline, and this because the craft and science of their art demanded rule and order.

Swashbuckling—aye, that is a good word for Zairians.

We trotted our sectrixes down the slope. Duhrra had come into all of Naghan the Show's possessions, and the cash was used to buy what was necessary for our journey. I found I

still did not like the sectrix. This was the first of that species
of six-legged saddle animals I had encountered. The nactrix is
found in the hostile territories. The totrix in the lands of the
outer oceans. Poor Rees! What had happened to his regiment
of totrixes? And to Chido? I must not think of them—
twenty-one years must have destroyed the last vestiges of
their feelings for Hamun ham Farthytu. I imagined Nulty at
Paline Valley would be the Amak in all but name by now.
These dusty memories enraged me, so I bashed the sectrix in
the flanks and we went careering down the last of the hill and
flying into the camp.

A group of men were formed into a ring and as I went up
and down in the saddle to the awkward, cross-grained gait of
the sectrix, I saw dust flying up from the center of the circle.

"Stand away there!" I bellowed. The sectrix was maddened
now, its head rearing up and sideways against the bit. On we
thundered. The backs of the ring of men came nearer and
nearer.

"Out of the way! Stand clear!"

Now one or two faces turned my way. The noise was really rather wonderful. The swods yelled. The ring of red backs
switched around. Faces contorted, mouths yelled, arms and
legs swayed up and out—and I was rolling past in a bellow
of noise. Then the stupid sectrix tangled all its six legs among
the gang of men struggling over the open ground and down
we all came in a whirling flurry of collapsing bodies.

Head over heels and away, rolling among a welter of red
uniforms and naked chests and a Pachak's tail-hand gripping
my arm and a pair of studded marching sandals beating a
tattoo on my head and—I surged up, gulping for air, stood
there with the Pachak bellowing angrily, the swods toppling
aside, the dust and noise in the sunshine perfectly splendid.

"Silence, you pack of famblys!" I roared. I took my left
hand to my right and removed the Pachak's tail-hand. He
coiled his tail over his head and glared about ferociously.

His red uniform was torn. He had a few cuts on his face.
I saw the faces of the swods, so I knew what was going on
here.

"Who in the name of Zogo the hyr-whip are you, you
rast?"

I jumped for the swod who spoke, took his throat in my

hand, squeezed—only a trifle—and bellowed: "Who I am is my business, you nurdling onker. But you speak to me with respect, or I'll ring Beng Kishi's Bells so loudly in your skull your brains will spout out your ears."

A couple of the men liked that image. They laughed. I let the man go and stepped back. To the Pachak I said, "Now is your chance to walk off with dignity."

Pachaks are diffs of middle height, with two left arms, a whip-like tail equipped with a hand, straw-yellow hair, an intense loyalty and a fighting capacity that has caused great argument among the professionals of Kregen.

The Pachak said, "I shall stay and fight them with you."

I said, "I do not intend to fight them, dom."

"A pity."

Then Duhrra rolled up on his sectrix and started edging the animal in through the ring. The dust was settling. An ord-Deldar appeared and began bellowing, as all Deldars bellow, and the men shuffled off. They cast longing looks back.

"You," I said to the Pachak, "will have some recreation if those fellows get off early tonight."

"They are apims."

I did not laugh. "So am I."

"True. But you have a heart that weighs its decisions."

The laugh was very near now, incongruously near. "If that were only so, then I would not be here."

"Nor me. I am Logu Pa-We. At the moment my nikobi is given to the Roz, Nath Lorft na Hazernal."

"I am Dak, and this is Duhrra." I let my glance dwell just long enough on the small gold zhantil-head he wore on a silk cord threaded through a top buttonhole. "You are a hyr-paktun, Logu Pa-We. We are honored."

His straw-yellow hair fell about him, ripped free of its braids in the fight. Now he swept it back over his forehead with a gesture of pride. Any man, no matter what race, who gains the coveted pakzhan, the gold zhantil-head that indicates his status as a highly renowned soldier of fortune, a notorious mercenary, will be proud.

"And you who call yourself Dak. You also are a paktun?"

I had to ignore his choice of words. "I have been a paktun in my time. . . ."

"Then you still are."

"But I have never worn the pakzhan." I couldn't add that during my periods of mercenary service I had, indeed, worn the pakmort, for he would never understand why I had taken it off, unless I had been disgraced. It requires a court of fellow paktuns to bestow the pakmort, and a court of hyr-paktuns to bestow the pakzhan. As for that wild and feral beast, the mortil, he is almost as large and powerful as the superbly impressive zhantil; he is just as savage and free.

This Pachak hyr-paktun fingered his golden pakzhan. The pakmort is fashioned from silver but it is also worn on a silk thread looped through a convenient top buttonhole or on the shoulder knot over armor. "You will drink with me?"

"Aye, gladly," said Duhrra.

The Pachak glanced at him and curled his tail in a single cracking acceptance. I have a great deal of respect for the Pachaks as people. I like to hire them as mercenaries, for they are intensely loyal to their employers and will fight to the death. So we three went off to the nearest tent offering refreshment. I demanded tea, that superb Kregan tea, for I was thirsty.

We talked as fighting men will talk, a rapid shorthand of professional jargon that conveyed much information in few words.

The army here was in trouble. The Grodnims always seemed able to best the Zairians in battle. "They lack discipline," commented the Pachak, Logu Pa-We. "I think I will not renew my nikobi when the contract expires."

"You would fight for the Grodnims?" Duhrra showed his ignorance then, as almost all Zairians were ignorant of the diffs of Kregen and their ways.

Logu flicked his tail-hand around his jug, but he answered equably enough. "That would not be ethical."

"You great onker," I said to Duhrra, and drank tea.

"Yes, master."

"And I'm not your master, by the diseased intestines of Makki-Grodno!"

"I do not agree with you in that, Dak."

The Pachak, evidently summing us up as just two more unstable and highly unprofessional Zairians, drifted into more general conversation. I learned what I could. When I said we

wanted to get through the lines and into Shazmoz he pursed
his lips.

"You would run great risks."

"There is a man I must see there."

"And I need a hook."

"Yes, there is a man renowned for that there."

The contract the Pachaks entered into with their employers
they called their nikobi. That is, it was a weak approximation
to the obi which gave authority and working arrangements to
my clansmen of Segesthes. It was half an obi. Chuliks and
Rapas and Fristles worked a different system. The myriad
different forms of human beings on Kregen never cease to
fascinate me. They are as different in their bodily forms as
they are in the working processes of their minds. Yet they are
all human and share human attributes. It would need an in-
sensitive clod of a very high order of cloddishness to regard
them as freaks, as candidates for a zoo or a menagerie. They
are men and women. How odd we must look, we two apims,
Duhrra and me, in the eyes of this Pachak. He would regard
us as being crippled. We had only one left arm each, and so
would always have trouble in taking powerful blows on a
shield. We had a bare bottom each, with no incredibly useful
tail with its grasping hand. He would find it laughable and
impossible that a whole world swung in space peopled by
cripples like us. I had the notion, fed by thoughts about the
Everoinye, that very possibly a world existed peopled only by
Pachaks. It made sense. No, the multifarious forms call forth
no slighting or disbelieving comments about inmates of zoos
or menageries; menagerie men contribute to the life and color
and adventure of Kregen. I would have it no other way, clods
or no clods.

The drinking was now bringing out the singing. Men love
to sing on Kregen, and women too, in their own way.

The suns were declining now and, in the casual way of the
Zairian military, the soldiers had had enough for the day.
The songs lifted. A group of Pachaks serving with Logu Pa-
We sang too, but the apims of the southern shore sang alone.

Logu was telling us of that remote and eerily mysterious
land of Tambu, off the southwest coast of the continent of
Loh. He was one of the very few men I had heard claim they
had been there. He was saying the experience had scarred

him in his ib. He would never go back. He was as well aware of the lands of the outer oceans as I was—better, probably— and it was clear he was now regretting his decision to bring his men into the inner sea. Or regretting that he had joined up with the reds instead of the greens. But his ideas of pak-tun ethics must be admired.

The Zairian swods were singing *the Destiny of the Fishmonger of Magdag,* a highly colored and lurid account and one calculated to bring mirth to the voice and tears to the eyes, with the crashing down of the jugs onto the sturm-wood tables on the refrain "For the fish heads came off red, came off red, the fish heads dropped off red, red, red."

The pang struck me then: what did these fine roistering fellows, snug in their inner sea, know of the fishheads of the outer oceans?

Panshi had told me there had been no further raids after the one in which I had gone wandering on my travels, as he had phrased it. But I knew the internecine battle between the red and the green, here in the Eye of the World, was of scant importance beside the greater conflicts waiting outside in the greater world.

That very snugness had, I know, been a great deal of the charm of the Eye of the World, of my affection for the Krozairs.

The Swifter with the Kink went up—how we all dreaded a swifter whose lines were not true, as with the galleys' inordinate length-to-breadth ratio they so often were! And then *the Chuktar with the Glass Eye* battered against the stars. Oh yes, the swods sang.

I caught Duhrra's eye and motioned. Logu caught the signal, for Pachaks are quick in these matters, and we three rose and went out, away from the campfires and the singing.

"So you wish to steal into Shazmoz?"

"That is our intention."

"Maybe a way can be found. You will need to be silent and quick . . . and to bear up."

I think Logu was going to say we would have need of courage, but he had the sense to halt himself.

"You must leave all preparations to me."

I thought it fair to warn him: "That is agreeable. But we

shall keep our fists upon our swords and the blades loose in the scabbards."

He chuckled and his yellow hair glowed strangely under the light of the moons.

We went through the moons-lit darkness toward the shapes of tents which seemed in less of a muddle than the others. A small body of Pachaks formed about us, grim men with blades already gripped in their tail-fists. It took very little time before we were all mounted up and riding softly out of the camp. This army of Zairians comprised detachments from many free red cities of the southern shore and other lands from further south; there were parties of Krozairs and Red Brethren also. We were able to pass through the last picket lines—these were men from Tremzo, stalwart fellows with pickled hides from drinking of their own produce—and so walk our sectrixes slowly off into the no-man's-land between the contending armies.

"You are determined to get your hook?"

"Aye, Dak. As you are to see this man you prate of."

In a little dell we dismounted and the Pachaks opened their saddlebags. I did not make a face, but the sight of the green robes and the green feathers filled me with disgust.

"It is necessary," said Logu peremptorily, "that you wear these garments."

We did so without arguing. When we resumed our movement we were a returning patrol of Grodnim scouts. I thought perhaps we were a little early for that, but after we had passed the first sentries with quick and harshly intemperate words from the hyr-paktun who led us, I realized Logu knew what he was doing. The way led us through a well-packed road where the moonslight glittered on the ruts of wheeled traffic. Supplies and varters. The damned Grodnims were organized. I knew how well they could handle slaves; even the Katakis could teach them little in that nauseating department of economics.

The breathing mass of a camp showed on our left. A few lights hung in regulation intervals. We pressed on. After a time we angled sharply to our right, toward the coast. Sand shushed and shirred beneath the sectrixes. A dark shape rose ahead to bar our path and the moons shone on a lifted spear. What Logu said in a whisper I did not hear, but we went on with the spear returned to the upright position and the sentry stepping back from our path. He was a Fristle, his cat-face and slanted eyes turning to watch us go. We passed in silence.

Presently Logu reined alongside me.

"My brother is near now. You swear that your mission has nothing to do with the armies here, with the fight we have?"

"Nothing, as Zair is my witness." It was true.

"And as Papachak the All-Powerful is mine, if you lie your tripes will spill steaming on the ground."

He meant it. I meant what I said. We understood each other.

His brother turned out to be cut from the same cloth. They conferred for a moment, their sectrixes close, and I caught the words ". . . paktun not in employment."

If you marvel that two brothers could serve in armies opposed to each other then the rigid system of mercenaries on Kregen has escaped you. If they met in battle these two would fight. That was a part of their mystique, why they were paktuns; if asked they would look puzzled and say, probably, "It is in our nikobi."

But they were human beings in these stark surroundings, and I saw the real affection these two grim fighting men bore for each other. Duhrra and I might pass on; Logu's brother would not, of course, in the ethics of nikobi, allow him to pass.

After that we were passed through and Logu's brother said in his gruff voice, "You had best leave your greens here."

We doffed the hated green and, once more clad in the brave old red, set forth into the darkness. In only a bur or so we came under the walls of Shazmoz and the first patrols. With many exclamations of wonder we were escorted into the encircled town.

The sight of a city under siege is unpleasant. The place moved with a sluggish air most displeasing. The men looked gaunt. We passed fires made from smashed houses and saw women there, poor bedraggled creatures who held out their hands to us. When a few gold coins were tossed to them they spat and hurled them back. Of what use gold? One cannot eat gold.

A Hikdar met us under the lamp over the citadel door.

Like any city that sought to exist on the coast of the inner sea, Shazmoz was heavily fortified, with a defended harbor. The citadel frowned on a hill above the nighted waters. I said, "It is necessary that I see Pur Zenkiren."

"Your business? You come from Roz Nath?"

"No. My business is private."

The Hikdar was not a Krozair. I wondered if I dared presume, but guessed the news of the disgrace of Pur Dray Prescot would already have been spread. He looked at us undecided. Duhrra moved uneasily on his sectrix and then dismounted.

"Hikdar, is there one here called Molyz ti Sanurkazz? Molyz the Hook-Maker?" And Duhrra held up his stump.

"Yes. He is here."

The Hikdar made no move to admit us. A guard party hovered near, bows drawn. This was an anticlimax. And yet who could blame the Hikdar? Strangers coming in the night through enemy lines demanding to see the general in charge of a besieged city? This stank of treason.

So I spoke a few short words that, whispered in the ear of a Krozair Brother, would apprise him that one of his fellows sought audience. The Hikdar nodded. "I will see. Stay here."

The wait stretched. Then he was back. "Come."

Many and many a time have I marched through a grim gray castle surrounded by guards. Often they have been my men, as often perhaps they have guarded me. Our feet rang on the flags. Torchlight flared and marked our way with fleering shadows. Up through the levels we marched, stairway by stairway, past guards who, every one, showed the ravages of hunger and privation.

Along a passage a carpet muffled the tramp of our feet, then we reached a lenken door bound in iron. The Hikdar bashed on the door; it swung back and we were ushered into an anteroom filled with aides, young dandified men wearing profuse red decorations. There was another door, another knock, a fresh entrance. I did not see the room. I did not see the furnishings. I was hardly aware of the guards crowding at my elbow, of Duhrra breathing hoarsely in my ear.

All my vision concentrated on the man who stood in the center of the floor, half turned to greet this importune Krozair Brother come so suddenly in the night.

Pur Zenkiren.

I stared at him. By Zair! I knew I had changed not at all in appearance from the man he had known and whom he had bid rememeree in Pattelonia far away on the eastern shore. But Pur Zenkiren! I felt the blood thump from my heart. Where he had been tall and limber, with a fine bronzed fearless face, now that face looked gray, with folds of sagging skin. The bold black mustache still jutted fiercely upward beneath the beak of a Zairian nose, but that nose was bone-fine, thinned down, razor-edged. His black curled hair was as profuse as ever. About Zenkiren there hovered the black vulture wings of defeat and despair.

He wore a long white robe and a Krozair longsword belted at his waist. The device of the hubless spoked wheel within the circle shone dimly on his breast, the threads dulled and the scarlet embroideries broken away. The hem of the white robe was caked with mud.

"You have important business with me?"

His voice had lost the firm ring of authority. In the lamplight—cheap mineral oil which stank in the chamber—he peered toward me. I stood positioned most carefully so that the shadow of the gross bulk of Duhrra fell over me, casting me into limbo.

"My name is Dak, Pur Zenkiren. I pray you"—and here I mentioned a word or two known only to the Krozairs—"hear me in private."

Whatever had befallen this man, he remained a Krozair. He waved his hand and the guards withdrew. He stared at Duhrra's stump.

"Yes, Jernu," said Duhrra, immense in the shadowed room, bending his head. "I seek a boon from Molyz the Hook-Maker."

"There was no need to ask me." He gestured at me, in Duhrra's shadow. "Stand you forth, you who dub yourself Pur Dak, and let me see you."

I said, "I did not presume to dub myself *Pur*, Jernu. But I must beg you to listen to what I have to say before you make a judgment. All men know of your wisdom and upright countenance. I humbly crave your indulgence."

This, I fancied, was how a man might think it proper to address a powerful lord who commanded a city, besieged though that city might be. I knew from old experience that Pur Zenkiren put as much store by flowery words as I did myself.

"You speak in riddles! Step forth so that I may see you. Instantly!"

There came the old hard smack of command.

Slowly I stepped into the light.

He stared at me for a long time.

Then he walked a few steps to a table cluttered with lists and maps and an empty bottle on its side, where the oil lamp trailed a thin plume of blue smoke. He put a hand to the wood; he did not sit in the broken-backed chair.

"Why do I not instantly call out for the guards? Are you broken from your ib and come to torment me? Is it you? No, it cannot be you."

"I stand before you, an innocent man adjudged guilty. Think back, Pur Zenkiren! Think back to the deck of a Magdaggian swifter running with the blood of the Overlords, and a slave with a brand in his fist. Think back to Felteraz and Mayfwy and the broad prizes brought into Sanurkazz. Think of Zy and loyalty and comradeship, and then tell me, face to face, man to man, looking me in the eye, tell me, Pur Zenkiren, if Pur Dray is or ever can be—"

He did not let me finish.

He lifted up his voice and shouted: "*Apushniad!*"

He had not let me finish; he had finished the sentence himself, and he had finished me.

Chapter Eighteen

A case for casuistry

A vision of Delia sprang into my head. Clear, distinct, infinitely appealing. My course was set.

The guards would come boiling in in the next mur. I leaped for Zenkiren and clapped a hand around his mouth and with the other pinned his right arm to his side. And I laughed. I roared with laughter, shouting my glee!

"Aye!" I roared. "Aye, Jernu, well may you laugh!"

Duhrra said, "Uh?"

I said, "Laugh, Duhrra, just a little." Then, in a heartbeat: "Thank you, Duhrra. Your laugh clinches all."

Zenkiren writhed. But his strength was wasted away. I held him. I bent and whispered in his ear.

"You will listen to me. We were friends once. We remain friends for my part. I know that if I said I would kill you if you cried out again for the guards, you would cry out, defying all, for the sake of the Brotherhood. This I know."

He rolled his eyes and we both knew I spoke the truth.

"The Azhurad was sounded. I did not come. I do not deny I failed. But it is the nature of my failure that needs examination." It is said on Earth that it takes a Jesuit to chop logic. Casuistry of itself forms little part of the techniques of dialectic of the Krzy, but intricately detailed arguments and debates that sweep away the confines of mundane limitations are a joy to them. The brain must be honed and sharpened to an edge keen enough to slip between reason and reason. I felt Zenkiren's interest as I went on to present the case. There were two impossibilities and each one negated the other. "I am—was—a true Krozair. I would slay any man who denied me that. And yet I did not hear the Call. How may such a dilemma be resolved, Zenkiren? And, in studying the problem, bear two things in mind.

"You must recall that day in Pattelonia when you asked me to help you in the fight in Proconia. You ordered out a liburna. We sailed and the storm rose and the thunder rolled and the lightning struck. You understood that at the time I was fated to journey east. You were to consult Pur Zazz on the matter. I do not know what he may have told you—" Here I felt a strong jerk from Zenkiren, as though he wished to speak. I gripped him fast and went on. "But it must be clear to you I am not like ordinary men."

When I said that I admit I felt like the cheating impostor I truly was. Duhrra let out a gurgling noise which I ignored. The stink of the mineral oil wafted across and the light wavered on the littered table, on the weapons in their racks, the draped alcove where Zenkiren slept.

"That is the first thing you must consider. And the second touches us both. Oh, yes, I know it is long and long since you and I met. I have been too many places and seen many wonders and done many things—aye, and many of them I would rather not have done. But through all my wanderings and in whatever place I have found myself, I have always thought of myself as a Krzy. Always. It has been the single most important fact of my life—always, as you will understand, after my Delia. You will not understand this, Zenkiren, but it is even of more importance than the Swinging City of Aphrasöe."

Even as I spoke I caught my thoughts treacherously swinging, as we used to swing from growth to growth, from house to house in Aphrasöe. After my Apushniad, how could this inner sea be of consequence to me? That was a garblish fool talking. It was not the Eye of the World that was important, it was the mystique of the Krozairs of Zy that grew to overtop the highest peak of the Stratemsk and their concepts of world-shattering import that drew me on. And they drew me on even then, even when I had appointed myself a meeting at the Akhram on the Grand Canal.

I moved Zenkiren, gently, preparing to ease him free.

"I mention this, but without weight in the argument or the dilemma. You may solve the dilemma how you will, riddle it how you may. But one thing I mention without influence: we were friends, Zenkiren, blade comrades. I have never forgotten you nor ceased to regard you with Brotherly affection. This may be a feather-weight, a passing cloud, a midge that lives a day—I can only speak for myself. For me it has been as the keel of a swifter that strikes cleanly through the seas."

Duhrra said: "Duh . . . by Zair, Dak! And you a—"

"Hold, good Duhrra. I love this old man, yet if he cries out to betray us he must be silenced."

The tides of my life on Kregen had moved me up and down, washed me this way and that, willy-nilly. Now I knew the ebb tide might turn. Now, perhaps, the flood might make.

I took my hand away from Zenkiren's mouth.

The presence of Duhrra could afford me no comfort now. I wondered if I could kill Zenkiren and knew I might have to silence him as I had before. He looked at me and slowly, slowly, wiped a hand across his mouth. His eyes melted into me.

"Pur Dray, and is there no lahal between us?"

"Lahal, Pur Zenkiren."

"A long time. I did not believe it could be you . . . and you Apushniad. That was no doing of mine, although my vote was cast against you."

"I knew it would be. You could do no other."

"But what you say . . . so long ago and yet only yesterday in vaol-paol. I imperil my vows talking to you, and yet is not talk better than skull-breaking?"

"Or ib-breaking. No, Zenkiren, you do not break your vows, for the judgment against me was false. I am still a true Krozair although unacknowledged and declared Apushniad."

Again Duhrra let go that gurgling grunt and again I ignored him.

Telling him anything now would only complicate the matter.

"What you say is of surpassing interest, for there is indeed in it the classic case of two opposites. . . ." We all know the various examples cited; here was another one. I knew the knot could not be untied but only cut, and dared I place the sword in Zenkiren's hand and indicate where he should strike? Would even *he* believe? I think, had I confided in old Pur Zazz, that he would have believed my story of Earth. He would have offered words of comfort. For better or worse I decided not to make Zenkiren the first person on Kregen I told of my Earthly ancestry. I knew who had the right to the first confidence. And if the knot therefore remained uncut and all that followed from it, then so be it. I was in a pretty ugly mood, I can tell you, and closer than I probably suspected to impatience and contempt of all the mighty and mystical Krozairs of Zy.

We talked for a while. No refreshments were offered. Shazmoz lay under siege and I knew Zenkiren well enough to know he would share the rations with his men. He said that among the Krzy present were none who had known me in the old days. Fifty years is a quarter of a man's life on Kregen. Despite their longevity, it is still a monstrous span of seasons. If I had not known who Zenkiren was, there is every probability I would not have recognized him. This dreadful alteration in his appearance was not so much the erosion of the passage of time, of course, but the immediate effects of the siege and the more subtle and far-reaching effects of his failure to be elected Grand Archbold.

He would not talk of that sad subject and instead launched into an impassioned tirade against this new leader of the Grodnims who led them from success to success. He was not an Overlord of Magdag. He had sprung up on the green northern shore like a weed that grows overnight and with leeching suckers strangles the plants that sustain it. And the name of this man, previously referred to by obscene and odiferous names in my conversations with the men of Zair, I now learned was Genod Gannius.

Genod Gannius.

I knew the name Gannius. I had held it in my memory against the day when I might begin to unravel the mysterious purposes of the Star Lords. Was this Genod Gannius connected with that Gannius I had first met in the Eye of the World?

My speculations on this point were shatteringly interrupted as I understood what Zenkiren was now saying. He had seated himself and he looked tired and worn, with only a flicker of that old martial blaze about him. Duhrra had gone to stand by the door, folding his brawny arms on his chest as he had done when Naghan the Show cried up his prowess. I realized Zenkiren had filed away the Krozair dilemma; he must have resolved the ultimate answer in my favor—for whatever reason—and would wait for a more opportune time to decipher the proof. Now he was talking about Genod Gannius and the armies of Grodnims, the forces he called the "new" armies.

As I listened my thoughts whirled and I felt the shattering effect of his words.

I will not repeat word for word what he said, although they lay graven on my brain. In effect, Zenkiren indicated that the Grodnims had developed a new and devastating form of warfare for which they owed nothing to the Overlords of Magdag. Whispers of it had seeped out. Then an army trained by this Genod Gannius had appeared and annihilated one of the typically sprawling, roistering, swashbuckling armies of Zairians.

The way of it was this: when the Zairians stirruped up and set spurs to their sectrixes they were met with a wall of enormous spears, held cunningly like a thickset hedgerow. When the infantry attempted to wade in with their swords flashing, the crossbows had loosed and the storm of bolts fell on them, piercing them through and mingling them with the wreckage of the cavalry. The crossbows had shot quarrel after quarrel. And then, at the end, a final deluge had strewed the field with red corpses. The green banners had flaunted high in victory.

And so it had gone on, on field after field, with the results that led up to the desperate straits the Zairians now found themselves in. When the red archers loosed their shafts they were deflected from the green ranks by that coward's trick, that despicable device, the shield.

I knew.

You who have heard of my previous sojourn here in the Eye of the World, and of my doings in the warrens of Magdag with my old slave phalanx, my old vosk-skulls, you will also know—and to my shame.

By Zair!

I had trained the slaves and workers to beat the Overlords. I had given them pike, shield and crossbow drill. We had been in the very act of thrashing the hated Overlords when the Star Lords had seen fit to snatch me away from Magdag and dump me down in Upalion in the far east of the inner sea. It had taken me no time at all, on my return here, to know that all my fears had been proved right and that the

Overlords had turned and beaten my friends, the workers and slaves of the warrens. They must have, else Magdag would have perished. And the inevitable had happened.

Blind! Onker! Stupid fool, idiot, idiot. A weapon given to my friends—a sharp, lethal weapon. Oh, what a cretinous object I was!

It had not needed a genius in war to seize on the devices used by the rebellious slaves, though from all I was to hear I think this Genod Gannius was a near-genius. It was Gannius, in his own hold, who had taken what I had given the slaves and molded it and trained his men and so taken Magdag. He had thrashed the Overlords, seized into his own hands all their power and wealth, and turned it to his own crazy schemes.

He had set himself up on the high throne in Magdag and all men bowed in the full incline before him.

"When I first heard of the new manner of war practiced by the rasts of Grodno," said Zenkiren, and he looked across at me with a slow reflective stare that made me extremely uncomfortable, "I was minded of a memory I had thought forgotten. I harked back to what I had been told of a Krozair Brother who roused the warrens in vile Magdag. It seemed to me he had told me something of training slaves to unseat Overlords in all their might and power, of sticking them through. I reminded myself of this, but I did not speak of it to a living soul."

"I had thought," I said, "that mayhap that was a further reason for Apushniad."

"No. To give sharp weapons wantonly to children is to invite being cut in return."

"Yet this dilemma of which I spoke is further enhanced by this . . . unfortunate . . . happening. For it is of a piece."

"I shall remember."

"There are powers, Zenkiren, over and above—I cannot speak of them even if I could, for I do not yet understand them." I would not tell him of my dreadful thoughts about this Genod Gannius. For the full horror of that I must wait until I learned the truth.

Duhrra was beginning to shift about, from one foot to the other, and he kept whistling thinly through his teeth, which were good and strong and yellow, so I knew he was thinking of his stump and the hook Molyz the Hook-Maker might fashion for him.

Zenkiren took up a pen—it was a quill and not a reed so he was keeping up some standards under siege—and wrote swiftly on the back of an old order, long since finished with and now in these stringent times pressed into service again. "Take this to Molyz ti Sanurkazz. He is authorized to use the necessary leather and iron."

"Thank you, Jernu." Duhrra took the paper and looked at me.

"I will meet you at the gate by which we came in, in time to depart."

"Zair keep you." Duhrra went out in search of a surrogate hand. The guards joked with him in desultory fashion. Though they were under siege and likely to starve to death if they were not stuck through first, yet they were still Zairians who loved a good laugh. My heart warmed to them.

Zenkiren took the opportunity to transact some business. The siege had become by now a matter of logistics, of empty storehouses, of morale and only occasionally of fighting. I knew if he asked me to stay and fight I would have to refuse. So much more of importance waited outside, in the greater world. He did not ask me. For that I was grateful, having no pride left.

We talked at length, for much time separated us. As with the other news I had gleaned I will apprise you of what matters at the opportune time. Suffice it to say I heard more bad news and it all centered on the new devil-given powers of the Grodnims.

"We can sustain very few further attacks in force. At least the Grodnims' new method of fighting does not aid them in siegecraft." He tapped his columns of figures scribbled over and over and altered often on the sheets of paper scattered on the table. "We have held them. No doubt we could hold them until the Ice Floes of Sicce go up in steam if we could eat. Unless they ship a larger army across we will not go down beaten in battle; only our unfortunate desire to eat will destroy us."

He cocked an eye at me. "And does not Roz Nath strive?"

Feeling the eyes of the Pachak, Logu Pa-We on me, I answered: "I do not think you should hold any hope in Roz Nath."

"Ha!" he said, a bark of sound, whether a laugh or a sob I did not know. "I have never reposed hope in Nath Lorft to march in and rescue us. But he performs a useful function, for Roz Nazlifurn will find his task that much easier." He stopped himself from talking then, stopped himself visibly. He rustled the papers on the table with his quill and said at random, "We grow less every day, less mouths to feed. We will last out."

His motives were transparent. There was a secret about this Roz Nazlifurn. I was going out of Shazmoz, through enemy lines, and might easily be captured. What I did not know I could not tell.

As though seeking to throw me further off, he added in a lighter voice: "We Krozairs do not put much store by titles and ranks of nobility. Would you not willingly trade a prince's crown, supposing you owned one, for membership of the order?" He pulled his lips back in a parody of a smile.

I did not smile. He did not know my history. The question hurt, stung. I surely would have, before the Apushniad! And now ... I rose from the chair and spoke politely. Now I had changed my priorities. I was hewing to my nature, as I then thought, doing the correct thing in difficult circumstances and to hell with anyone who thought otherwise.

"It is time to bid you remberee, Pur Zenkiren. I regret the long empty years. I made a mistake in not returning to the Eye of the World sooner. But bear in mind the Krozair dilemma. At the least, it will make a capital subject for debate."

He shook my hand as they do in the inner sea, and I felt again the old Krozair grip. He smiled, this time a real smile. "See, Pur Dray. I call you Pur and I give you the right hand of fellowship. I have decided the Apushniad was incorrect. Now it remains to prove it."

I felt this keenly.

"You do me great honor, Zenkiren. I have been an onker, and yet the slaves in Magdag ... they are human and needed to be set free. I did what I thought correct, according to my lights."

"Zair holds dominion over all and if it is His will—" He

shivered and plucked at his gown, feeling the emblem stitched there, making me plainly see why it was so threadbare and worn. "Good will come of all this. Zair would not will it otherwise."

"Rememberee, Pur Zenkiren."

"Rememberee, Pur Dray."

So I went out and through the nighted streets and soon found Duhrra walking up to the gate. He carried his right hand inside his folded blanket-cloak. The guards brought our sectrixes. They wished us well. We rode away from doomed Shazmoz with the star glitter high above and a small moon skimming past above our heads.

The Pachak hyr-paktun Logu Pa-We and his brother would see us safely back. There need be no alarms on that score. I rode the damned sectrix in his ungainly waddle and I thought.

I could live with what I had done with the old slave phalanx and my old vosk-helmets. Then we had fought for our lives and liberty. What followed later was not of our doing. But . . .

But when I had first been transported here into the Eye of the World by the Star Lords their clear command had been to save the lives of two young people from the hideous rockapes, the grundals. This I had done. I had ensured that Gahan Gannius and Valima should live. They had lived. They had married and begotten a son. That son must be Genod Gannius. I, Dray Prescot, had directly brought doom and destruction upon my beloved Zairians!

Chapter Nineteen

A brush with risslacas and a sighting at the Akhram

My Deldars had been ranked, as we say opening a game of Jikaida, and now I must press on and push all the spidery shadows of past follies behind me.

By the Black Chunkrah! What a nurdling onker I had been! For all the kindness Pur Zenkiren had been able to show me, I knew, and this without rancor or disappointment too great to be borne, that he would in all probability be quite unable to resolve the riddle. The two impossibilities canceled each other out; the Krozair dilemma remained. I would remain Apushniad. I had resigned myself to that. And then, gladly, fiercely, I declared that it was not a resignation but a joyous awakening to the true values of my life on Kregen.

"Down there, master!" said Duhrra, pointing. "Zair-forsaken Grodnims, may Uncle Zobab rot their livers and fester their tripes."

I spoke somewhat sharply as we rode the high bluff trending toward the sea, with the suns' radiance all about us and the thin piping of birds to keep us company. "What color do your wear on your back, oh Duhrra of the Mighty Muscles?"

He looked suitably discomfitted and resentful.

"The damned green, master. And an itchy, vile, mean and crawling color it is, to be sure."

I was not going to argue with him. We had said remberee to the Pachaks and ridden off, going west, wearing the green over our reds. Now we had almost reached the farthest point of the Eye of the World. Before us would soon appear the

Grand Canal and the Akhram, and, if we went that far, beyond them the Dam of Days.

Our sectrixes paced on. We kept to the wending ridge of bluffs above the narrow coastal strip for, however much we might wear the green and pass ourselves off as mercenaries, the ever-present danger was that Duhrra would explode into action against the Magdaggians, and I would be scant murs after.

Green is a charming color and restful to the eyes. There are a number of fine uses for green: it is the color of rifle regiments, of racing cars, of Robin Hood; I have nothing against the color itself. Had the Grodnims chosen to wear red and the Zairians green, my sentiments would have remained as they were, against what would have been the cramphs of red Grodnims. I did not forget what went on in their monstrous ziggurats and megaliths during the time of the green sun's eclipse.

A war party below, trotting their sectrixes parallel to us, had seen us; we must keep steadily on and give them no cause for suspicion.

In Havilfar, that progressive and yet barbaric continent, one of the most widespread of religions was that of Havil the Green. Havil, named for the Havilfarese word for Genodras, the green sun. How, you might ask, could anyone worship the small green sun when confronted with the magnificence of the huge red sun? The answer is simple and yet profound, and one that has made me ponder long. During eclipse, the red swallows the green utterly. There is no longer a green sun. But, eventually, lo! the green sun emerges, newly born, fresh, refulgent, a bright new sun eternally young. Oh, yes, rebirth and recreation play as significant a part in the religions of Kregen as of Earth.

Duhrra began to hum softly, *the Chuktar with the Glass Eye,* and we rode carefully, shading the liquid gleam of our eyes as we looked down on the war party pacing us below.

I shook the reins. "I think we had best join them. They will wonder why we ride aloof in this dangerous land. You, Duhrra the Mighty Mangler, must keep a straight tongue in your mouth."

He grew affronted when I taunted him with that old title

he tried to forget. He humped and grumped and then came out with: "And you, a Krozair Brother!"

"I may have been." He knew enough now to desert me or remain; he had chosen to stay with me.

"My twin was a Zaman to the Krozairs of Zamu. The zigging Grodnims captured him and tortured him and slew him. I do not forget that."

"I lost a good friend under the whips of the rasts of Magdag."

"Then let us join them as you suggest and as soon as we are able let us slay every one, every last cramph."

"If we have to, we will, but our purpose is to reach the Akhram. Your hook depends on it, you tell me."

"Aye." He favored his stump. "Aye, master, it does."

I licked my fingers and stroked my mustaches. "Pull those damn bristling mustaches of yours down, Duhrra. We will have to wear a hangdog down-dropping Grodnim pair if we are to pass muster."

We stroked the Zairian mustaches into hangdog Grodnim mustaches. It pained us, but it was necessary.

When a Grodnim strains tea or soup through his facial hair a good Zairian has to decide whether to laugh or throw up.

So we rode down the slope and joined the Grodnims. They were not Magdaggians, being from the free Grodnim city of Laggig-Laggu, a large and prosperous conurbation some twenty dwaburs inland of the northern shore of the Laggu River. Hard, businesslike warriors, they handled their sectrixes with confidence and I took note of their weapons. There were ten of them and their Deldar told us they were joining the Chuktar of the west. We nodded as though understanding.

Where we marched was the southern shore. It had belonged to Zair. Now followers of Grodno rode confidently there. From the very last western extremity of the Eye of the World right up to Shazmoz, the green flaunted triumphantly over the red. This area had always been relatively deserted, the haunt of wild beasts, used for hunting.

My own plans were now settled. Duhrra needed to go to the Akhram, for there were to be found associated with the Todalpheme, who monitored the tides, doctors of a higher quality than the usual. His stump was not yet ready to accept the chafing of a leather socket and hook, so Molyz the Hook-Maker had told him, and the doctors of the Akhram would advise him further. So that was why Duhrra rode. As for me, my plans envisaged waiting, and damned impatiently too, for a ship of Vallia to pass through the Grand Canal bound back home. The galleons from Vallia carried on trade with the Eye of the World, as I have said, and I was confident one would eventually arrive. The voller was gone, and riding, walking, climbing and, in the end, crawling, over the Stratemsk, the hostile territories, the Klackadrin and then eastern Turismond would take far, far longer, if I survived it.

"Risslacas!" shouted the Deldar, yanking his longsword out, sticking his stirrups in and racing away at the head of his squad. We followed, keeping closed up. On the ridge above us two risslacas hopped along. They were carnivorous and no doubt regarded us as juicy dinners. This was obviously their territory. They were big, with enormous rear legs and haunches, pear-shaped bodies with neck frills of spines, two small grasping forelegs apiece and heads that could gulp an entire sectrix.

The sectrixes knew it. They were terrified. They bounded along on their six legs, letting terrified snorts of panic blast from their open mouths, not conserving their energies to run. Damn stupid sectrixes. Had I been riding a zorca it would have flown like the wind, everything concentrated on galloping. Had I ridden a vove I would have had to restrain it from going up the slope and knocking the risslacas over.

"May Grotal the Reducer wither their bones!" yelped the man riding by Duhrra. Sheer panic hit these Grodnims. The enormous size of the risslacas and the sharp glitter from their teeth and eyes were enough to unman them. I cocked an eye up the slope, knowing the sectrix, maddened with fear though it was, would not put a foot wrong now. The fur of the risslacas, a slaty brown ocher, fluffed as they cooled their laboring bodies. Fur and feathers are used to protect from heat as well as to conserve it. The two main families of risslacas, the cold-blooded and the warm-blooded, are well represented on Kregen, as I have said. It is a fair scheme to assign dinosaurs a class of their own, distinct from reptiles, birds and mammals. Their expenditure of energy would heat their bodies quickly and then they would have to rest to dispose of all that body-heat if they were cold-blooded. The sectrix had no doubts what they were. It ran with its blunt head outstretched and its six legs pumping, pumping, its body convulsing with effort.

The men of Laggig-Laggu carried short bows cased at their sides. By some considerable effort I edged my mount alongside the man who kept calling on Grodno and demanding that Grotal the Reducer deform, wither, plague, the risslacas so that he might escape.

"Let me have that, dom." I slid the bow from the case and with it a handful of arrows. The bow was a poor thing if one thought of the longbow of Loh—or of Valka now!—but it would serve. Duhrra saw what I was doing.

"No, master!" he bellowed. "You have no chance!"

"The risslacas were designed by—" Then I rephrased that, for the name of Zair instead of Grodno had almost slipped from my babbling lips. "They hunt sectrixes. That is how they eat."

He couldn't argue. The sectrix wouldn't stop no matter how much I banged it, so I did not try. I turned in that damned uncomfortable seat and slapped an arrow into the bow, prepared to see if I might win approval in the eyes of Seg Segutorio, who is, I believe, the finest bowman of Loh of them all.

I do not claim to be as fine a bowman as Seg. That would be prideful folly. We have shot many a round and sometimes I win. The lumpen, ungainly, impossible gait of the sectrix made accurate shooting almost impossible. By calculation, riding the humps and bumps, the yawing and swaying, I fancied I would hit a risslaca eventually. There were only two weak points, the eyes. There were too few arrows to risk the chance. When Duhrra saw me cock a leg over the high wooden saddle he fairly yelled in outrage.

"Go on, Duhrra and, if I live, make sure you come back for me."

I slipped off and the sectrixes were gone in a billow of dust before he could answer. I turned.

By Krun!

They were big! And they were close!

The first arrow spit from the bow. I would not miss at a time like this. Two arrows whipped from the bow and the leading risslaca went crazy, screaming, pawing with his ridiculous little forelegs, waving that enormous head from side to side. From each eye an arrow sprouted. The second dinosaur came on. He was, if anything, larger than the other, and cleverer or luckier, for he moved as the third arrow shot and it chingled and broke against his snout.

He was almost on me, snorting, spurts of steam belching from his gappy nostrils, his mouth wide and cavernous and blood-red, ringed with fangs. I shot again and his left eye went black for him. There was time now only to leap to that side, into his blind spot. His head swayed. I ran off, turned, notched the last arrow. His head swayed around; he saw me with his remaining eye; he charged. The arrow shot spitefully.

He shrieked and ran, ran in circles, colliding with his mate. Then, maddened by pain and unable to see, the two dinosaurs fell on each other, biting, clawing. It was hideous and pathetic and disgusting. I felt no flush of victory. I felt sorry for them, for they had been hunting, doing what nature had intended they should do. It was their misfortune that they chose to hunt Dray Prescot.

Somewhat glumly I left them and walked on in the trail of the sectrixes. It took three burs before Duhrra came back for me. He was cursing and swearing and when he saw me he looked like a man who sees a ghost, a broken ib returned to Kregen, all ghastly and gibbering.

I mounted up.

"Thank you for coming back, Duhrra. There may be others."

"Those Grodno-gastas! Refused to return, said we were no business of theirs! Rode on, quaking, the cramphs!"

The sectrixes were still nervous, sweating, trembling. We galloped them a little, to ease their fears and to stop them from catching cold. They would have to be coddled this night.

"That rast of a Grodnim swod will have a good story to account for the loss of his bow."

"Aye, master. And I will have a story that tells of how a maniac called Dak acted like a—uh ... no one will believe me."

"If the risslacas had not been stopped," I said, letting my mount gallop ahead, "no one would have told any stories."

"That is true, by Zair!"

So it was in a growing spirit of comradeship, for all that Duhrra insisted on slipping the odd "master" into his sentences, and occasionally letting fall that idiot's "duh," we came at last to the Grand Canal, after a long enough and tiring journey.

There was no sign on the southern shore of the Grodnim army.

The northern shore, as I well knew, had a thriving series of communities held together in service to the Todalpheme, those wise men who calculate the tides and send warning, causing the Oblifanters to issue instructions to the workers for the Dam of Days to be opened or closed. I had never seen the Dam of Days. My Delia had, for she had accompanied my sons Drak and Zeg when a galleon from Valka had brought them here to sail to Zy for their education. I would take ship and sail home to Valka, and if I never saw the Eye of the World again it would be too soon.

Missals grew brilliantly along the upper level of the Grand Canal where the grass was cropped short. I stared at a particular grove of the missals, seeing their pink and white blossoms, thinking back. Duhrra sensed my mood and remained silent.

Slowly, I walked toward the edge of the Grand Canal. The last time I had come this way Waterloo had been less than a year gone.

How I remembered! The sweltering Bombay night, then Kregen, glorious Kregen with the streaming mingled sunshine, the air like nectar and a whole world in which to go adventuring. Well, I had been a long way since then and done many things and seen many wonders. Then I had been callow in the ways of Kregen. Now I felt myself not wise so much as indoctrinated. I knew in my heart that I was just the same nurdling onker who would rush headlong into incredible danger where the prudent self I now imagined myself to be would hang back. It is all in the situation.

Over there I had seen a dying Chulik stagger from the bushes, his face ripped off by the teeth of the grundals. Lower down the cliff face flanking the Grand Canal I had fought the grundals and so saved Gahan Gannius and Valima.

Saved them at the behest of the Star Lords, for I had been in mortal fear lest the Everoinye fling back to Earth a pawn who disobeyed. I had saved them for the day they could marry, mate and so bring forth the suppurating evil that to-day was called Genod Gannius, the man who ate up the Zairians, their lands, beliefs and spirit. Truly the Star Lords planned long and long into the future. I stood there thinking back on my handiwork and I realized afresh that each person with whose destiny I had meddled at the orders of the Star Lords must play a part in the greater destiny of Kregen.

Even my own part, which I had then thought worthy, of creating a slave phalanx of my old vosk-skulls and thrashing the hated Overlords of Magdag, had been turned against my Zairians by the machinations of Genod Gannius. Perhaps the Star Lords had seen what I would do. I could not believe that, for it had not been a thing of careful edges; rather it had grown and accreted of itself. No wonder the Star Lords had snatched me away in the moment of victory. A puzzle that had been with me for many years and seasons on Kregen had been solved.

Duhrra coughed, a hugely artificial cough, and said, "The suns decline, master. If we are to reach Akhram before night-fall . . ."

"Aye," I said, somewhat heavily. "I have been thinking what a gerblish onker I am, when the Deldars are ranked."

He didn't bother to reply and I saw by the way he twitched his stump he did not agree. We went down the staircase cut into the wall of the Grand Canal and our sectrixes followed down the angled sloping paths cut for animals and swam the blue water; we climbed the other stupendous wall and came to Akhram.

The top of the Grand Canal was five miles across, flanked by cut steps a hundred yards broad, a mile or so deep, with something like forty steps of varying heights around a hundred and fifty feet average. The sheer colossal size of this man-made artifact impressed me all over again, as it had be-fore. The perspective dwindled out of sight to the west. At that end of the Grand Canal lay the Dam of Days. For the simple satisfaction of actually seeing it I knew I would go there very soon. Duhrra and I approached the portal of the Akhram on this northern bank. Once again I saw that confus-

ing collection of domes and steeples and minarets clustered
within the stone walls. Once again the bronze-bound lenken
door opened and the Todalpheme in their blue-tasseled cords
and yellow hooded robes approached, bearing torches, making us welcome.

Their smooth skins showed the ministrations of oils and
strigils, their faces fleshed with good living and yet ascetic
with the mysteries of their profession. The Tides of Kregen
are monitored by the Todalpheme. It is an art and a science.
They had asked me to join them and I had refused. The old
Akhram, the leader, was dead, and a new old Akhram lived
in the chief place in his stead, as he had told me would happen.

There is little to say of that night. Duhrra and I were made
welcome, appointed a chamber, given food, were sent packing to bed. I lay awake for some time, pondering long on
what had happened to me since I had last been here. It was
incredible, but it had all happened.

The following morning after breakfast I walked with the
Akhram, trying to recapture those old feelings of mine. He
remembered my walking with his predecessor for, after all, it
had been merely a quarter of his life span ago. I glanced up
as a shadow fleeted below the suns.

I gaped.

A voller speeded up there, a fast two-place scout, quick
and nimble. It vanished toward the west, flying fast and low.

The Akhram folded his hands within the sleeves of his
robe, his face smooth and yet knowing. "A flying boat, yes,
of late we have seen it a number of times."

"You are surprised?"

"Yes. We know of Vallia and Donengil here, of Wloclef
and Loh and Djannik and a few other places. We have heard
tales of boats that fly."

I rubbed my chin through the beard I had let grow. I did
not like the look of this. "You have heard of Havilfar?"

He regarded me gravely. "Had you asked me that question
but a sennight ago, I would have answered no. Today I must
answer yes."

I felt the black bile, the anger, the remorse that I had
stayed so long here in the inner sea. My place, I thought

then, was at home countering the wiles of Hamal, the rich and evil Empire of the continent of Havilfar.

"We Todalpheme, as you know, take no part in the struggles between the green and the red. Our own people support us, and wear brown. They are raided—you will, I think, remember one such raid?"

"Yes."

The Todalpheme, because of their vital function, were taboo subjects over most of Kregen. No man would strike one down, lest the next tide should sweep him, his family and home away to watery destruction. I glanced up. Clouds massed before the suns. The temperature dropped markedly as we walked back along the battlements of the Akhram.

Akhram went on speaking: "We hear that this Genod Gannius has enlisted new allies in his struggles against the Zairians. He has brought new fighting men and weapons, and he has asked for a quantity of these wonderful flying boats."

I stared at him. Again the sense of vast unseen struggles enveloped me. The shadowy purposes of the Star Lords had, it seemed to me, been made a little more plain. They had used me to save Gahan Gannius and Valima and thus ensure the creation of their son Genod. What Genod was doing, therefore, must be desired by the Star Lords. I did not know why they should wish the green of Grodno to overcome the red of Zair, here in the Eye of the World.

The Akhram was still speaking, his face shadowed as the clouds grew over the bright face of the suns.

"We predict a great tide and the representatives of Genod Gannius have asked us to make sure a convoy of ships bearing the flying boats is allowed through the Dam of Days before we close the caissons." He glanced obliquely at the clouds. Already I, an old sailorman, had sensed the gale brewing. "If the storm breaks with the tide the ships will be safely inside the Grand Canal. We could not refuse Gannius, for he brought an army with his request, and they guard the Dam of Days now, to enforce their orders."

If I seem to you particularly stupid in that I did not at once seize on these facts and construct an impressive theory, I must plead only that I had taken a savage whirling in the blasts of fate and now I only wished to turn my back on the inner sea. Yes, I would feel a terrible grief when the red of

Zair went down, when Zy was destroyed and Sanurkazz ravaged. But they were merely small places in a small locale hidden from the rest of Kregen. My place lay in Valka and Vallia, maturing our plans to withstand the insane ambitions of the Empress Thyllis of Hamal, or in Djanduin with my Djangs, or taking hard steps to combat the raids of the shanks from around the curve of the world. I also had to visit Strombor in the enclave city of Zenicce and assure myself that my house prospered. And I would then go on a visit to my clansmen of the Great Plains of Segesthes, my wonderful clansmen of Felschraung and Longuelm. So there was much I must do in this marvelous and terrible world of Kregen. The inner sea shrank in my estimation of the important things in my life.

But Havilfarese vollers, here, in the Eye of the World! Manned by the cramphs of Magdag and all the other rasts of Grodnims, swooping down to destroy the red of Zair. How the Krozairs and the Red Brethren would fight! It would be a wonderful ending to all, to join them and roar out the battle songs for Zair and so go down fighting into the Ice Floes of Sicce.

Sanity returned. That would not help Delia. She might sympathize with my emotions, but I could not destroy her out of sheer warrior's pride.

Already I had spent far too long dillydallying in the Eye of the World when I should be actively seeking out a galleon from Vallia, not meekly sitting here waiting for one to sail past. There would be galleons in Magdag. I must go there, find one and give orders to her skipper, in my capacity as Prince Majister of Vallia, order him to bear me home to Vallia without delay. Yes, by Vox!

But I thought Delia would allow me one look at this marvel, this Dam of Days. Just one look. Then Magdag, Vallia, Valka, home!

I said to Duhrra: "On the morrow I visit the Dam of Days. After that I go where I fancy you will not wish to go."

Duhrra replied comfortably, "I do not think there is such a place, master."

Chapter Twenty

The Dam of Days

"Why do you call yourself Dak, when our records show your name to be Dray Prescot?"

Akhram looked up at me with his wise gaze frank and open. We sat in his study with all the old familiar paraphernalia of ephemeris, globe, table and dividers spread around. Here I had talked for many burs one time with his predecessor, the old Akhram. I had been invited to join the Todalpheme and had rejected the offer, hungering for my Delia.

I said: "There have been many events in my life since last I passed this way. The name of Dray Prescot is well known on the inner sea ... well ..." Here I paused, thinking I boasted. To correct that impression, I said: "I am a hunted man from one side and, if the other side knew I still lived and was here, I would be the target for instant destruction. The name Dak is an honored one. I do not treat it lightly."

"We are aloof from the red and green. But we understand the passions that rule men within the Eye of the World. And, yes, I will arrange for you to visit the Dam of Days. And, yes, you may rest assured your name will remain Dak with us."

"You are most kind."

So Duhrra and I and a small escort of three of the younger Todalpheme rode out astride sectrixes for the western end of the Grand Canal. We carried supplies carefully wrapped in leaves. By walking the sectrixes and not galloping hard the journey would take about fifteen burs. I thought Delia would allow me fifteen burs there and fifteen back out of my burning urgency to return to her. Looking back, I think I sensed more in this journey than a mere excuse to my Delia. So we rode.

You who have followed my story this far will know that some other and altogether more evil and more Dray Prescot-like motive inspired me. Those ships carried Havilfarese vollers. I fancied they would be Hamalese rather than Hyrklanan or some other of the smaller states of Havilfar manufacturing fliers. So there might be a beautiful opportunity for me, the old reiver, the old render, the old paktun, to steal away a voller and fly directly back to Delia. That would be like the Dray Prescot I hoped I still was.

The water in the Grand Canal was low, barely half a mile deep. That was the usual depth the Todalpheme, through their agents the Oblifanters who ran the Dam of Days, attempted to maintain. When the tide smashed in against the outer coast I knew from the defenses of Zenicce and Vallia the level could go up in a Bay of Fundy maelstrom. These matters are a question of science, the suns and moons acting together producing spring tides, the neap tides falling about a lunar quarter later. With seven moons acting with and against one another and the two suns, for this purpose calculated as a single gravitational source, the possibilities were fascinating, susceptible to interesting calculation and extremely fraught. The Todalpheme earned their inviolability from the crude external pressures of Kregen.

I had much to occupy my mind as we jogged on. Duhrra had been measured up for his hook and the doctors had pursed their lips over his stump, commenting acidly on the butchery of whoever had amputated. Duhrra had thrown me a comical glance and I had told the story, which brought forth, as I had expected, a genuine desire to overcome the handicap of botched work. If they had deemed it necessary to amputate further they would have. Luckily for Duhrra—and me—they did not.

So, in the fullness of time, we came in sight of the Dam of Days.

How to describe it?

In rhapsodic terms, glowingly referring to the size, the splendor, the majesty? In scientific terms, the cubic volumes enclosed, the tons of water passing, the mechanisms of the caissons? In economical terms, for although electricity was not generated here—and I knew nothing of it then—the megawatts available would have lit up the inner sea.

In artistic terms, when the suns shone on the stone facings of the rock fill and glowed with all the flowerlike glory of an Alpine garden?

The Dam stretched across the mouth of the canal, which had widened into the bay. The bay enclosed a vast sheet of water. The Dam towered in size, rising to a stupendous height, and yet, when the eye's gaze traveled along the length, from headland to headland, the Dam appeared a long low wall against the sea. I think a Hollander would have appreciated that great work, or any man who has worked on a dam, anyone, actually, who had heart and imagination for the work of man's hands. The Dam had been built by the Sunset People in the long ago. Now I had learned—on Earth, on Earth!—that the Savanti of Aphrasöe were the last remnants of that once proud and world-girdling peoples. They had built well and to last. Yet their cities were tumbled into ruin in many places of Kregen; in the Kharoi Stones of my island of Hyr Khor in Djanduin were to be seen the fragmented particles of their glory.

Yet the Grand Canal and the Dam of Days glowed with the newness of building. The Sunset People had loved them.

"You see the waterfall, tumbling down into the sea by the northern headland, Tyr Dak?" The young Todalpheme pointed. He was a novice, learning his trade. In a hundred years, perhaps less if he was astute, he might become Akhram. I nodded. The waterfall fell into the sea and beyond it, inland, there was the glitter of a lake.

"When the tide rises the water fills the lake, so the river has merely to top it up. That is the reservoir from which comes the power of the Dam of Days."

We jogged on. Camped on a wide flat area rose the tents and huts of a sizable force. They were Grodnims. Duhrra hugged his detested green robes closer to him. I knew that we stood in some real danger of being accosted as slaves or runaway slaves, and was ready to be unpleasant in any event to any damned Overlord.

The three Todalpheme, although entirely unconcerned for they were secure in their immunity, angled away before we crossed the Dam. They were upset that naked force had been used here, where the pure light of science, as they said, should reign supreme. I could tell them about science, thinking back to my frustrating experiences on Earth during that twenty-one years of torment. I could also tell them about the uses of naked force.

Across the Dam the vistas were immense. On our right hand the greenly gray sea heaved away to a wild horizon. The gale was surely coming. On our left hand the waters, although separated only by the bulk of the Dam, yet showed the bluer color of the inner sea. We crossed halfway and stood for a while, lolling on the high parapet, looking around, marveling, silent. At intervals the Dam of Days was pieced by openings. There were arranged to resist the push of water from east and west and not from one side only like a lockgate. They were fashioned in the form of gigantic cylinders rising and falling in open masonry guides. A modern analogy I can now give is to liken them to pistons. When water from the lake was introduced from valved pipes they sank and so effectively blocked the openings.

The lifting of these caissons, although essentially simple, demanded a level of technology beyond that of the current manipulators. That only one caisson rope of steel wire had ever broken is a tribute to the building of the Sunset People. Next to each caisson in the Dam was sited an enormous reservoir tank. This was free to move up and down in guides. Many steel cables passed over central pulleys from caisson to tank. When the tank was filled with water from a separate valved and piped supply from the lake, it would descend. Because the tank size was greater than the amount of caisson under the sea level, the tank would haul the caisson up as it sank. Vents in the caisson valved open to let the water run out. Because the caisson, when high and empty, was itself larger than the amount of water left in the tank after that level equaled the sea level, the caissons would fill and sink, thus hauling up the tanks. All very neat and economical, the power being supplied by gravity through the falling water.

Finally, I should say that the Oblifanters kept hordes of workpeople busy greasing everything to ensure that it ran sweetly. To allow the caissons to move up and down their guides against the enormous differential of water pressure, a whole series of wheels were fitted on each side, to resist pressure front and back.

This made me think. The Todalpheme gave their orders to lower or lift the caissons to regulate the level of water flowing into the inner sea. Usually the high tides would cause them to close the gates. Why should the Sunset People bother to arrange wheels to resist pressure from the back of the dam? I suspected that in those long-gone days the dam was employed for more than merely regulating the tides.

One of the young Todalpheme novices shaded his eyes, looking out to sea. "I believe . . ." he said, pointing. I looked.

This young Todalpheme was used to poring over papers indoors. My old sailor's eye picked out the familiar shapes. Argenters, their sails board-stiff, riding the brushing skirts of the gale, rushed headlong through the tumbling whitecaps. I studied them, the wind in my face, wondering how many of them would smash to pieces before they negotiated the gates of the dam.

I saw the flags fluttering.

Four green diagonals and four blue diagonals slanting from right to left, the blue and green divided by thin borders of white.

Menaham.

That made perfect sense.

When mad Queen Thyllis, as she was then, had invaded the island of Pandahem she had overrun country after country until her victorious armies and air service had been stopped in the Battle of Jholaix. Of all the nations of Pandahem she had made allies of the Menahem. I had remorseful memories of my treatment of young Pando, the Kov of Bomark, and his mother, Tilda the Fair. They lived side by side with the people of Menaham, and they called them the Bloody Menahem. Even when Thyllis of Hamal had been forced back, made to conclude a peace with Vallia and those nations of Pandahem she had overrun, still she continued the alliance with the Bloody Menahem. Hamal possessed few ships. Pandahem was an island center of commerce, as was Vallia. So what was more natural than that Hamal should use ships from Menaham?

If you ask why bother to use large, slow argenters to transport vollers when they might fly, you forget the ways of

Hamal, the cunning of those cramphs of Hamal and their
treacherous vollers. I knew well enough that the fliers in those
ships would work well for a while and then break down. Oh,
yes, I knew that! Would the Hamalians risk a flight from
Hamal to the inner sea in suspect vollers?

And, of course, Genod Gannius, like us in Vallia, would
be so anxious to lay his hands on fliers he would accept the
probable defects as part of the price he must pay. This was
what Vallia had done, what Zenicce and all the others who
bought vollers from Hamal had done. Otherwise, no fliers.

So I stood no longer lolling on the high parapet-walk
watching those ships standing in. They were handled smartly
enough and they negotiated the wide openings superbly. They
rode the waves like great preening swans. All their flags fluttering, the sails cracking and billowing as the hands braced
the yards around, the ships aimed for the gaps, the white
water spuming away from their forefeet. They breasted the
waves and sailed through the Dam of Days into the bay leading to the Grand Canal.

I walked across to the other side of the dam and watched
them, their motion much easier in the enclosed water. They
made straight for the canal. They would probably lie up in
the harbor halfway through, or in the harbor at the eastern
end, depending on circumstances. Then the vollers would be
brought up from those capacious holds. The air service men
from Hamal would give then a final check and hand them
over. No doubt Genod Gannius had made arrangements for
his men to be trained in their use. And then . . .

I had an apocalyptic vision of hordes of Grodnims descending from the skies, first to smash all resistance in
Shazmoz, then other cities along the red southern shore, then
on and on, razing Zy, on and on, finally taking Holy Sanurkazz.

Well, the vision was apocalyptic, but it was no further
business of mine.

And Mayfwy and Felteraz?

I bashed my fist against the stone of that high walk. I
cursed. Why must I remember Mayfwy and Felteraz now?

Of what value were they, set against my Delia?

But they were not set against her.

One value could not destroy another if there was no conflict of interest. Wouldn't my Delia tell me—demand of me—that as a simple man, let alone a one-time proud, high and mighty Krozair of Zy, a man who professed Opaz—when it suited him, to be sure—my obligation was to protect Mayfwy, who was our friend?

But I wanted none of the inner sea. I wanted to go home. Sight of those argenters of Menaham had kindled the spark of deviltry. I would sneak down there by the light of the moons, steal a voller, and so fly back to Valka. I might set one argenter alight; that would be reasonable, though I did not think I would care to attempt to destroy them all. Genod Gannius struck me as the kind of general who would take care of such possibilities in his planning.

A brisker gust of wind blew against the back of my head. I turned. The sea was getting up and the whitecaps were now rolling in thickly, with here and there a spume lifting and billowing away downwind. The air was noticeably colder.

Men in the brown of the workers were crowding past, down on the main road across the dam. I saw an Oblifanter directing them, a tough commanding figure in brown with a good deal of gold lace and gold buttons, with the balass stick in his fist.

"We must return, Tyr Dak," said the novice. He shivered. "The tide is making. They will close the gates now that the ships have passed. We must go back."

"And about time, too," said Duhrra. He had no idea what those ships carried, that they spelled doom to him and his kind. "We have seen this marvel, Dak my master. Now, for the sweet sake of Mother Zinzu the Blessed, I would like to see about my hook."

Slowly I climbed down off the high parapet and trailed on after the others. The novice called me Tyr Dak—sir. And Duhrra called on Sweet Mother Zinzu the Blessed, the patron saint of the drinking classes of Sanurkazz. Wouldn't my two favorite rogues, my two rascals, my two oar comrades, Nath and Zolta, also be caught up in the catastrophe if these vollers fell into the hands of Genod Gannius, the Grodnim?

The coils of unkind fate lapped around me then. Uppermost in my mind, the tantalizing thought of Delia drove out all other thoughts—almost. Nath and Zolta, Duhrra ... and Mayfwy. It was not fair. But then nothing in this life, either on Earth or on Kregen, is fair. Only a gerblish onker would imagine otherwise.

When we had escaped from King Wazur's test, there on the island of Ogra-gemush, Delia had had to instruct me. I had been all for leaving the Wizard of Loh, Khe-Hi-Bjanching, and Merle, Jefan Werden's daughter, in the pit. Delia had made me, all wounded and half dead as I was, climb down there and drag them out—twice. If Delia were here at my side now, wouldn't she demand the same chivalry, the same conduct, damned stupid though it might appear to one unversed in the mysteries of the Sisters of the Rose and the Krozairs of Zy?

That I was no longer a Krozair of Zy had nothing to do with it.

Cursing, in the foulest of foul moods, I stamped along after the others.

The tide was making rapidly.

The Oblifanter, a bluff, weather-beaten man twirling his balass stick, was most polite to the Todalpheme, novices though they were. To Duhrra and me he extended a distant politeness that reflected his opinion of Grodnims who sought to take his functions into their hands. We walked on. The wind blustered past above the parapet. Flags were snapping and then standing out stiff as boards. The sea must be covered in white now. Inland the bay remained calm. The argenters were sailing into the cut, the wind on their quarter, under reduced canvas.

A giant creaking, groaning filled the air, like the ice blocks of the Floes of Sicce grinding against each other.

The Oblifanter cursed and ran to one of the tall chain-towers. He was yelling, "Put some grease on the ropes, you nurdling onkers!"

I wondered, if he kept up that tone to a Hikdar of the Grodnims, how long it would take for him to lose his teeth and have his nose broken. The Grodnims are a barbarous lot.

When we reached the spot the noise had sensibly reduced. We could look over and see the brown-clad workers perched on a spider-walk tipping buckets of grease onto the thick steel cables as they passed over the pulley train. Close by, the monstrous bulk of a caisson lowered slowly into the sea, while on the other side the equally monstrous bulk of a counterbalancing tank lifted up in its guides. The whole spectacle would have delighted the very hearts and souls of all Victorian engineers, who doted on gigantism within the context of wrought and cast iron. I walked on.

It was no business of mine.

The image of Delia floated before me. Now that image looked scornful. Her glorious face filled me with the kind of feelings a rope's end might have after a manhound puppy has finished with it.

A rope's end does not have feelings, although it can impart them smartly enough in the fist of a boatswain's mate, and it would be in shreds after a manhound had finished with it, puppy or not. In much the same kind of shreds as my emotions . . .

The valves controlling the pipes to the caissons lay grouped together under a stone shelter, built as an integral part of the dam. I stopped there, watching the brown-clad workers turning the handles. The Todalpheme ahead swung around and motioned me to follow. The Oblifanter whisked his balass stick over the rump of a worker who was clearly not putting his heart into the work.

I said, "Oblifanter, you would oblige me by opening the valves to the tanks and closing the valves to the caissons."

He gaped at me.

I said, "Be quick about it, dom, for my temper is short."

He started waving his arms about. His face assumed that red sometimes seen in a malsidge trodden on in a dopa den.

"You cannot do that! The gates will open—the tide will flood through!"

"Nevertheless, that is what you must do."

"But the tide! The *tide*!"

"You will let enough through to do as I desire. When that has been accomplished you may lower the caissons again, so it will not be enough to sweep on through the Eye of the World. It will expend itself before it reaches Shazmoz." I thought about that, of the Grodnim ships hovering like sea-leems off Shazmoz, preventing communication. "We had best leave the caissons up until the tide reaches Shazmoz. Yes." I felt remarkably cheerful. I did not smile, but I felt amazingly active and energetic. "Yes, that will serve admirably."

"You are mad!"

"Do not doubt it."

"Here!" yelled the Oblifanter, his eyes fairly popping from his head. He shouted to a group of Grodnims sauntering off with the workpeople not laboring at the valves. "Here! You! Earn your keep, for what good you do here! Stop this madman—"

He said no more for I put him to sleep gently and lowered him to the stone-flagged roadway. I stared at the group of workpeople at the valves. Their faces looked back blankly, like calsanys'.

"Shut the caisson valves and open the tanks. *Jump!*"

They saw my face and they shivered and began to do as I said.

The Grodnims walked back, puzzled by the shouting, and saw what the workmen were doing. The Todalpheme stood to one side, quite unable to grasp what was going on. Duhrra looked at me hard and then sauntered across.

The day was darkening over, the clouds massing. The wind blew keenly. The gale would strike very soon now. And all the time the tide rose, one of those enormous Tides of Kregen that could wash away all before it like a tsunami, leveling and destroying, save where the hand of man placed obstacles in its path to protect his property and life.

"What's going on here?"

It so happened that there was a Jiktar among the Grodnims. A Jiktar has come a long way in the chain of command, for he commands a regiment, a swifter or a galleon; when he has worked his way through to zan-Jiktar, he may reach the highest military rank of all, that of Chuktar, above whom there exist only generals of the highest rank, princes, kings and emperors.

"Stand aside, rast!" He spoke quite matter-of-factly. He shouted at the frightened workpeople. "Shut the tank valves at once."

I said, "Open the tank valves."

The Jiktar did not hesitate. That was one reason why he was a Jiktar.

"Seize him!" he said, again quite normally. "If you have to slay him, you have to. But I would like to put the madman to the question."

He'd really like that, enjoying himself.

The Grodnims came for me with their longswords swinging. I was not overly fussy about how many got themselves killed.

There remained one item to be finalized, no, two, for I saw Duhrra start fumbling about under his blanket-cloak.

"Stand away, Duhrra!" I yelled. "Don't get yourself killed."

He did not reply.

What I must do was position myself in front of the workers so as to cow them and assure them of unpleasantness if they did not continue to fill the tanks, and I must prevent the Grodnims from getting past me at them. The fight looked promising. The immediate future appeared somewhat scarlet, lurid and highly diverting.

The impressions of the moment burn bright still: the wind beginning to build up into a howling torrent rushing across the high loft of the Dam of Days; the frightened workers in their brown smocks frantically turning the valve wheels as I glared at them; the clatter of the soldiers' studded war-boots as they ran on the stone flags of the walkway; the glitter of their mail and the bright sheen of their green as they advanced ample excuse for swordplay; the sight of Duhrra hopping about beyond them, his face a maelstrom of emotions that in another place and another time would have proved comical in the extreme; the feel of the longsword hilt in my fist. This was a cheap weapon, not a Krozair longsword, with a cross-guard and grip of iron, the grip covered in sturmwood, the blade true enough but the whole brand lacking the superb balance of the genuine article. The grip spanned only two hands' breadths so there was no chance of spreading fists in that cunning Krozair fashion. This sword was designed for the bludgeoning, hacking of men-at-arms in the melee. Well, it would serve.

The Grodnims at first thought simply to overawe me, so they rushed up swinging their swords, yelling, ferocious. It seemed unchivalrous, unsporting, not Jikai, to slay the first of them, so I parried his blow and cracked him across his mail coif. He went down like a log. The second pair came in together, abruptly shocked, ready now, in the swift way of the men of green, to slay me and have done.

Their blows hissed past and I cut once, backhanded once

and leaped clear of a third who sought to drive his point beneath my breastbone.

My sword took off the side of his face. I whirled blood-drops at the workers who had stopped turning.

"Turn, doms, turn! Fill the tanks!"

The blood spattered brightly across them and yet, in the instant I swung back and engaged the next pair, that bright red darkened and dulled as clouds drove beneath the suns.

More men ran up, shouting, as the Jikar, fairly foaming with rage as the outrage he felt, bellowed them on. I cut down the two before me, finding the clumsy sweep of the longsword some impediment. I had used a longsword like this many times. Perhaps employing the magnificent Krozair longsword weakened a fighting man when he was forced to use lesser weapons. So I leaped and ducked and fought, hacking and thrusting when the opportunity offered, for these men wore mail. I had noticed on this second period in the Eye of the World that the Grodnims affected a second sword scabbarded at their waists, a shortsword. Perhaps this was the handiwork of Genod Gannius. If it was, he would have turned purple with rage that his men stubbornly stuck to their familiar longswords now. I was unarmored. A shortsword man might have been able to drive in under my longsword and finish me. The shortsword has, as I have said, advantages in some combats.

A Grodnim Deldar, raving to get at me through the press of his own men, abruptly stiffened, rearing upright, his eyes popping. I saw a sword smash down on that juncture between neck and shoulder where the mail spreads, battering its way through. The Deldar fell. Duhrra, the sword in his left hand whirring up for another blow, appeared bright-eyed, furious of face, yelling.

"Hai Jikai!" bellowed Duhrra, laying about him. "Hai Jikai!"

The wind blustered past above us. Mailed men screamed and fell as our longswords bit. Duhrra took a glancing slice on his right arm—only a slicing glance. In combat of this kind there are seldom wounded men, not for very long anyway. A blow from a longsword, which is really a sharpened length of tempered iron, will do a man's business for him with certitude.

The longsword possesses awful smashing power. I took a

man's arm off and whirled to deface his comrade, leaped and ducked and so roared in to get at the Jiktar.

He saw me coming and jerked his sword up. Two more men went down before we could meet. Duhrra took out another and then the stone-flagged walkway contained only the brown-clad workpeople, the three Todalpheme, the Grodnim Jiktar—and a quantity of dead Grodnims scattered about.

The Jiktar said, "You are assuredly mad and will die for this."

I would not have replied anyway, but as I closed I saw a wide-winged shadow on the stones. The sun had shafted through for an instant, the green sun, for the red remained swathed in cloud. If this was an omen I would have none of it. In that ephemeral shaft of green sunlight the shadow of a hunting bird lay at my feet. Before I looked up I leaped out of reach of the Jiktar's sword.

Yes. Yes, up there, the damned scarlet and gold raptor, the spying Gdoinye of the Star Lords!

The sight enraged me more than the fight had been able to do.

And then . . . and then!

A blue radiance began to seep in, to encompass me. The vague outlines of that giant Scorpion appeared before my eyes. I tried to scream out violently and managed a whisper, feeling myself falling. The blue radiance hovered. Someone—a long time ago and a long way away—had said that by willpower I might avert the call of the Everoinye. I tried. I struggled. I do not think that I could have succeeded alone.

The harsh bite of the stone flags against my knees told me I still remained on the high Dam of Days. There was still a fight to be fought and won, a Jikai to create. The blue radiance changed, swirling, coiling. I sensed an unease. A tinge of yellow crept into the blue. I did not ever remember seeing yellow when I was transmitted to and from Kregen.

"I will stay here, Star Lords!" I roared. I struggled to rise. I could hear a strange tinkering sound, as of water hitting a tin cup. "Leave me be, you kleeshes! I stay here!"

The blue wavered; the yellow prospered.

The enormous form of the phantom blue Scorpion assumed vast, grotesque proportions—and then it burst. A blaze of pure yellow exploded about me, with the sound as of cymbals clanging in the High Pantheon of Opaz in Vallia.

I knelt on the stone flags of the walkway across the Dam of Days. I looked up. The Jiktar was in the act of ferociously smiting at Duhrra, whose left arm lifted his sword at the last moment. Duhrra's sword showed a succession of savage dints along both blade edges. He was finding extreme difficulty in settling to a rhythm and swinging. That he had fought as well as he had with his left hand testified to his extraordinary physical strength and to the resolution of his will.

With a beast's roar, a roar as of the leems being let out into the Jikhorkdun, I gathered my feet under me and sprang.

The Jiktar's head flew high as his torso toppled.

"You are unharmed, Duhrra?"

"Aye." He panted now and lowered the sword. "I thought you done for, although I could not see . . ."

"No." I looked at this hulking man-mountain with the idiot-face and bulging muscles and the useless stumped right arm. Very gravely I lifted my bloodied sword in the salute.

"Hai Jikai, Duhrra. Henceforth, I think, I shall call you Duhrra of the Days. Hai Jikai!"

He gaped at me, amazed. The reference to the Dam of Days was clear enough.

"If you . . ." He started over. "It is for you . . ."

I swung the sword at the pipe valve wheels. The workers, freed by the fight from oppression, had all run off. They had closed the valves down. I could not blame them. I walked across.

The moment I began opening the valves again to let water flow from the lake reservoir into the tanks and so lift the caissons and open the gates, the three Todalpheme hurried across. They had been shaken by the savagery of fighting men; but this business now, they conceived, concerned them.

I disabused them.

As gently as possible, I said, "If you seek to stop me I shall knock you all down."

They appeared to understand.

The flat rather than the edge sometimes works as well.

One said, "The tide is rising fast and the storm comes on apace. If you open but one gate the water will—"

I finished with the valves, for I had spun the wheels with savagery, and said, "The water will serve Zair. After that, you may close the tank valves and open the caissons'."

They knew I would stand by the wheels with a naked sword in my fist until I was ready. The blood had ceased to drop from the blade now, but the length was shining red and evil in the light.

Tremendous power was to be unleashed in the next few murs. Water from the lake reservoir ran through the multi-branching pipes and past the valves I had opened, filling the counterweighting tanks. The wind tore at us, streaming our hair, screaming past our ears. The roar of the waters mounted. The tanks began to sink. The weight of water pulled them down and the steel wire ropes groaned under the strain. Duhrra put his sword down and ran to slop grease onto the series of pulleys, using the flat wooden spatula with his left hand, the grease-bucket caught up under his right arm stump.

"Pour it on, Duhrra!" I bellowed in my foretop hailing voice. He barely heard. He upended the bucket over the pulleys.

The caissons began to rise. I knew that if they did not rise sufficiently for my purpose before the full weight of the tide bore against them they would not budge thereafter. On the coast of Scotland the measurement of breakers has revealed a stunning effort of six thousand pounds per square foot. So I stood while we opened a door to hell.

Clouds blew furiously overhead, drowning the faces of the suns. Up there the moons were lining out in that deadly conjunction which would certainly spell destruction and might mean death for many a seaport city around Kregen where the seaward defenses had been neglected. Even the three smaller moons, which hurtle frantically low over the face of the planet, were in conjunction. The first and largest moon, the Maiden with the Many Smiles, the two second moons, the Twins, and the third Moon, She of the Veils, all were exerting their gravitational pull together with the Suns.

When no moons are in the sky of Kregen—when they cannot be seen, that is—that is called a night of Notor Zan. When all the moons blaze at the full, when even the three smallest join with the major four, that is called the Scarf of Our Lady Monafeyom. We could see nothing overhead but the dark swirling clouds lowering down, but we knew what was going on out there as we knew how the waters of the ocean were responding to the titanic forces.

The Dam shuddered.

All that monstrous construction thrilled to the shock, alive with the vibration.

The wind tore the reason from our skulls.

The tide burst through.

The gale broomed its own violence and added to the pell-mell tumult. I hung onto the guardrail, my hair blown forward over my face, staring at the mouth of the Grand Canal.

The opening was small at this distance and the argenters appeared like dots in the gloom, but I have imagination and the whole scene was described vividly to me later by one who was there and saw it all at close hand.

Across the bay leaped the tidal bore.

A wall of water, tipped with the vicious fangs of breakers, towering, cresting, blowing, omnipotent in its might. How tall was the eagre?

The famous Severn bore rushes up at the equinoxes to heights of five to six feet. Good friends have told me that in New Brunswick they have seen the daily tidal bore roaring up the river from the Bay of Fundy in a mightily impressive sight: a genuine wall of water simply rolling up the river with the floodwater following directly behind. The rise and fall of the tide in the Bay of Fundy is known to every schoolboy. At the head of the bay the tidal height reaches a fantastic sixty-two feet and even halfway up, at Passamaquoddy Bay, it is twenty-five feet. The force and power of millions of tons of water rolling along with the fang-toothed eagre at their head are enough to convince the most sceptical of mortals that in sober truth nature is the lord and master of the worlds we inhabit.

All this power and smashing violence, the colossal movement of water—with only one sun and one moon!

How high?

I stood there as the Dam thrilled to the vibrations of untold millions of tons of water smashing at its ancient structure, as the water spumed through the opening I had made shuddering under the shrill of the wind.

How high?

I saw the small shape of an argenter lifted up and up and up. It broke apart. It flew apart as a barrel flies apart when its hoops are broken through. Planks, timbers, bundles—dark, pitiful objects—whirling and smoking through the frenzied turmoil of the waves, with the spume covering all with a white confetti of death.

Horrible, terrible, malignant. I would prefer to pass lightly over that destruction of a fleet, for I am an old sailor who has a love for ships.

But the ships were broken and riven. Crushed against the hard stone of the terraced Grand Canal, tossed up like chips to fall, cracking open and spilling shrieking bloody things that had been men, the ships died. The wind lashed the sea and drove relentlessly on. The bore sliced through the Grand Canal and the waters boiled and roared and fought as they cascaded on.

On and on through the cut smoked the waters.

The tide had struck and destroyed, shouting in its strength.

How high?

High enough for death.

High enough to claw up past terrace after terrace of the Grand Canal, filling the cut with the violence of unleashed waters, rolling remorselessly on and on over the wrecked remnants that had once been a fleet proud with flags.

So, I thought, ended Genod Gannius' plans to use vollers from Hamal against Zairians.

The sight of those broad comfortable ships, those splendid argenters, being smashed to driftwood did not please me, even when I knew what they were and what errand they had been on.

I, an old first lieutenant of a seventy-four, am sentimental in these matters.

Against the shriek of the wind Duhrra's voice reached me thinned. "It is time we moved on, Dak my master. I see the green moving in the shadows beyond the Dam."

The darkness pressed down as the stormclouds boiled. The Todalpheme were anxious to lower the caissons once I gave them leave. I stepped past the body of the Jiktar. He had been a Ghittawrer, a Grodnim member of a green brotherhood that attempted to ape the ways and disciplines of the Krozairs. His sword would be of fine quality. Duhrra and I would leave the novices; we must find our own way out of this situation. I turned back.

"One boon I ask," I said to the novice. "The tide will reach Shazmoz but will scarce do further damage. Do not tell the Grodnims the names you have heard us use."

"Then what names shall we tell them? They are hard men and will be exceedingly angry."

"Say you heard us call each other Krozairs."

The Todalpheme's face betrayed his speculation through the continuing shock. "That will make them even more wroth."

Then I laughed. "I shall be sorry to miss that pleasant sight."

So, laughing, Duhrra and I ran rapidly from the Dam of Days.

Once we had slipped into the storm-shadows at the far end we were able to circle and mingle with the Grodnims, securing ourselves from all possible suspicion. We were merely two paktuns, serving Grodno the Green.

I had stooped to take the longsword from the Jiktar. It was a fine weapon. Its pattern was startlingly similar to a true Krozair longsword, but it was not. Its edge was dented in only two places, where Duhrra's common blade looked almost like a saw. He too possessed himself a fine new blade. All the common longswords bore on the flat of the blade below the guard the etched monogram G.G.M. I remembered that. The Jiktar's sword bore a device I knew, a lairgodont surmounted by the rayed sun. The lairgodont, a most ferocious carnivorous risslaca, is known over much of Kregen but is most numerous in northern Turismond. So I kept the hilt of the longsword, with its device and decoration of emeralds, hidden under a flap of green cloth, for that symbol denotes a green brotherhood devoted to Grodno.

We took our chances, Duhrra and I, and we passed through the encamped army of Genod Gannius, commanded by his Chuktar of the west, and so came at length free of them and to the east of the Grand Canal, on the northern shore.

"I am for Magdag, Duhrra. There I shall find a galleon, a great ship of the outer oceans. I shall bid you remberee."

"We shall see," he replied. He was altogether too complacent. He had said that idiot "duh" barely half a dozen times since I had dubbed him Duhrra of the Days.

Truth to tell, after the visitation on the Dam I had been hourly expecting the return of the damned Gdoinye and the apparition of the blue Scorpion. I felt sure I had not beaten the Star Lords and I expected them to whisk me away. If they chose to hurl me headlong into fresh adventure on Kregen, well, that had been the pattern of my life and I would do what I could to fight through and reach Valka and Delia. If they chose to toss me contemptuously back to Earth I felt I might truly go mad. I did not think I could face another spell of twenty years on the planet of my birth.

We had stolen three sectrixes and had enough plunder loaded on the third to last us. We rode gently, for we had a way to go. The gale had passed, scouring the sky. With a new day the Suns of Scorpio flamed above, casting down their mingled streaming light. We rode in an opaline radiance.

The sea glittered to our right and the deserted countryside about us testified to the savagery of man in the inner sea. Also, I realized, it indicated that the sea could turn savage and cruel if the Dam of Days did not regulate the Tides of Kregen. Ahead of us a little knoll posed the usual problem. I said, "We are two greens, Duhrra of the Days, lest you forget. We may ride up boldly."

"Aye, Dak, my master. But if they be not too many . . ."

I glanced at the stump. In his saddle bag he carried the leather attachments to buckle on, the hooks and implements given him by the doctors of the Todalpheme. We had paid for them with golden oars taken from a Grodnim who lay in the bushes with a slit throat.

"You must wait to test your new hook, Duhrra of the Days."

"May Uncle Zobab quickly smile upon my stump then, for I long dearly to . . . uh . . . prove . . ."

The sectrixes stopped in mid-stride. Duhrra sat erect in the saddle with his big moon-face arrested with down-dropping jaw. I looked at the knoll.

A scarlet and golden figure sat a zhyan there.

The enormous pure white bird with the scarlet beak and claws took to the air and with a few lazy beats of its four wings settled at my side. I gazed at the woman seated on the zhyan's back.

She smiled gently at me.

"Lahal, Pur Dray."

"I am no longer Pur Dray, Madam Ivanovna."

"And on Kregen I am not Madam Ivanovna. You may address me as Zena Iztar."

Her robes sparkled in the light of the suns. All scarlet and rose, crimson and ruby, with golden tissue vestments and sumptuous gems and trappings, she presented a dazzling sight to an old sailor who was no longer a Krozair of Zy. She wore armor, golden plates cunningly fashioned, fitted to her, making me see the full voluptuous figure, the strength, the lissomeness, the lithe power in a seductive frame. I did not return the smile.

"Why do you seek me out, Zena Iztar?"

"Didn't the yellow overthrow the Scorpion's blue?"

"Aye."

"Do you not then owe me gratitude?"

"I waited three damned long years after you visited me in London."

"Aye."

We stared at each other.

Then, touching her red lips with a painted and gilded fingernail: "You are no longer a Krozair of Zy."

"No. It is of no consequence now."

"I think you lie."

I did not think I lied. "No, I do not lie. If those Zair-forsaken cramphs of Star Lords do not catch up with me I intend to sail to Valka. There is where my labors are required."

The marvel, the magic, the sheer wonder of this visitation, this apparition, had no power to move me now. I was sullen. I knew what I wanted to do at last—about time too—and I suspected most evilly that I was to be prevented.

I repeated, speaking so that she gazed down haughtily at me, although she did not flinch by more than a slight shifting of her head: "I am for Valka."

"And what of the Eye of the World? What of your friends here? What of Zair?"

"I am Apushniad!"

"Yet we both know that Dray Prescot is a man who could alter that, if he willed."

"He does not so will."

"I feared this. I had hoped—"

"Look, Zena Iztar. I want to go home! I want to see Delia again. Is that so strange? I have been tossed around, made slave, pranced about with these disgusting greens of Grodno—now I want to go back to Delia again."

"She is safe and well in Esser Rarioch."

"Aye! And that is where I want to be also."

"Why did you open the Dam of Days and destroy the vollers from Hamal? Was that a rational act of a man who does not care?"

"I am not a rational man! I thought to strike a blow for Sanurkazz and Zy and Felteraz. That is all."

"It is not all. I must leave you now. But I will tell you this: in your stiff-necked pride and in your selfishness you will fail. You will not be allowed to return to Valka."

"By the Star Lords?"

"No."

Before I could roar out a fresh question, for I was exceedingly angry, as I felt I had every right to be, the zhyan clashed its four wide wings, raising a whirlwind of dust, and rose into the air. I watched it fly up. The scarlet and gold figure leaned out and down, looking at me until vision was lost. Even then, I suspected, this hulu of a Madam Ivanovna, this fancy Zena Iztar, could still see me, a hulking great fighting man, hot with the lust to bash something around because he could not go home to his wife and children.

". . . uh . . . to prove I can take a swordsman with my right hand."

"Do what?" I said.

"Master! What is it?"

I forced myself to sit in the uncomfortable saddle, take up the reins and try to make the stupid sectrix behave.

"Nothing, Duhrra of the Days. A vision. It is passed. I still ride to Magdag and I will still find a galleon. There is much to be done in the outer oceans. I will shake the dust of Grodno and Zair from my feet and say good riddance."

Much had been explained to me, if not in words, but a very great deal remained; there were yet mysteries to be solved. I'd think about them when I reached Valka and once more held Delia in my arms, my Delia of the Blue Mountains, my Delia of Delphond.

"Uh ... I shall never say good riddance to Zair. But I think I will go with you across the wild and wonderful outer oceans."

I recollected myself. What the hell did I think Duhrra was going to do if I left him stranded in Magdag, the fortress city of the megaliths, the home of the Overlords of Magdag, the archenemies of all Zairians? I glared at him.

"Very well, the Duhrra of the Days. You come with me." I could not smile, but I said, "And right gladly will you be welcome."

"Uh," said Duhrra. "I think perhaps tomorrow I will try my new hook."